Men of Metal and Crosses

History of Spain's Exploration and Conquering of Mexico

What men among you have not thirsted for glory and riches?

Donald L. Ensenbach

Men of Metal and Crosses: History of Spain's Exploration and Conquering of Mexico

Other books by Donald L. Ensenbach

Kokopelli: Dream Catchers of an Ancient
Shadows Through a Spirit Window
Whispering Winds Remember
When the Spirits Move: A Native American Creation Story
The Quest: Footsteps of Change

Print ISBN 978-1-949267-39-6
eBook ISBN 978-1-949267-40-2

STAIRWAY PRESS—Apache Junction

Front Cover Painting by Trisha Dreyer
Cover Design by Guy D. Corp, www.GrafixCorp.com

STAIRWAY PRESS

www.StairwayPress.com
1000 West Apache Trail Suite 126
Apache Junction, AZ 85120 USA

Introduction

HISTORY IS AN important part of who we are because of whom were here before our time. By understanding the trials and tribulations our forefathers experienced, we come to the realization of why, where, and how we are today. Understanding the people around us, black, brown, red, white, or yellow, and what each of them and their ancestors lived through brings us to where we are now. Meeting each other in peace and war was part of each person's heritage, in history and now.

Each of us have stories of past successes and failures in meeting and connecting with other people, just as all people came to this land of opportunity with one thought uppermost in their minds, to better themselves and their families. The people whom they met here were interested in protecting that which they had used, settled or mobile, for centuries before these foreigners arrived, taking away that which they considered theirs.

This book tries to define the acts of both, and provide the reader with a short history of how the Americas, North, Central, and South, changed over four hundred years. This is a great time to turn back the pages of time to the 1400's with Spain removing by force the Moorish Islamic people, leaving their shores to discovering and conquering new lands, the "new world" which they called "New Spain."

Christopher Columbus, while searching for a shorter route to "the Indies," discovered many islands and harbors located in the Atlantic Ocean and the Saragossa Sea. Discoveries led to exploration, then to conquering the land and people in search of treasure and wealth. Upon arrival, governors were appointed, who in turn, gave out land grants to favored arrivals within their domain, and if native slaves had been taken, they were given to serve the landowners.

Other explorers followed shortly thereafter, with Grijalva, Cortes, and Coronado conquering land and people, while Fray Marcos de Niza, Father Eusebio Kino, and Fray Junipero Serra attempting to convert the "heathens" to Christianity.

Join with me now and explore the deeds of our forefathers, both conquerors and conquered. I truly believe that no one goes anywhere at any time to do harm to another person if it were not for fame, fortune, or land. And, there is no one who wouldn't fight to retain what they have if given an equal chance to hold it.

I sincerely hope that you find this book enlightening, thrilling and worth the price you paid for it. Thank you for your interest.

—Donald L Ensenbach, author

Acknowledgements

THIS NOVEL IS written using several historical books in the research for its content including books by Bernal Diaz de Castillo, Alvar Nunez Cabeza de Vaca, Samuel Elliot Morrison and John Francis Bannon.

Descriptions from these authors were used in assembling facts in support of the stories of discovery and conquests by Christopher Columbus, Hernando Cortes, Cabeza de Vaca, Fray Marcos de Niza, Father Eusebio Kino, Francisco Vasquez de Coronado, Fray Junipero Serra and Don Juan Batista de Anza.

I owe so much to all readers for your interest in the books I have written. I do feel this, being the last book in the series *Whispers from the Past*, is the best I have ever written, although it is less fiction and more history than any of the previous books.

So, thank you, one and all.

My wife, Opal, who has been my constant companion and guiding light for the past 60+ years, has the patience of a saint as she sees me so little when I am writing. In fact, while writing this book, she came into my office each evening and told me when it was time for the 10 PM news, which I try to never miss. Thank you, Opal, for all of your understanding, and stand-by-me faith in my writing.

Our children, Cheryl, Toni, and Greg deserve a thank you also, as because of my writing and appearances around primarily the Southwest, we get to see them usually once a year when we travel to Wisconsin for the Threshold's Showcase of Authors which I organize and sponsor in my hometown of West Bend.

The cover of this book was an acrylic painting contest held and sponsored by me by Trisha Dreher, an art instructor at Friendship Village, Mesa, Arizona. Thank you for your wonderful effort in bringing my thoughts to the cover.

The editing of this book, as well as the five previous books, was done by Keith Ougden, a part time resident of Mesa, Arizona, but a very knowledgeable and well-traveled resident of Cyprus. In fact, he does most of the editing while he and his delightful wife, Virginia, cruise around the world most of the year.

My next effort in writing will be finishing a history of my mother's family, who helped build the city of Cedarburg, Wisconsin. Following that, I plan on writing a book on the many industries of West Bend, Wisconsin followed by bringing my autobiography up to date.

Thank you again for your interest in my interests, as that is what I try to write about.

—Donald L Ensenbach

Chapter 1—Queen Isabella and Christopher Columbus

IN THE YEAR 711 AD, a huge number of Islamic Muslim people from North Africa stormed the southeastern part of Spain, overrunning the many small local fiefdoms, and killing many of the Spaniards who practiced Catholicism.

This forced priests of that religion to take the many gold candelabras, chalices, and other valuable relics from the churches and try to hide them from the attackers.

It was said that these valuable pieces were placed onto ships that carried them far to the west, and allegedly were taken across the seas to a new world beyond the ocean to be hidden in the seven cities of Cibola. These attackers were known as Islamic Muslim Moors, who ruled the southeastern part of Spain until the 1400's, when they were driven from the country.

According to historical accounts of that time, there was a Spanish sheep herder, Martin Alhajo, who was herding his sheep in the Sierra Morenas mountains area when he came across a small, unguarded pass leading toward the Moorish army camp. He left a cow's head and a pile of rocks at the entrance to the pass, which directed the Christian army to the unsuspecting Moorish troops who were defeated there at the battle of Las Navas de Tolosa on July 16th, 1212.

The defeat led to the end of the Moorish presence in Spain. Martin Alhajo was honored by being given the honorary title of Cabeza de Vaca, meaning the head of a cow. His descendants kept the honorary title as the family grew.

During that span of seven hundred years of the Moorish reign, there were some things they taught the Spanish people, among them knowledge of architecture, astronomy, mathematics, navigation by boats, and the building of many beautiful villages and homes, mostly in the color white. The Spaniards had protected and ruled some of the land to the north during those seven hundred plus years, mainly in the areas of Castile and Aragon.

In 1469, Isabella, an eighteen-year-old daughter of the king of Castile, married a seventeen-year-old son of the king of Aragon, Ferdinand. Isabella was crowned queen of Castile in 1474 after the death of her father.

During her early years of rule, many fiefdoms within Spain became troublesome as they warred against each other. But as Isabella exerted pressure through various methods of persuasion, the fiefdoms were united under her rule by 1479, and she became Queen Isabella I of Spain in that year. Ferdinand became king of Aragon in 1479 upon the death of his father, and became the king of Spain upon the death of Isabella in 1504.

A young Genoan Italian adventurer by the name of Christopher Columbus took to the sea at a very early age and accompanied other adventurous seamen to ports in Portugal, Ireland and Iceland.

On his voyage to Portugal, the boat on which he was a seaman was attacked by many French warships, although there was no war between the countries at that time. The boat he was on was sunk, but he grabbed some wooden planks and paddled his way six miles to land, where because of wounds he suffered in the battle, he was cared for until he could once again board another ship.

This was a very advantageous misadventure for the young seaman as Portugal was the center for learning the languages of Portuguese and Castilian, Latin to read the geographical maps of the past, mathematics and astronomy for celestial navigation, rigging and shipbuilding, and above all, discovery.

Through the many voyages he made, he accumulated some ideas on how to navigate ships for long distances using the stars and sun to follow latitudes and had heard about the Norse villages on

Greenland, indicating there were lands west of Europe. This encouraged him to find a way to find adventure and hopefully the riches he expected to find there.

The Orient beckoned.

It was in 1492 that a young Christopher Columbus beseeched Queen Isabella I of Spain to pay for and permit him to sail westward across the ocean and find a short way to India. She allowed that and paid for three ships to be outfitted with rigging and the latest navigational tools, along with food and water for an extended period of time. The ships were the Santa Maria, Columbus's flagship manned by fifty-two sailors, and the Nina and Pinta, manned by eighteen sailors each. Columbus departed the mainland from Cadiz, Spain on August 3rd, 1492.

The queen had bestowed "Admiral of the Ocean Sea" to his reputation, and granted him the honor of being named as governor-general over all mainlands and islands he should discover or acquire in the said seas by his labor and industry. Also, he should take and keep a tenth of all gold, silver, pearls, gems, spices and other merchandise produced or obtained by barter and mining within the limits of those domains, free of all taxes.

He was awarded the title with all rights and prerogatives appertaining thereunto his heirs and successors perpetually. He quickly sailed to the Canary Islands where he picked up additional provisions and left that port on September 6th, 1492. It was a long voyage without maps, sailing across the Atlantic Ocean into the Saragossa Sea, and his crews became ready to mutiny against him just days before a man in the forecastle of the Nina, Rodrigo de Triana, spotted land at 2 AM on October 12th, 1492.

Columbus and his crews arrived on an island he named San Salvador as a landing place which, undoubtedly, was one of the islands that make up the Bahamas now. Since there are over 700 small islands in the Bahamas grouping, it is impossible to ascertain exactly which was the first to be spotted, but the one most talked about is now called Watlings Island. He and his men began exploring the island, and resumed sailing southward along the eastern contour of what is now considered Cuba (Espanola), to an island they called Hispaniola, an island that now contains Haiti and the Dominican Republic.

Columbus left a contingent of about forty men there when he sailed back to Spain in 1493 aboard the Nina, his favorite ship. Also on board were slaves captured from the indigenous people he found there. The slaves were put into the services of the more well-to-do residents and governmental people of Spain.

By September 24th, 1493, Columbus had assembled seventeen ships and approximately 1,200 men to accompany him on a second voyage to Hispaniola. His intention was conquering the Taino tribe, colonize the area, bring the Catholic faith to the people he would find there, and acquire for Spain and himself the wealth he expected to find.

Among the men who made up the crew on his own ship, which was again named Santa Maria, were a medical doctor and two of the men who had been taken as slaves from Hispaniola, who, while in Spain, had learned to speak the language and had been baptized into the Catholic religion. Sailing to the Canary Islands from Cadiz, Spain, acquiring additional supplies, and sailing off from there was the plan. The great fleet left Cadiz on September 25th, arriving at Grand Canary on October 2nd, but sailed on to San Sebastian, Gomera where they anchored on October 5th.

The fleet was met with celebratory cannon fire and fireworks, and they were welcomed with open arms. Columbus had met the widow of the ruler of the four main Canary Islands, Dona Beatriz de Peraza, during his earlier voyage, and fallen in love with her. But, because of his already having been married, and the fact that the young widow would have wanted a new husband to remain at her side rather than sailing away to other places, it is unclear if they met other than when the fleet put into port.

After taking on fresh supplies and live animals to start flocks and herds in Hispaniola, the ships left San Sebastian between

October 7th and 10th, with the animals penned on the decks of the ships, as no animals would have survived below decks. Every captain of every ship received sealed instructions on what to do if the fleet were to be separated.

As the fleet moved west-south-westerly, Columbus had been talking with the two slaves who were familiar with the island chains around Hispaniola, and they told him about the beautiful arc of Caribbean islands east and south of Hispaniola.

While on the earlier voyage, Columbus had observed man-o'-war birds flying in that direction. According to the words of Dr. Chance, the surgeon on board, Columbus...

> *...rectified his course to discover them, because they were nearer to Spain, and the route thence to Hispaniola was direct.*

Although not realizing it at first, this route shortened the voyage by at least one week. This voyage across the ocean was uneventful, as the hurricane season had preceded the sailing by about one month. Actually, the Santa Maria was slower than many of the lighter ships, and the captains of those ships had to trim their sails in order for the flagship to stay with them.

Finally, at 5 AM on November 3rd, 1493, a pilot watching from the forechains of the ship Mariagalante spotted a black cone rising from the water pointing upward into the dome of paling stars. He climbed up the mast for a better look and called out, "The reward! We have land."

The call went from ship to ship, announcing the words that all of the men were waiting for, some more impatiently than others.

Columbus summoned all men on all ships above deck to a prayer led by one of the Franciscan friars on board the flagship. Columbus named that island Dominica, as they had seen that beautiful island on a Sunday. Shortly after sunrise, a second island was seen, and that island was named Santa Maria la Galante by

Columbus after the ship on which he sailed. So on his second voyage, Columbus discovered the shortest and best route from Europe to the West Indies. The island chain was named the Virgin Islands after the mother of Jesus.

After days of sailing through the many islands that made up the Virgin Islands, the seventeen ships arrived on the eastern shores of Hispaniola on November 22nd, 1493. Not recognizing that side of the island, they sailed around to Samana Bay, the place from which the Nina and Pinta ships had departed on January 16th on their return to Spain earlier that year. Some of the soldiers were left ashore seeking the garrison that Columbus had ordered to be built by the forty men left behind before he sailed back to Spain, but all they found were a few decayed bodies.

Arriving at the entrance to the bay in which the original Santa Maria flagship had struck rocks and sunk, Columbus decided not to proceed until daylight, November 28th. Anchoring outside the entrance to the bay, the cannons were fired in the hopes that the garrison would fire back, but no answering fire was heard or seen.

A canoe skillfully drew up alongside Columbus' flagship, and a man who had been seen with the chief of his tribe at a meeting between the chief and Columbus on his previous landing, requested he be seen by Columbus. This meeting occurred, and Columbus was told by the man that a warring village came to fight with the men in the garrison, and his chief was wounded trying to protect the Spaniards.

All of the Spaniards were killed by the other tribe, according to the man's story, and the reason the chief couldn't come to the ship to speak to Columbus was that he was still recovering from his injuries.

The following day, Columbus did go into the village and meet the chief, who was recovering from the injuries, but the story changed a bit when Columbus talked with him. It was said that some of the Spanish soldiers took advantage of some of the island women, which caused some jealousy in their husbands and fathers. Some of those women were from another tribe, and that tribe was responsible for the murders of the Spaniards, although the chief had tried to defend the men remaining inside the garrison.

During this meeting, Columbus had sent out two light ships to locate a position in which to locate another garrison.

Upon reporting back to Columbus, the ship commanded by Melchior Maldenado sailed through a bottleneck entrance into Fort Liberte' Bay where they anchored and received a message to visit from the chief of that village, who had been introduced to Columbus on his previous voyage.

That chief considered Columbus as a good friend, and Columbus decided to visit the chief with all of his many soldiers dressed in their brilliant uniforms and armor. After a very amiable meeting, the chief was invited to the flagship for dinner, where he saw the very first horse he had ever seen.

After leaving the ship, Columbus, his officers, and Fray Buil, one of the Franciscan priests on the voyage, discussed the matter, and everyone other than Columbus suggested that the chief should be captured and put to death, but Columbus showed restraint, and said that more evidence would show the chief to have told the truth.

Which is the way it turned out.

As the story unfolded, some of the men of the garrison began fighting amongst themselves, and some were killed. The remaining men began taking up with many women of the island and even jealousy between themselves led to more deaths. The other tribes did take offense at the way the Spaniards treated women and killed the rest.

In looking for another place for building a garrison, Columbus decided to locate it closer to where the gold mine was to be found. The people and animals on the seventeen ships were weary of sailing against the wind as they searched for a decent place to land, finding a lee in a wooded peninsula, and a level plain that looked as though it would support a permanent city.

Columbus called it Isabella, after his patron, Queen Isabella. However, it was not a very good place to build a garrison. The closest drinkable water was over a mile inland away, the harbor did not offer the depth to accommodate ships the size of those in his fleet, fishing was not good in the harbor, and the gold mine the Spanish sought was not in the immediate area.

As in many other cases, including Jamestown in Virginia, sea captains and their men lived differently than did the people who lived on land, and were not aware of these issues until after they had made their hasty decisions. Upon their arrival, a temporary church was assembled, and four days later, on the Epiphany, January 6th, 1494, Fray Buil conducted the first Mass in the new world, attended by the entire fleet.

Immediately thereafter, Columbus selected a man by the name of Alonso de Hojeda to lead a group of men, guided by a group from the native tribe, toward the area of the gold mine. The group was very successful, finding a village where a goldsmith was working on intricate gold-leafing, and who presented Hojeda with three large nuggets of gold, which Hojeda took back to the town-site of Isabella.

On their way back to the town the river which had to be crossed had swollen, and the returning party waited as the natives brought large canoes in which the Spaniards sat while the natives swam behind, pushing the canoes across the river, arriving at Isabella on January 20th.

During the time the group had been out searching for the gold, the men who were erecting the buildings and planting the crops became ill. Because of the change in diet, mosquito-borne sicknesses, and working conditions, the medications that had been brought from Spain were exhausted.

Columbus wanted to stay and collect more gold and other valuables, but because of the health of his men, he decided to organize a return voyage to Spain, not returning himself. Aboard the returning vessels, he loaded 30,000 ducats of gold, cinnamon, and bell peppers in shells, white sandalwood, sixty parrots of different colors, and other species of birds from the area.

What was of most interest were twenty-six natives of different islands and languages, among whom were three cannibals who lived on human flesh. Columbus left five vessels at Isabella, including the stout little Nina. Two of the ships left there included artillery in case of attack by natives or mutiny by the Spaniards. After the ships' departure, Columbus organized another search for the gold mine, taking all but a few men who were building the structures in Isabella, or were sick.

There were cavalry men with horses, crossbowmen, sword-wielding foot-soldiers, artisans including carpenters, axe men, masons and ditch diggers, with implements and tools with which to dig for gold and build a fort.

They found a beautiful valley in which the fort was to be located, and Columbus left men there to build it. Returning to Isabella, Columbus found a large number of men who were anxious to return to Spain, causing much trouble for the workers, and beginning to mount troubles in and around the town. He found that he had to discipline the offenders, some quite harshly, in trying to quell the uprising.

He decided to send Hojeda, along with some of the trouble-makers, to replace the man he had left in charge at the fort, but on his way, Hojeda became aware of a village which had captured a few of the Spaniards, stripped them of their clothes, and killed them. Hojeda captured the chief of the village and two of the chief's warriors, and brought them back to Isabella, where Columbus ordered them to be beheaded in the village square.

One of the chiefs from another village pleaded their case, and the chief and his warriors were released. But, this was the first in a long series of disagreements leading to bloodshed in the new world. This discipline by Columbus, of Spaniards as well as natives, led to grievances presented to the sovereigns back in Spain.

Next, Columbus sailed three of his ships and their seamen to both Cuba and Jamaica, leaving his brother, Don Diego, as president of the council for the city of Isabella. His other brother, Bartholomew Columbus, accompanied him on this exploration voyage. They explored many parts of both islands, but did not completely encircle Cuba, and reported that it was a peninsula rather than an island.

He used his favorite ship of this voyage, the Nina, as his flagship. Returning to Isabella, Columbus found that there were many issues caused by Spanish hidalgos and soldiers against the natives, and the natives' retaliation presented him with more problems than he could handle. He realized that some of his most influential personnel, including Fray Buil and Mosen Pedro Margarit, who had commanded the first fort in the interior of Hispaniola, had returned to Spain and would testify that Columbus had been unjustly punishing both Spaniards and natives.

He made preparations to return to Spain and try to clear himself of their claims.

On March 10th, 1496, Columbus boarded the Santa Clara (the renamed Nina) and sailed back toward Spain accompanied by the Santa Cruz, a ship that had been built from the remnants of several ships that had been broken apart in heavy winds at their moorings near Isabella. Along with him sailed two hundred twenty-five Christians wishing to return home, and thirty natives being taken as slaves below the decks.

This was far from the seventeen ships that Columbus had led from Cadiz in 1493, but it was all that he could raise. The route this two-ship fleet took led them to their first port of call, Puerto Plata of the now Dominican Republic, with the view of making it the capital. However, Bartholomew, Columbus' brother, reported to Columbus that the water found there was not good, but he had stayed there, and was taken back to Isabella by land to resume a lesser leadership role there.

Columbus next sailed for Guadeloupe, but anchored off Mariagalante, an island which Columbus had taken formal possession of during his first voyage. The Spaniards on the ship were unable to find any native foods to bring back to the ships, and the ships sailed on to Guadeloupe the following day. Upon landing, and sending some soldiers toward the village they saw there, a large number of women came from the village sending waves of arrows toward the soldiers.

Columbus sent some of the native women on board to ask the village women for food, but were told their husbands were on the north of the island and would be happy to furnish food for the vessels. Traveling northward, they came to another village, which again greeted them with waves of arrows, but the soldiers fired their guns, scaring the natives into the hills.

There were some people captured from the village, among them the wife of the chief. There was bartering done after that, but all of the captives were sent back to the village other than the chief's wife. Some food was obtained through bartering, and the two ships resumed their sailing toward Spain. Many weeks later, on June 11th, 1496, the ships entered the harbor at Cadiz, Spain. It had been a long and treacherous journey, but the "Admiral of the Ocean Sea" had guided the ships and the people who survived the long trip to his home port.

Being advised that the king and queen were at a city called Valladolid, a long procession of the Spaniards and native dignitaries plodded their way to that city. Whenever they entered an important city, the native chief wore colorful clothes adorned with gold, and the native chief's brother a large gold necklace.

Parrots and other birds and animals not common to Spain were included in the procession. Columbus also looked forward to seeing two of his sons, who had been honored to be pages to Queen Isabella upon meeting with the king and queen.

Presenting Queen Isabella and King Ferdinand with a handful of gold nuggets the size of pigeon eggs, he was greeted with much courtesy. He began petitioning the royal couple to outfit another expedition, this time asking for five vessels, to which they agreed, ordering him to assemble three hundred colonists to occupy Hispaniola at royal expense, and include thirty women who would not be paid, but would work their way aboard the ships and marry some of the colonists upon landing at Hispaniola.

The largest number of colonists were made up of prisoners who were offered pardons if they would be willing to become colonists, as traveling to the new world was not considered to be an opportunity to become wealthy as much as an opportunity to be released from prison.

Two of the ships, the Nina and the India, left Cadiz in January, followed shortly thereafter by three ships with supplies. The five ships met in Seville, and left that port sailing southward to Sanlucar da Barrameda, where Columbus boarded his favorite, the flagship, the Nina.

In sailing southward, he expected to find more gold near the equator, and hoped to find a settlement on a heretofore undiscovered continent. Having stopped at several ports to replace provisions that were being used on the expedition, while in the middle of the sea, the breezes that filled the sails became nonexistent for several days. Through the prayers of the many people aboard the ships, the breezes resumed, and Columbus redirected the ships northeastward on the morning of July 31, 1498.

Later that day land was spotted by a servant of Columbus, a man named Alonso Perez. Having dedicated this sailing to the Blessed Trinity before leaving Spain, when it was seen from the ship that there were three hills on the land they were approaching, Columbus called the land, Trinidad.

The next few days were used as vacation days for the crews and colonists. Washing the salt from their bodies in the cool, clear, fresh waters of the island occupied part of the time offered by Columbus, while fishing and oyster gathering were other projects that were undertaken.

Meanwhile, Columbus was making plans for discovering and exploring the land that could be seen to the west of there, that being less than 7 miles from the western shore of Trinidad. That was where Columbus directed his ships to sail after a large tidal wave caused by a volcanic eruption almost upset one of the ships carrying provisions. Steering northward around the northern shores of the island of Trinidad, and approaching the west side, Columbus found the greatest of his discoveries, the coastline of what is now Venezuela of the continent of South America.

Finding a cove with a sandy beach and huge boulders on each end, Columbus made for that place, landing there on Sunday, August 5th, 1498, and naming it Ensenada Yacua. Seeing a thatched house with a fire burning, he and his men approached the hut, but found that the people had fled. The entire area around the hut was filled by chattering monkeys, and since there were no other people other than the Spaniards to witness his taking formal possession of this land for the king and queen of Spain, he postponed that duty for another day.

Two days later, a number of friendly natives returned to the area of the hut, and trading began between the natives and the Spaniards.

Columbus was having trouble with his eyes, sending his senior captain, Pedro de Terreros, to take formal possession of this land, which the natives called Paria. It is still called the Paria peninsula of Venezuela. After preliminary gifts were given by the Spaniards to the natives—beads, sugar, bells, and other trinkets—natives rowed their canoes out to where the ships were anchored, bringing foods, fruits, and a beer called chicha fermented from maize.

As he continued to explore along the coastline of Venezuela, he stopped at a place where the women came on board wearing pearl necklaces, which were of great interest to the Spaniards. The women gladly traded them for the beads the Spaniards had brought with them, and the women were asked to collect more pearls for the next time the ships would stop there.

Continuing along the coastline, they sailed up to a great river leading into the interior of the continent, with fresh water flowing toward the salt water of the ocean.

Wanting to investigate part of the interior, the ships were directed into the large river channel, where the people on board saw native gardens and groves of mahogany and yellow fustic trees. It was like another world to the Spaniards, but as they sailed further into the interior, there were rocks that would have damaged the ships' bottoms, so Columbus had them turn around and head back into the ocean waters. From the exit of the river, another island was sighted in the distance, and Columbus chose to name it Assuncion as it was first seen on the eve of the Assumption of Jesus.

We now know that island to be Grenada. The following day, another island was seen, which he named Margarita, after the charming and witty daughter of the king of Austria. Columbus made a large mistake in judgment at that time.

Instead of taking the time to collect pearls and other items of wealth in order to give them to the king and queen, he hurried to return to Hispaniola, where by that time, men who were dissatisfied with their lives in that country, had sailed back to Spain, telling anyone who would listen of the harsh way the Columbus family treated both Spaniards and natives.

So much pressure was placed at the feet of the king and queen, that they appointed a royal commissioner, Francisco de Bobadilla, with the authority of unlimited powers over persons and property, and sent him to Hispaniola.

Upon his arrival at Santo Domingo on August 24th, 1500, the first thing Bobadilla saw was a gallows from which seven Spaniards were hanging. The only Columbus brother in that city at that time was Diego, who told him that there were five men to be hanged on the morrow. Without waiting for the reasons why these men were sentenced to be hung, Bobadilla confined Diego in the brig of his ship, and sent out a letter ordering Christopher and his brother Bartholomew to return immediately to that city.

Not wanting to defy the royal authority of Bobadilla, the two brothers submitted to their incarceration ordered by him. Having won the loyalty of the citizens of Hispaniola by offering freedom to collect gold and other wealth from wherever they could find it, and other freedoms they had not had while being under the rule of the

Columbus brothers, Bobadilla set about sending the brothers back to Spain in chains.

Appearing before King Ferdinand and Queen Isabella, Christopher and his brothers were not given the attention they needed to plead their case of the many accomplishments they had brought to the country of Spain. The royals were too busy to hear of the founding and the formalizing of taking possession of the lands which Christopher had located for Spain, and all of the wealth they had brought back to the royal couple.

Finally, after six months of being incarcerated and made to look foolish, the royals released them and encouraged Christopher to return to the new world for more exploration. Returning his admiralty in title only, there were four ships provided for his fourth voyage.

On May 11th of 1502 Christopher left Cadiz, Spain for his fourth and last expedition to the new world. Because of his age and health issues, Christopher did not command the vessel in which he, and his twelve year old son, Ferdinand, were transported, however, it was Christopher who directed the four ships, all caravels, along their journey.

Some of the men who accompanied the expedition had been on Christopher's earlier voyages, such as Diego Tristan, captain of the ship in which Christopher and Ferdinand sailed. Bartholomew Columbus, Christopher's brother, was said to be captain of the ship he sailed on, but the true captain was in fact Francisco Porras, with his brother, Diego Porras, sent along as auditor, chief clerk and crown representative.

The third ship was captained by Pedro de Terreros, who had accompanied Christopher on his three previous voyages, while the owner of that ship was Juan Quintero, the man who was boatswain of the Pinta ship during Christopher's first voyage.

The fourth and final ship was captained by Bartolomeo Fieschi, a friend of the Columbus family before Christopher was born. This was a special fleet for Christopher to direct as he had always expressed a preference for lighter, more maneuverable ships, and three of the four were of that type.

After leaving Cadiz, Christopher directed the ships to a Portuguese fortress at Arzila, as he had been asked to stop there to help the Portuguese fort stave off an attack by Moors. By the time the ships arrived there, the Moors had left the area, and the ships sailed on to Grand Canary arriving there on May 20th, a route of six hundred seventy-five miles.

Taking on wood and fresh water, they set sail for Hispaniola, and took the same route as he used on the 1498 voyage. The trade winds helped the ships to the fastest ocean voyage Christopher ever made, reaching Martinique in twenty-one days. There he took three days to have his men rest, bathe and wash their clothes of the salt from the ocean spray.

Leaving that anchorage, the ships stopped at Dominica, passed by the Leeward Islands he had discovered during his second voyage, passed by the southern coast of Puerto Rico, and entered the Ozama River leading to Santo Domingo, the new capital of Hispaniola.

Although Christopher had been told by the royals not to return there until he was on his return trip to Spain, he expressed reasons for stopping there anyway. He said that the main reason was to have letters he had written to his family back in Spain placed on ships that were scheduled to depart for Spain.

However, his real reason was to be able to trade one of the four ships he found lacking in performance, and hide from an oncoming hurricane he felt was ready to strike. He sent Captain Terreros with a note to the governor, requesting permission to come ashore, and urging that the homeward bound fleet be detained until after the hurricane had passed, but the requests were turned down. The outbound fleet left port, but as they reached the Mona Passage, the hurricane winds hit the fleet, sending twenty-five of the twenty-nine ships to the bottom of the sea.

By coincidence, Bobadilla—the man who had replaced Christopher as governor, being the royal commissioner, and who had

Christopher and his brothers arrested and sent back to Spain in chains—was on one of the ships that went down.

All of the men aboard those ships were drowned. Amongst the cargo were two hundred thousand ounces of gold including one nugget, the largest ever found in the West Indies, which was said to weigh 3,600 ounces.

The ships of Christopher's fleet were badly beaten about in the terribly fierce winds and the heavy rains, but they all survived because of the shelter they had sought and found before the storm struck. After the hurricane had passed, Christopher took the time to have each ship repaired to the condition they were before the storm and before leaving the harbor, and allowed the sailors and soldiers a few days of rest.

Many of the men fished off of the ship, catching a manatee, which Ferdinand correctly categorized as a mammal, not a fish. One of the men aboard another ship spied a lazy sting ray resting on top of the water. Taking a harping iron, he deeply penetrated the skin, and the ray began swiftly towing the ship around the harbor. The men on the other ships were amazed at the speed at which the ship was traveling without sail or rowing. The sting ray died while towing the ship and was brought up onto the deck by tackles. These events occurred at Azua in late June or early July, 1502.

Departing from Azua, they sailed around Beata Island and the Alta Vela rock, where the Columbus expedition landed in 1498, but anchored in Jacmel, as Christopher recognized the indications of another storm approaching the area.

After the storm had passed, he decided to take a western route to explore the western Caribbean, hoping to find land and be able to explore the shoreline of whatever he found.

After three days, the ships approached a small group of islets called the Morant Cays, where by digging into the sand, they found fresh water. With the wind picking up, the small fleet sailed three hundred sixty miles in three days, at which time they approached an island called Bonacca off of the coast of Honduras.

There were natives living there, but because the island was small, they had nothing of great value to trade. The many tall pine trees growing on the sides of the hills were the only things to be seen from their anchorage, but the Spaniards mistook terra calcide (similar to iron pyrite) for gold.

That turned out to be fool's gold, and was hidden from view as it was forbidden to privately trade in gold. While there, a large canoe was rowed out to the ship in which Christopher was transported. It was about thirty feet long and eight feet wide, carried twenty-five rowers, numerous women and children, and carried a large number of dyed and woven cotton-made shirts and coverings, shawls worn by the women, long wooden swords with flint fitted into the edges, copper hatchets, bells and other curious items.

The canoe was easily captured, the Spaniards took whatever they pleased of the contents, and the elder of the group inside the canoe was taken to become a translator for the Spaniards.

He turned out to be an intelligent and helpful man, whom the Spaniards baptized and renamed Juan Perez. Later, when Columbus and some of his men had returned to the royal courts in Spain, many questions were asked of the men who had been with Christopher at the time of this landing as to the people who met them and the type of life they represented.

The items which they included in the canoe indicated an advanced civilization such as the Mayans, but there was no indication of any ties to that civilization, but rather to the Honduran roots near where they lived. Trading between the civilizations is highly likely, as traveling traders covered many miles throughout North and South America in earlier times.

Also, the natives of Central and northern South America smelted gold, silver, and copper, designing and manufacturing items in metal that were the equal to those of ancient Mexico.

It was in early August that Columbus headed his fleet toward the shores of Honduras, finding there the same type of civilization as that of Bonacca. The place at which they anchored was named Punta Caxinas after the type of fruit tree growing along the beaches of Honduras. The men of that area wore thick cotton jackets that were sufficient protection from penetration of arrows. Following the shoreline windward, they anchored near a river which Christopher named Rio de la Posesion, as he took formal possession of that land for the king and queen of Spain following a Mass performed by Fray Alexander.

Many of the native peoples came to witness the various customs of these foreign visitors, and much trading took place after the solemn Mass and possession performances were concluded. After resuming their sailing, Christopher became sick, and the men on his ship designed and erected a shelter for him on the deck, from which he could continue to direct the captains on the route he wanted to take.

Much of the time was spent in driving rain, heavy seas and strong winds which drove the ships close to the rocks near the shores during the days, so Christopher looked for protected coves in which to anchor at night. This weather lasted for twenty-eight straight days, causing the crews and everyone aboard the four ships to suffer from depression.

One who was not affected as much as the others was Christopher's son, Ferdinand, who seemed to help lift the spirits of the men aboard the ship on which he and Christopher sailed. The depression of the men got to be so bad they took turns confessing their sins to one another in hopes of earning their rights to heaven if the craft would be torn apart or settle into the sea, and they were to die at sea.

During all of this foul weather, Columbus could have given in to changing course and sailed into smoother waters, but he would not give up. His intention to find the strait that would take him to the other side of this continent, to areas where no other Spaniard had yet seen, remained firm. Finally the weather lifted to find sunny warm days and beautiful starlit nights, and the ships fairly flew along the coast heading south.

There came a time when the coastline fell to the west, offering a fair breeze and in giving thanks to God, Columbus named the cape Gracias a Dios, or Thanks be to God.

Following the eastern shore of what we now call South America, he came into the area now known as Nicaragua. They came to a harbor leading to a large river opening. Columbus chose that place to anchor for a short while in order to give time for the men to bathe, wash clothes of the salt, and replenish the food and fresh water provisions.

It was there that one of the small boats was capsized by a wave, and two men drowned. For that reason, Columbus named that place Rio de los Desastres, or River of Disasters. Exiting that anchorage, the ships picked up a southerly flow of air sending them one hundred thirty miles south along the coastline bringing them to the shores of what is now Costa Rica.

On September 25th, 1502, the ships found a beautiful, wooded island, behind which was space to anchor all of the ships, and a great beach at which to bathe, wash clothes, and rest, as Columbus knew that each was needed by all. The natives called their island, Quiriviri, but Columbus named it La Huerta, the Garden. A great number of men, women, and children gathered upon the shore, the men carrying bows and arrows, spears tipped with sharp fish bones, the women and children dressed in woven cotton clothes.

The natives boarded small boats rowing out to the ships with the intention of trading with the Spaniards, however, Columbus seeing they brought no gold in the small boats, ordered the natives be given small tokens of beads and bells of little worth, then sent them back ashore. The natives did not give up however, sending two virgin girls to the ships, which Columbus ordered to be clothed and returned to the people waiting on shore.

The natives were very impressed that the Spaniards had treated the young girls with such dignity, offering them clothing and food, before ferrying them back to shore. It impressed Ferdinand,

Christopher's son, seeing the goodness of his father and the command he had over the men in his expedition.

The following day, Bartholomew, Christopher's brother, was rowed ashore, and with paper and pen, was about to write about them, but the natives thought it was witchcraft, running from him, and throwing a powdered herb into the air to dispel the magic.

On October 2nd, 1502, Columbus sent a group of Spaniard soldiers to investigate the island, and they reported back to him that they found an abundance of flowering plants, and they had seen many deer, pumas, and a strange turkey-like bird with feathers that looked like wool. They found a great wooden palace covered by cane stalks, and tombs, within one of which was a mummy wrapped in cotton cloth, and over each tomb was placed a stone tablet carved with figures of beasts.

Some tombs were carved with effigies of the dead person adorned with necklaces of beads and other items the person would have most valued.

Upon their return to the ships, they brought along two native men they captured for use as translators, for, as they passed from the area that Juan Perez could translate from the language he understood to Spanish, he was released to return to his people. The people from whom these two men were taken, sent out gifts as though paying a ransom for the return of the two men. One of the gifts were two wild pigs, called peccaries, one of which was very aggressive.

One was returned to the natives. The other chased the men around the deck of the ship, with its sharp teeth nipping at heels, and chasing the wolfhound owned by Christopher below deck where it remained until the wild pig met its match.

A large spider monkey, which had been shot by a crossbowman and had one foreleg cut off, coiled its tail tightly around the pig's snout, seized it by the neck with its remaining fore claw, and began biting the pig into submission. The men aboard that ship watched with glee as kindness to animals was not practiced at that time. Columbus included the incident in his letters to the king and queen.

On October 5th, the expedition sailed from La Huerta heading southward again, still searching for the strait leading to the western shores of this continent, and to the ocean that assaulted its shores.

They found a great channel leading Columbus to think that he had found the strait at last. But no, once more it proved to be a huge bay, spotted with islands so close together that when sailing between them, the rigging on the ships were brushed by branches and leaves from the trees and bushes lining the banks.

The sailors made their way through the maze of islands, at last coming to a huge land-locked lagoon, thirty miles wide and fifteen miles wide at the entrance.

It was beautiful, but not the strait for which Columbus searched.

Another great disappointment, yet it yielded the first sign of fine gold to the Spaniards who had joined the expedition for the purpose of enriching themselves.

In that bay, now called Almirante Bay, a native wore a large medal around his neck, made of fine gold estimated to be worth a large amount of money, which he traded to the Spaniards for three small hawk's bells worth about one cent.

In Columbus' time, explorers took directions from native people's gestures, as each tribe seemed to have different languages, none of which were understood by the explorers. Given gestures that indicated places for which the explorers were searching, the returned gestures were to places that had no relation to those for which they were searching.

This time they were directed to another place that according to the native giving directions was understood by Columbus to be the passage to India. That place turned out to be named by Columbus as Alburema, known as Chiriqui Lagoon as it is called today.

It was there that Columbus and the men who had sailed with him were rewarded with gold for which they traded goods of little value. These people wore little clothing, painted their faces and bodies with black, red and white watered resins from a variety of leaves from bushes and trees.

The only covering was over their genitals, and that was usually a thin woven cotton string, like a bikini. Much wealth was traded for, and much information was gathered by Columbus and his captains.

It was there that Columbus learned he was on an isthmus, not realizing he was just miles from where the Panama Canal would link the Atlantic and Pacific Oceans many centuries beyond his time. Columbus and his ships were anchored there from October 6th to the 16th, 1502, bathing, eating, fishing, hunting, requesting information, and trading with the natives.

This then, was the very best of Columbus' fourth trip to the new world. From the time he left his Alburema, there is no record of him mentioning the strait for which he had been searching since April of that year. He was resigned to the fact that there was no strait leading to China from where he was.

He began his search for the second object of his fourth voyage to the new world, that of gold.

On October 17th, 1502, Columbus left the lagoon, passing by the entrance guarded by the Tiger Channel, so named because of the two islands of a red hue at the entrance. Sailing around Punta Chiriqui, they were heading into the harborless Golfo de los Mosquitos, or Gulf of Mosquitos.

Anchoring off the mouth of a river called Guaiga, the ships had entered the region known by the natives as Veragua, a very important source of gold. After several days of anchorage there, during which the Spaniards hoped to establish contact with the natives, their wishes were brought to fruition.

The Spaniards took to their small boats rowing them to the shoreline. Over one hundred natives rushed from the brush and trees running into the water up to their middles, waving spears, blowing horns, beating a drum, splashing water toward the men in the small boats. Some of the men in the boats were smart enough to wave some of the hawk's bells and beads that shone brightly in the sunlight, enticing some natives to trade sixteen pieces of gold to them for the cheap items the Spaniards had brought into the boats with them.

Returning to their ships, the Spaniards made another attempt to meet and trade with these natives, but once again were met with threats. One of the men had brought a musket with him, and after firing it once, the noise so frightened the natives they ran for the woods along the beach.

Columbus and his men made a few trades, but the natives complained that they were protecting their land, and had not brought gold to trade.

Christopher made his intentions of locating areas in which gold was mined known to his men, and they sailed on. Unfortunately, they found no harbors in which to anchor in this beautiful, but unhospitable gulf.

From their ships, the men could see sandy beaches, much beauty in the bushes, flowers and trees beyond the beaches, and colorful mountains further inland as they continued to sail by. Finally, there was an inviting harbor spotted by one of the men on the ship carrying Christopher, and they anchored there. It was called Cativa by the natives, and these people rushed to the waters, sounding their alarm with drumming and trumpeting, but soon became interested in what the Spaniards were willing to trade for the gold they offered.

Their chief, who was protected from the sun by men carrying a big leaf offered one of his own gold disks in trade. According to Ferdinand, Christopher's son, who wrote notes of the expedition, this was the first native village that had used stucco in their buildings. A piece of the stucco was taken by Columbus to show the king and queen upon their return to Spain. As he continued to sail past the rest of Veragua, he passed out of the area in which gold was mined and refined.

Entering the territory of Cobraba, which is what the natives called it, there was no harbor in which to anchor, so no investigation of the land was undertaken. But Bartholomew, Christopher's brother, kidnapped a native as an interpreter. A terribly long storm season fell upon the area in which Columbus tried to hide his ships, and the storms lasted a total of two months before the fleet could sail again.

As they were leaving that landing, another violent storm drove them without allowing any of the ships to seek shelter. After the storm subsided, a large harbor opened to the fleet at the time they needed one.

Christopher named it Puerto Belo because it was quite large, fair, inhabited, and encompassed a well-tilled countryside. The anchorage was close to the shore, but the ships could make a fast run to the mouth of the harbor if necessary.

The country about the harbor was well cultivated, and the houses were only a stone's throw apart. Yes, this was a very perfect setting, except for another storm which arrived, shutting down any sailing for seven days. During those seven days there was much trading between the native farmers who traded food and skeins of fine spun cotton for small brass items. Upon leaving that pleasant port, they sailed eastward for nine days before running into another storm which pushed them backwards about thirteen miles.

Putting in at several islets which happened to be full of maize, this area was called "harbors of provisions." Remaining there for twelve days, the ships and casks were repaired.

Leaving the protection of those harbors, the fleet of four ships ran from the approach of another storm, finding a small but snug cove which protected the ships well. The ships were wedged against the high banks of the cove Columbus called Retrete, known today as El Portete. Since the ships were nestled right up to land, and since the homes of villagers were near, some of the Spaniards would slip away during the night, trading with the natives.

At times the Spaniards took more than the natives liked, so there were fights between them. Although Christopher tried to keep peace, he prepared the cannon on board to fire without a ball being inserted to fire. The sound of the powder exploding scared the natives, but they returned to their positions threatening the ship. This time a ball was loaded and fired.

The natives had learned their lesson and did not bother the ships or Spaniards again. Ferdinand mentioned for the first time in his notes regarding Retrete that "there were large lizards, like the crocodiles of the Nile in the waters of this strange place." Finally leaving Retrete, the ships headed back to Veragua, as Columbus discovered by this time the only thing the royals were interested in was the gold brought back to them.

That had been the village that was mentioned each time by natives of other villages when gold was spoken about. According to those natives, it was there where gold was mined and made into gold mirrors. He was tired, sick, and was thinking about his home, wife and family. If he could trade for enough gold to satisfy the king and queen, he would be set for life.

The storms had depressed the crews, the soldiers, and even himself, but there was one chance to save his expedition, and that was to get more gold. Storms continued to buffet the fleet of four ships, and the seas rose up as wave after wave struck the tiny group, while lightning and thunder rolled across the skies.

The torrential rains swept through the entire fleet of ships, drenching everyone aboard.

The men's faith and determination suffered greatly, with almost all of them thinking of dying rather than surviving. During this storm a waterspout rose with water being drawn into the clouds that were hanging low in the skies. As the waterspout danced along toward the four ships, it made a sudden turn, and danced across the waves to the portside of the lead ship disappearing into the pelting rains coming from the opposite direction. Columbus, having been told of the waterspout began reading a verse from the Bible, which seemed to turn the waterspout away as he began reading aloud, "be thee gone."

A narrow escape to be sure.

As the skies cleared and the rain abated, a large swarm of sharks surrounded the four ships, and the men took to striking the ones that came to the top of the water with chains, and shooting arrows at them. Shark steak was not their favorite food, but it was fresh, and took the place of the hunger pangs they were suffering.

Putting into a harbor the Indians called Huiva, they repaired the rigging and checked the ships for seaworthiness as well as resting, regaining strength, and ridding themselves of the depression of the past several days.

Also provisions were taken aboard, and the men relished the change in diet. Columbus ordered the four ships to leave the place he called Puerto Gordo after three days, but once they hit the open sea, another storm hit them, blowing them back to the same anchorage they had just left. It was fourteen days before they were able to leave that place on January 3rd, 1503. Upon departing Puerto Gordo, another storm blew in, and it took three more days to find a harbor in which to anchor.

It was on January 6th that the ships sought refuge in an outlet of a river, which Christopher called the Rio de Belen, after Bethlehem, as they had landed there on the feast day of the Three Kings. After making soundings at that river site and at the Rio Veragua which was found to be just a league, about three and one-half miles, from Rio de Belen, Christopher decided to make Rio Belen his headquarters from which the expedition would search for gold, then begin mining.

As the native population found out about the Spaniards, their ships, and their interest in mining or trading for gold, the main chief of the Guaymi villages agreed to meet with Christopher. This was after one of the interpreters convinced his tribe and the chief that the Spaniards meant no harm, and wanted to trade with them. The ships were moved back to the Rio Veragua to meet with the chief, whose men moved and cleaned off a great stone on which the chief sat while speaking with Columbus.

As things had been discussed and understanding was mutual, Columbus moved the ships back and along the interior using the Rio de Belen as the first route to explore. On January 24th, a deluge rushed down the river, sending the ship, Capitana, the ship carrying Christopher, Ferdinand, and other men, into the nearby ship, Gallega, breaking the cables and anchor chains, and carrying them together toward deep water.

The men worked hastily aboard both vessels and were able to separate them from each other and retake command and redirect the ships to another mooring. Driving rains, flooding, and the seas breaking over the entrance to the river kept the men from doing any exploring, but did give them the opportunity to repair the lines, the rigging, re-calking the sides and inside of the ship and the other damages done by the deluge, rains, flooding and winds.

By February 6th the weather had calmed down, and Christopher ordered the resumption of exploring. Guided by some of the Guaymi men, an area was found from which the Guaymi tribe had been able to collect gold without much digging.

Samples were taken to Christopher and happily, he decided to set up a Spanish community near the place where the gold was found, leaving his brother Bartholomew in charge, while he would return to Spain for reinforcements.

By February 14th, Bartholomew and fifty-four Spaniards rowed twenty-two miles westward along the coastline to a river the natives called Urira. There they met a friendly reception led by the high chief, and spent the night within that village.

Bartering for gold, the natives traded gold disks to Bartholomew, which were sent back to the ships, stored with the intention of taking them to King Ferdinand and Queen Isabella. Upon Bartholomew's return to the Capitana, where Christopher and Ferdinand waited along with the men in the two other ships, work was started on the settlement that Christopher wanted built, and which was given the name of Santa Maria de Belen.

After ten or twelve buildings had been erected, homes and warehouses for necessary supplies, the rains stopped and as the land around them dried up, so did the water level in the small harbor diminish in depth.

The ships were unable to leave as there was less than two feet of water above the sand bar at the entrance. Unfortunately, some of the Spaniards made uninvited visits to the Guaymi village, taking advantage of the women, married or unmarried, bartering or stealing gold from the natives, which made the natives angry.

There were more visits by the natives, not only the Guaymi warriors, but also surrounding tribes' men. Ferdinand, Christopher's young son, wrote in his notes that they had to pray for rain, just as they had prayed for rain to stop during the rainy season.

Provisions were running very short.

Diego Mendez, a gentleman volunteer aboard the ship Santiago, volunteered to row along the coastline toward Veragua to find out more about the native men who were threatening to make war on the men aboard the ships. He had taken it upon himself to learn the language of the natives of this area, as they had spent much time there. He found an encampment of over one thousand warriors just a mile or two from where the ships were trapped.

Calmly stepping from the canoe he had been rowing, he asked them of their plans, and because of their superior numbers, they told him they would be attacking the four ships in two days. Having been prepared for trouble, he had told them he was going to treat an arrow wound their chief had sustained and was granted access to the chief's quarters.

As he was leaving the hut, a great noise emitted from the crowd, and he knew he was in trouble. He had planned to present something very different for their benefit, and he pulled out a mirror and scissors and began cutting his own hair, which was something none of the natives had ever done, or seen done. After that, he asked the warriors that had witnessed the haircut for food and drink, which were brought to him, and which he consumed. Leaving the camp of the native warriors, he rowed back to the ships of Columbus and told him the news.

After hearing the news, Columbus and his leaders decided to

capture the chief and some of his leaders, holding them as hostages. This they did, with Columbus and Diego approaching the hut of the chief without being challenged, while the rest of the soldiers surrounded the camp.

Upon their entry into the hut, a Spanish soldier fired his musket as a signal. The chief and thirty leaders, wives, and children were captured and escorted down to the small boats in which Columbus and eighty soldiers had arrived at the village, and took them back toward the ships. The chief slipped out of his bonds and jumped overboard, swimming back to his village.

While this was happening, there had been enough rain to allow the ships to sail over the sand bar, leaving Bartholomew, Christopher's brother, Diego Mendez, a small contingent of twenty soldiers, and a wolfhound to protect and govern the small village of Santa Maria de Belen.

The chief assembled another attack on the community this time, and shot arrows, slings with rocks and stones, and spears at the small community's buildings, killing one and wounding several more, but with the help of the crossbowmen and musket fire, the defenders put the native warriors to flight, with the wolfhound chasing them into the surrounding woods.

Unfortunately, Captain Diego Tristan, the main captain of the ship Capitana, had been sent ashore with the purpose of bringing fresh water to the ships. Having been ordered for that purpose only, he and his men did not take part in the defense of the community, but continued on to get the water.

After leaving the scene of the fighting, his small ship was rowed to the area where there was a fresh water stream. From the woods native warriors sprang and attacked, killing everyone but one man who dove into the water swimming underwater to safety. He returned to the ships, telling the men of the attack and demise of everyone but him.

There were other issues that prevented Columbus to leave that area immediately. The fourth ship, the Gallego, had not been towed over the sand bar, and the one remaining small boat was the only serviceable boat with which one could approach shores, no matter the anchorage around the world. It could not be lost in trying to pull the Gallego across the sand bar, nor to pick-up any additional sailors or soldiers on that boat or in the community.

Over the next eight days, the native warriors retired after being made aware of the superior weapons of the Spaniards. Three ships were still anchored in deep water outside the sand bar, and the worm-infested Gallego floated inside the sand bar. A volunteer, Pedro de Ledesma, using the last small boat, rowed up to the sand bar, swam to the shoreline, and entered the community.

Finding the men quarreling among themselves, asking for transportation to rejoin the ships outside the breakwater, Diego Mendez had begun constructing a raft with which to carry the men over the sand bar to rejoin the reduced fleet of three ships.

The community of Santa Maria de Belen was abandoned, all of the men who had been left behind to defend that community had been brought out to the ships by raft, and Diego Mendez was rewarded by Columbus by being named as captain of the Capitana, the ship aboard which Christopher rode. The three ships left that location on April 16th, 1503, expecting to reach Hispaniola, but the ships were in bad shape. Ship worms had eaten the ships innards, and leaks sprang everywhere.

They sailed eastward, because to have sailed northeastward would have sailed them into the teeth of the wind.

They arrived next at Puerto Belo, in present day Jamaica, where they had to abandon the ship Vizcaina, which meant the men aboard that ship moved to the other two ships. Diego Mendez mentioned in his notes of those days that all men aboard both remaining ships were put to work bailing water that rushed through the worm holes below decks. On the night of June 22nd, the two ships were nestled as close to shore as possible in a place Columbus had named Puerto Bueno, with three pumps and kettles still bailing water from the sinking ship.

On June 25th, 1503, the two ships picked up enough wind to push them twelve and one-half miles eastward to a harbor enclosed by reefs Columbus had named Puerto Santa Gloria in 1494 during his second voyage to the new world. That was the final resting place for the two ships, the Capitana and the Santiago.

After arriving at that port, the remaining provisions were taken ashore in the only remaining small boat. Anything that would be of any use to the marooned Spaniards was saved, which wasn't much. Columbus then ordered the ballast to be thrown overboard to lighten the ships, and they were pulled ashore to be used as homes and a fortress until palm tree homes were constructed.

There were two streams of fresh water located nearby, and a large native Indian village was just beyond the streams. The most immediate need was for food after having located the fresh water. There were only one hundred sixteen of the one hundred forty men who had been with them before reaching Veragua, but all of them were hungry and needed food badly.

Once again, Diego Mendez and three of his men, volunteered to go out to meet with the native people, hoping to find help with food and other necessities. Luckily, the people of the closest village were friendly, inviting him and his men to eat with them.

Making an agreement with the natives to supply food for the men with the Spaniards trading the beads, bells, and other trinkets, Mendez sent one of his men back with the news and some food. Proceeding to the next village, he made similar agreements with the people of that village, again sending a man back to the Columbus group with food and that information.

Going to a third native village, he became good friends with the chief, even exchanging names with him, and convincing the chief to have a very good canoe and six rowers provided to him and his last remaining man, with more food aboard, rowing them back to the place where the two ships had been beached.

To obtain that canoe, Mendez traded a brass helmet, a cloak and shirt. As the Spaniards were forced to remain in the area of the two beached ships and the few houses they had erected, Columbus began to worry about the men mutinying, leaving the area and defiling the villages, women or children, thus possibly forcing the native Indians to make war on the tiny settlement.

Consulting with Diego Mendez as to suggestions on what to do, Columbus decided to seek a volunteer to try to row the 105 miles against the wind to the western shores of Hispaniola, then 305 miles to Santo Domingo, but no one but Mendez volunteered. After fixing a false keel to the large dugout canoe he had purchased from the chief of the native people, then pitching and greasing the bottom, raising washboards on bow and stern to keep out heavy seas, and fitting a mast and sail on the canoe, he took one experienced Spanish sailor and six native rowers with him as they set forth.

Stopping along the way at a small harbor, walking into the woods looking for water and food for the other people and himself in the canoe, he met a group of native warriors intent on killing him.

While the natives played a game of chance to decide who would kill him, Mendez stole away, returning to the canoe, which was rowed back to Santa Gloria. Reporting to Christopher that he had failed to get to Hispaniola, Columbus asked that he try again, which he agreed to do, but asked for protection until he could clear the island of Jamaica.

This was provided by a fleet of canoes manned by Bartholomew, Spanish soldiers, and friendly native rowers. Also, a close friend of Christopher, a Bartolomeo Fieschi, the captain of the ill-fated ship Vizcaina, accompanied Mendez and his native rowers in a second canoe.

Each of the two canoes carried six Christians and ten natives in the hope that at least one of the canoes could make it Hispaniola. If both made it successfully, Mendez was to try to get to Santo Domingo and request a ship be dispatched to pick-up Columbus and the men who were stranded there. Fieschi would sail back to Santa Gloria to tell Columbus that help was on its way.

It took over three days of rowing to approach a small island where fresh water was found in the clefts of rocks. Some of the native rowers drank so much that they died. Off in the distance they could see Cape Tiburon, which was the closest point of Hispaniola, which was still thirty miles distant.

During the cool of the evening, the canoes were launched and by mid-morning both canoes had safely landed at that cape. Resting for two days before setting off on their different voyages, Mendez left toward Santo Domingo and Fieschi was to have started his return toward Santa Gloria.

However, the Spaniards who had accompanied him would not enter the canoe to return to Santa Gloria, and seeing their refusal to return, the natives wanted to remain there also.

Mendez made his way to Santo Domingo, hoping to find the governor Ovando so he could order ships to rescue Columbus and what was left of his expedition. However, Ovando was off in the interior putting down a native uprising. Upon following Ovando into the interior and catching up to him, he told Ovando of the trouble Columbus was in, which privately pleased Ovando. He saw Columbus returning with glory and gold, and regaining the governor's appointment.

This would send him back to Spain without any important position. Also, at the time there were no ships in port at Santo Domingo to send to affect a rescue, so he made Mendez wait impatiently for a ship to be sent to rescue Columbus and what was left of his expedition.

Back at Santa Gloria, as months passed, the Spanish men were getting upset as Columbus ordered them to remain in the beached ships and buildings that had been erected. Food was still being brought by the natives, but in diminishing amounts as the Spaniards ate more than ten times the amount the natives ate.

The fields the natives planted, weeded, and harvested were not able to support both groups, and they began to put food away for the winter for themselves.

Stirred up by Francisco de Porras, the captain of the ship the

Santiago, and his brother, Diego Porras, the crown representative and comptroller of the expedition, a mutiny was formed, and forty-eight of the one hundred or so men remaining on the island with Columbus joined the uprising.

Many questions were asked of the brothers by the men, and were answered with themselves being the ones who would benefit the most. Storming into the room of the Capitana in which Columbus laid in bed suffering from an arthritic condition, the Porras brothers asked Columbus why, while the ships were still floating, were they not headed to Hispaniola?

Not admitting that the ships were taking on more water through the holes below deck, and that it would have led to all of them drowning as they tried crossing many miles of roiling sea, they kept on saying that they would take the ten dugout canoes and head for Hispaniola, but after they left in the canoes, with native Indians doing the rowing, they quickly found out that good weather never lasts long on an ocean.

As they rowed eastward the winds sent them backward, and finally the attempt was given up. They had arrived at another landing on Jamaica, and began walking back to Santa Gloria to rejoin Columbus. They began abusing the native tribes as they walked toward Santa Gloria, and upon their arrival there, they did not join the group loyal to Columbus, but set up a camp nearby.

Months passed, and the food that was being brought to Columbus and his group that had remained loyal to him was reduced by the native villages, as the crops were not enough to feed their own people and Columbus too.

A strange thought came to Christopher as he was thinking how he could increase the loyalty of the native villages and perhaps bring additional loyalty from his group as well. Remembering one of the books he had brought with him, one called "Ephemedes" which included predictions of upcoming eclipses, he read that in three days' time, on the night of February 29th, 1504, a total eclipse of the moon would occur.

He sent an Indian messenger to the chiefs of the villages of the area requesting a meeting with them on the day of the predicted eclipse. Admonishing them for the diminishing amount of food they were bringing, he told them the God of the Spaniards was upset and the God of the Spaniards rewards the good and punishes the bad. To illustrate, Columbus told them the men who rebelled and tried to leave by canoes were kept from leaving the island, and had come back in defeat.

As for the natives, he pointed out how negligent they had become in bringing provisions to the faithful, and how that evening the God of the Spaniards would begin to punish the native population for their negligence.

He spoke of the rising of the moon as bloody and inflamed.

The chiefs left the meeting, some with disbelief, and others scared, but all willing to wait and see. As the moon rose, with the natives all watching, they returned to Columbus with fear in their eyes, willing to improve their care of the Spaniards, bringing food with them as they implored Columbus to intercede for them.

As the eclipse was at its peak of hiding the moon, Columbus did get down on a knee, and his words spoken to God were two-fold, one thanking God for the eclipse and the other for the fear the eclipse put into the natives. Columbus had accurately calculated the beginning and ending times of the eclipse to fit within the time during which the fear of the natives rose within them through the time to gather foods to bring to Columbus, to the time they asked Columbus to request God to return the moon to its regular appearance.

After he had shown them the humility offered to God, they believed Columbus had great powers to make great things happen.

The fantastic voyage by Diego Mendez, and the message and request of Columbus, raised curiosity in Ovando, the governor of Hispaniola, so he sent a very small caravel to Santa Gloria captained by Diego de Escobar, a man who had been a rebel under Roldan. That captain brought a message from Diego Mendez that he had been successful in reaching Hispaniola, but had not been able to purchase a ship to sail to Santa Gloria.

He was hoping one would become available soon. Columbus had just time enough to write a short note to the governor, thanking him for the courtesy of letting him know of the success of the voyage by Diego Mendez's journey, and hoping for the help of God and the governor.

Diego de Escobar dropped off some wine and a slab of salt pork before departing that evening—leaving behind all of the homesick Spaniards.

Ovando undoubtedly hoped that Columbus would have been found dead, which would leave his position as governor safe. The men in the camp of the Porras brothers had not seen the caravel approach the camp of Columbus, so were not aware of its arrival and departure.

Columbus told the men who were with him at Santa Gloria that he had chosen to stay with them until a ship could be found by Mendez to transport all of them back to Hispaniola. This calmed the loyal men at Santa Gloria, and Columbus tried to get the rebels who had gone with the Porras brothers to acquiesce and rejoin the group loyal to him. He sent some salt pork to their camp, but the brothers began asking for more food and clothing, more space on the rescue ship when it would arrive, and other favors.

The messenger got so disgusted, he returned to Columbus with the rebels close behind. A fight took place with the loyalists winning, capturing Francisco de Porras, putting him in chains, a few were killed, and others injured. Most of the fighting was done by swords, so there were many sliced bodies.

Meanwhile Diego Mendez awaited the arrival of ships from Spain, as Ovando would not allow him to use any of the caravels in the Santo Domingo port for a rescue mission. Three ships arrived, one of which Mendez was able to charter.

He outfitted and provisioned the ship under the command of Diego de Salcedo, who had been a loyal servant of Columbus.

Mendez boarded a different ship bound for Spain, with the letters Columbus had written to the king and queen, padre Gorricio, and Don Diego, his son who was by this time part of the queen's bodyguard, as had been ordered by Columbus. Salcedo steered his ship to Santa Gloria, picking up the one hundred Spaniards left alive there, and headed back to Santo Domingo, but the ship began to leak badly.

The voyage was against the wind, and had to put into port at Puerto Brazil, then Beata Island, where Christopher wrote a thank you letter to Ovando. Finally reaching Santo Domingo on August 13th, 1504, Ovando made great pretense of joy at seeing Christopher, inviting him to his home, but setting the Porras brothers free.

Another ship was chartered, and Christopher, Bartholomew, and Ferdinand Columbus were boarded, and they sailed back to Spain departing Santo Domingo on September 12th, along with twenty-two other passengers. Most of the men who sailed on Columbus's fourth voyage chose to remain in Santo Domingo, having had enough sailing for a while. Some of those later became the first settlers of Puerto Rico.

The voyage that the Columbus family took had many troubles on their way to Spain. On October 9th the mainmast broke into four pieces. Between the three members of the Columbus family, they built a jury mast from the longest piece, braced it well with the other bits, and that was enough to get them to port at Sanlucar de Barrameda on November 7th, 1504. Queen Isabella was on her deathbed, so no summons to her bedside was offered Christopher.

No opportunity to offer her any of the golden gadgets he was able to bring back with him. No opportunity to complain of the indignities he suffered at the hands of Ovando, the mutiny led by the treasurer and his brother, Diego and Francisco Porras, nor the many perils the entire expedition suffered during the four years of the voyage. None of that mattered to the people closest to the king and queen.

Why be bothered by the tales of the old seaman?

Queen Isabella died on November 26th, 1504, dismissing any chance for Christopher to be recognized for his accomplishments he had made essentially in her name. She had always believed in him, had backed him with her own money, and had consoled him in his adversity. King Ferdinand's ideas of royal policy left him with no place for sentiment.

Ovando was sending back to Spain much gold from Hispaniola, and public sentiment had little love for the man who had been sent back to Spain in chains for being too harsh on misbehaving Spaniards and rebel natives.

However, Christopher was well taken care of by the ten percent of the wealth that he had sent to the royals for safe keeping, as well as the wealth Ovando was sending from Hispaniola. Christopher was too sick to attend the funeral of Queen Isabella, and lived the rest of his life in a hired house in the parish of Santa Maria, Seville, Spain.

On May 20th, 1506, Christopher, surrounded by family and friends, heard a Mass, received Communion, said a prayer, and died from a heart attack at the age of 55.

There is no doubt that Christopher Columbus was deeply religious, but ruthless.

Chapter 2—Vasco Nunez de Balboa & Juan Ponce de Leon

1493-1513

DURING THE FOUR voyages of Christopher Columbus, other adventure and wealth-seeking Portuguese and Spaniards left Portugal and Spain to travel to the "new world" they called New Spain.

Columbus had found and declared for Spain the place they called Hispaniola, now known as Santo Domingo, of the Dominican Republic. Juan Ponce de Leon, having been noble-born, and having been a successful soldier when the men of Spain defeated the Islam Moorish armies in early 1492, would have been seeking fame and fortune after the war was won.

He accompanied Columbus on his second voyage, arriving in Hispaniola late in 1493, after having stopped for a short time at Anasco Bay on the western coast of Puerto Rico. Having had the opportunity to have seen the rich soil, the gently rolling hills, and the limestone available for building great homes, de Leon may have developed the plan of returning to Puerto Rico one day, to withdraw from this island the natural wealth it contained.

During his time in Hispaniola, Ponce de Leon remained in the Spanish army as a captain under the command of Nicolas de Ovando, who had been named royal commissioner of that land. De Leon's bravery, courage, and leadership suppressed an Indian uprising. He was rewarded by Ovando by being given a land grant and being named the governor of an eastern province of Espanola called Higuey.

The horrible sounds of battle, the explosions from cannon and muskets, the twang as arrows left bows and crossbows, the clash of lances, swords and knives hitting and tearing flesh, separating bones, and the screams and shouts of terror as these weapons of war injured or killed the adversaries; for the first time ever, neighing of horses being ridden toward the native warriors who had never seen horses before were heard by native people.

As these battles ended, the cries of the injured or dying left an indelible mark on those who fought the wars, be they victors or vanquished. Surrendering lives or taking lives is a haunting experience, then or now. As governor of Higuey, Ponce de Leon used the natives as field hands in agriculture, as miners in the gold mines he founded, as well as personal servants to his family and other Spanish gentry.

Seeking other worlds to conquer including riches that might be claimed in them, he remained in Espanola until 1508, when he set out with the approval of Ovando to explore other lands, eventually returning to, and with purpose to, investigate the island of San Juan Bautista, now known as Puerto Rico.

Having heard of great riches to be found on the island of San Juan Bautista, he led an army of one hundred soldiers transported aboard one ship on an expedition to that island, establishing a settlement called Caparra, on August 8th, 1508. Building homes there and assigning men to watch over the settlement, he returned to Spain in 1509, seeking King Ferdinand II's authority to be named governor of Puerto Rico, which he received.

Upon his return to Puerto Rico, he found the settlement of Caparra overrun and deserted, as the native people had risen up, killing or setting to flee the remaining Spanish residents. He immediately began building a new community nearby, which is now called San Juan, Puerto Rico. During the five years of his residency on Puerto Rico, Ponce de Leon used Puerto Rican natives as slaves, working in the fields planting, weeding, and harvesting crops, and working in the gold mines he discovered on that island, as well as utilizing servants for himself and other Spanish gentry.

In 1511, there was an uprising, possibly caused by one of de Leon's captains, a Cristobal de Sotomayor, and much warfare took place until the Spaniards were again the winners. A strange story about this warfare was a dog which could smell the difference between a friendly and an enemy Indian, but the dog was finally killed by the enemy Indians.

Also in 1512, de Leon was replaced by another governor, Diego Colon, brother of Christopher Columbus, allowing de Leon to become anxious for other adventures. Returning to Spain at the invitation of King Ferdinand II after he was replaced as governor of Puerto Rico, he came under the good graces of the king, who gave him permission to find other places he could bring under the banner of New Spain.

Hurrying back to Hispaniola, he waited for word of new places to sail to with the intention of winning a new governorship. Then in 1513, Ponce de Leon heard the legend of a fountain of youth to be found in Florida, thought to be an island at that time, but is now the state of Florida. Gathering an army and ships with which to travel the relatively short distance from Puerto Rico to Florida, Ponce de Leon first landed on a beach near the present city of Saint Augustine, in eastern Florida. He established that settlement, calling it Saint Augustine, which over time became the oldest of any continually lived-in settlement by Europeans in North America. Only the Native American settlement of Oraibi in northeastern Arizona precedes that settlement, as it was established during the 1100 AD time frame, and continually lived-in until recently when the Hopi people who lived there gave up the village for modern conveniences such as electricity, running water and toilets.

Ponce de Leon never found the legendary and mythical fountain of youth, despite many years of searching. On his voyage to return to Spain he sailed through the Bahamas, along the east and west coasts of Florida, and as far west in the Gulf of Mexico to became the discoverer of the Yucatan Peninsula, which became part of the great empire of Mexico. In 1520 he returned to Florida, where he was fatally injured in combat, then taken back to Cuba where he died in 1521.

Another vastly-known man of that time in history was Vasco Nunez de Balboa. Born in approximately 1475 in the area of Castile, Spain, and being related to Bernal Diaz de Castillo through the Nunez family, he grew to be a man seeking fame and fortune in the name of the Spanish Queen Isabella and King Ferdinand. He set off from Spain in 1500 on a ship commanded by a captain named Rodrigo de Bastidas, arriving in Hispaniola later that year.

Given a land grant to live on and farm, he was a complete failure at farming, owing everyone from whom he borrowed money. As these lenders began foreclosures on his property, he wrapped himself in a container that was deposited in the hold of a ship captained by a man by the name of Enciso in the port of Santo Domingo. That ship was going to transport reinforcements for the Spanish colony on the Gulf of Darien.

Balboa was discovered as a stowaway, but when Enciso found the port to which he was to deliver the provisions and reinforcements deserted, Enciso didn't know what to do or where to go. He listened wisely to Balboa, who had overheard the talk of two sailors who had been at the deserted port, saying that the western side of the gulf was inhabited by natives that did not use poisoned arrows or darts.

There, Enciso founded the settlement of Darien in 1510. Enciso sailed back to Spain, leaving Balboa in charge. Balboa made friends with the chief of the tribe who lived in the area of Darien, and married the chief's daughter. The tribe was helpful in supplying much of what the settlement needed, and even brought as much as four thousand ounces of gold to Balboa. As the gold was being weighed, a son of the chief broke into the group who were weighing the gold and broke the scale.

The son screamed at the Spaniards saying that Christians only wanted the gold to ingratiate themselves and the king of Spain. If that is all they want they should go over the mountains to the south where the large ships of other people sail or are rowed. That is also where the great waters are.

Balboa followed the son's directions southward, scaling the series of mountains before entering the Isthmus of Panama, and was the first European to see the Pacific Ocean. He had taken one hundred ninety soldiers and several hundred native guides and porters with him in September, 1513. These natives used machetes to cut open the pathway through the tropical rain forest.

It was a great sight to see this huge expanse of water, and as the men made their way back to Darien, a new governor had been appointed and was also on his way there. He was a barbarian, Pedrarias, who shortly after his arrival, treated the natives cruelly, incarcerated Balboa, charged him with treason and murder, and sentenced him and four of his companions to be beheaded.

This sentence was carried out.

About the year of 1525, Pedrarias left Darien, and it returned to its earlier state of uninhabitable jungle.

Chapter 3—Hernandez de Cordova, Juan de Grijalva and Bernal Diaz del Castillo

1514 to 1517

THE BIRTH OF a boy to the family of a magistrate named Francisco Diaz Del Castillo and his wife, Maria Diez Rejon, took place in Medina del Campo, Spain in 1492. His name became Bernal Diaz del Castillo of Medina del Campo of Castille, a soldier who was to write the early history of Mexico in the "new world."

He was the second-born son of that family, which meant that he was not willed the fortune, nor title, accumulated by his father. As second-born son, his life was an option between a religious life as a priest, or as a soldier for his country of Spain. His ambition and courage sent him to schools where he excelled in reading and writing, becoming infatuated with the fiction of that time.

This led him to a military career and becoming part of the expeditionary forces sent to the new world in 1514 under the command of Pedro Arias de Avila, the newly appointed governor of Darien. A few months after their arrival at Darien, many people were sickened and many died. A dispute between Arias, the governor, and his son-in-law, with the governor fearing an uprising, led to his son-in-law having his throat cut along with some of his top officers.

Diego Velasquez, governor of Cuba, was a kinsman to Bernal Diaz del Castillo, and so Bernal decided to request permission to sail to Cuba, which he received, and he sailed off to join Diego later in 1514. He was greeted warmly by Diego, given land on which to live and given a promise of native slaves when they became available. Upon three years passing by without the benefit of slaves, Bernal joined a group of men who were also without slaves.

That group was headed by Francisco Hernandez de Cordova, a man well suited to lead an army of discovery and conquest. Upon requesting the permission for this venture from Diego Velasquez, Cordova was granted permission with the request that, upon conquering the natives, they were to bring some as slaves to Velasquez, to be given to residents for their use. Knowing that this was against the teachings of the Catholic Church, that request was declined by Cordova.

As Velasquez was fearful that the men might mutiny, he helped pay and outfit one of three ships on which the group sailed. A priest, Alonso Gonzales, agreed to accompany them, along with a man whose job it was to collect for the king's benefit one-fifth of all valuables the group was to acquire.

The group left a northern port of Cuba on February 8th, 1517 sailing past Cape San Antonio, turning westward and reaching an uncharted land after twenty-one days. Approaching the land, the captain of the two ships that drew the least water watched for rocks or anything that might hinder the ship from movement forward or aft. The people on board saw a large town located about two leagues from the shoreline, a town the size of which had not been seen since leaving Spain.

Several very large canoes, able to accommodate as many as forty people, were rowed out toward the two closest ships, with the people appearing to be receptive to seeing the white faces on board. The natives wore woven shirts and small bands around their waists. The people on board the three ships waved toward the natives as they approached. The natives were welcomed aboard and given small gifts of colored beads and woven colored cloth, for which they appeared appreciative.

As they walked around the ship looking at things they had never seen before, and through their excited talk, although not understood by the sailors and soldiers on the boat, it was easy to see they were impressed. Through hand and body motions, they invited the crew and soldiers on the ships to come into their village before they left the ships. The following morning, the natives brought out to the ships some smaller canoes, and the chief who rode in the leading canoe kept shouting, "cones catoche", so Cordova named that landing as Cape Catoche. As the Spaniards learned later, "cones catoche", meant "come to my houses."

Seeing the friendly gestures and smiling faces, the smaller boats were lowered from the ships and the sailors and soldiers slid into them, while some slipped into the canoes. As they approached the shore many of the natives, men, women and children lined the shallow water. Waiting for the chief to lead, the men followed him toward a large thicket of woods behind which a large number of warriors appeared and began shooting arrows toward the sailors and soldiers.

The soldiers had taken their guns with them, and the cold steel of their swords killed about fifteen of the native attackers before the noise and the effects of the guns sent the natives fleeing for their lives. Their arrows, lances, and stones from their slings injured about fifteen of the men from the ships, but as the natives fled, the men from the boats saw the adobe homes in the village and began to search them for gold or other valuables.

They found a few items made of inferior gold and copper, with a number of ceramic idols of their gods inside wooden boxes. Also, two prisoners were captured and taken to the boats, where they began learning Spanish so they could act as interpreters. Later on, after they were baptized, one was named Julian and the other Melchior.

After everyone was aboard, the ships set sail westward along the coastline for fifteen days, at which time the fresh water supply needed to be resupplied. A landing place was spotted, and the two ships with the lightest draw carefully drew into the lagoon, from where a village was seen, with a pool of fresh water in the front of the village. The men sent out to get fresh water were protected by soldiers with guns and swords, but there was no need for them to use the weapons as some of the people of the village came out to welcome them, asking what they were looking for.

Some called out, “Castilan,” but the men were not familiar with the sounds of the native voices and did not understand what they were trying to communicate. The natives indicated by gestures for the men to follow them into the village, and this time they were very friendly. Then, as the men entered the village, many women and children mixed in with the sailors and soldiers, making them feel more comfortable. Suddenly, ten men emerged from one of the buildings, most likely the building in which the high priests of their religion lived. Their heads were matted with blood, so much it could not be combed out unless cut, and they brought incense out to fumigate the men, and through their actions, threatened the men to leave the island before the fires they had set in front of the men burned out, or they would be attacked.

The men marched back to the area where the water casks had been laid, loaded the casks and entered the small boats, rowing out to the ships. They set sail again to the west and it was six days before a bad storm washed over them for a period of four days before subsiding.

Again, the three ships sailed west, looking for another area where they could refill the water casks, as the casks were leaky, and the storm had the ships pitching and rolling leading to spillage. The ships came upon a bay with a native town about a mile from the shoreline, and there was a river running into the ocean.

The ships could not get too close to the shore, but anchored about a half mile out. The small boats were lowered and all of the men jostled among themselves trying to become the first to board so that they could walk on solid ground again. Rowing to the river outlet, the men noticed with alarm a large number of native archers, men with lances and shields, some with large double-edged swords, and others carrying slings and stones, all marching behind men carrying banners with feathered crests.

By sign language motions and shouting words the men from the ships could not understand, they seemed to be asking if the ships had come from the east, and the men gestured in agreement. The natives turned and marched back into their town. Not knowing whether this action by them meant good or bad things, the men of the ships decided to spend the night on the beach rather than rowing back to the ships.

They filled the water casks and set them near to the small boats, and slept fitfully that night. In the morning, with great noise from whistles, banging of drums, and continuous shouting, a much larger group of natives, armed as before, surrounded the men from the ships and began shooting the arrows and stones into the circle of men who were outnumbered by as many as two hundred to one.

The arrows pierced many bodies in areas their armor did not cover, not once but many times, but not all injuries were life threatening. Fifty of the soldiers were killed on that field of battle, but the rest used their guns, and, as the encirclement closed in, their swords, to open a pathway through the encirclement toward the small boats, and were able to escape.

A decision was made by the ships' captains and Cordova to scuttle one of the ships before returning to Cuba, as some of the injured sailors could not perform their duties, and Cordova had been hit by ten arrows, and almost every person who had been on the beach had been hit multiple times. The water casks had been left behind, so it was dry sailing all the way back to Cuba.

A few days later, as they sailed eastward, five of the men who had been hit by arrows in their exposed necks were given a burial at sea. On the way to Cuba, one of the ships sprang a leak, and although the pumps pumped out some of the water, it was decided that a closer port would be in Florida, as one of the ship's captain had been with Ponce de Leon when he discovered Florida.

The two remaining boats sailed to Florida, where temporary repairs were done on the leaking boat, and then the two were sailed to Cuba. Landing in the port now known as Havana, Cordova went to the land which had been given to him when he first arrived in Cuba, but died from his wounds just ten days after arriving there. The rest of the men reported to Diego Velasquez, who was happy to get the gold and other booty the group had taken, and immediately arranged another fleet of four ships to return to the lands that Cordova had discovered with hopes of receiving more gold and other items of worth, including slaves.

Another group of sailors and soldiers were outfitted under the command of Juan de Grijalva as captain general, with three other Spaniards captaining their ships which they outfitted with their own money. Bernal Diaz Del Castillo was assigned to be the ensign for this endeavor. Two hundred forty men who were without Indian slaves signed on, having heard of all of the valuables that might be had from this sailing.

All of the men who signed on also paid what they could for additional guns, ammunition, food, and trinkets with which to barter with the people whom they were to meet. The fleet set sail on April 8th, 1518 heading due west, but because of the winds, the fleet ended near the south shore of the island of Cozumel.

As the fleet passed by on the southern shore, a town was spotted, near which a good anchorage free from reefs offered a good place to stop. Grijalva led a large group composed of both sailors and soldiers to shore, but found that the natives had all run away to hide after seeing the ship under sail, something they had never seen before.

As Grijalva walked toward the town, two old men hidden in the field of maize were brought to him by one of the sailors. With the help of the two Indians, Julian and Melchior, who had been taken from their village during Cordova's earlier venture and then baptized and educated to the Spanish language, the two men were told to bring their chief to speak with Grijalva, but after they left, they did not return.

While waiting for the chief, an attractive native woman appeared and began speaking in the language of the islands of Jamaica and Cuba, which Bernal and several others of the group understood.

She told them that the residents were scared and had fled into the woods. She was asked to contact the people of the village and ask them to come to meet the Spaniards, but after she had talked with the people, none were willing to meet the men. The woman was taken out to the ships and sailed with them.

Eight days later, the ships approached Champoton, the village at which the natives had surrounded and mortally attacked and killed fifty of the soldiers, as described earlier.

This time, the natives waited on the shore, feeling quite proud and confident that they could rain death upon the soldiers who were sent ashore with guns, crossbows, falconets (small birds that were trained to attack,) and lurchers (a wild attack dog.)

The natives put up a good fight, killing six soldiers, wounding Grijalva three times and over sixty of the men were wounded, but the natives were put to flight, entering the swamp behind the village, not to be seen again while the soldiers remained on land.

Unfortunately, one of the lurchers was left behind when it ran into the swamp and did not return. Having stayed three days at that town, and having found little in the way of value inside the homes, the group sailed away.

Many days later, after following the contour of the land, the four ships approached a river that opened to the ocean. The larger ships anchored in deeper water while the lighter ships were able to get closer before lowering boats for the soldiers and Julian and Melchior to approach the native warriors. Julian and Melchior relayed the message that the Spaniards were not there to attack them but had gifts to give them.

As they understood what had been told to them, four canoes

with thirty men in each approached the strip of land on which Grijalva and his men had landed. After seeing the beads offered them, the natives became friendlier, but warned that they had heard what had happened at the previous town, and had many more warriors ready to fight, and they were much braver and more ferocious than the natives the Spaniards had faced earlier.

The group spent the night on the beach, and the next morning the chief of that town, along with a number of other residents, came to the place where the group was camped. They brought mats on which they laid food, and some items made of lesser valuable gold, cloaks and skirts such as they wore, and jewelry—the total not being worth too much.

However, the challenge of meeting and introducing these native people to the outside world was extremely rewarding to Grijalva and his group. Through Julian and Melchior, Grijalva told the assembled natives that the Spaniards had a very powerful chief, and the natives should recognize the Spanish chief as their lord. They replied that they already had a chief, and since the Spaniards just arrived, they did not know their people yet.

The following day, the four ships cast off, and following the contour of the land they came to the mountains on which snow is found year around, now known as Edzna.

It was at that time that Grijalva decided to send word back to Diego Velasquez of the condition of the group and request help. Captain Pedro de Alvarado, captain of the ship called the San Sebastian, was chosen to return to Cuba with the message. He left for Cuba, with the men on his ship glad to return to a safer place. That ship delivered gold that amounted to an equivalent of sixteen thousand dollars to Diego Velasquez, who was very happy with the initial return on his money.

Continuing along the nearby shoreline, the now three ships came to another river that flowed into the ocean, and on the shore were many natives waving long poles with white cloths attached to the tops. Grijalva decided to send a group of soldiers under the command of Francisco de Montejo.

The group included Bernal Diaz del Castillo and Julian, the native translator. However, these native people spoke a language of Mexico, and Julian was unable to understand them. Through hand motions, de Montejo was able to ask them to bring gold with which to barter for the blue and green beads the natives craved.

After de Montejo had sent word to Grijalva that the people with whom he met were peaceful, Grijalva anchored the ships, and accompanied the remaining soldiers to the landing site, bringing a store of beads from the ships. Realizing that Grijalva was the chief of all of the Spaniards, the natives paid him the greatest respect.

Eventually the Spaniards learned that Montezuma, the high chief of all of Mexico, had learned of the defeats of the native villages by the Spaniards, the terrible weapons they carried, and decided that his position was in peril. It was his will that his people treat these new arrivals with great respect, giving them much gold, and trying to appease them from harming the great civilization he had assembled.

This, then, was the beginning of the end of the great Aztec civilization that had overthrown the Mayan civilization seven hundred years before. A legend told to the Spaniards was that their arrival in this land had been foretold by a native high priest many years before, and that their arrival and conquest of these people had been widely announced and expected.

It was their pride and honor that made them fight for their land and lives. After six days of eating and trading, Grijalva pronounced the land to be part of New Spain by planting a Spanish flag, and began re-boarding the ships prepared to sail further into Mexico. Picking one of the men from the native tribe, they took him along, teaching him the Spanish language, baptizing him and changing his name to Francisco, expecting him to become another interpreter for the Spaniards.

The Grijalva expedition continued on for another month, stopping to exchange the beads for gold, getting additional fresh foods and water, but they approached a very wild current near a river which turned one of the ships into a set of rocks, damaging the ship.

As the group repaired the ship, natives from a town upriver brought food, and other things of worth including gold to the men of the ships. After the repairs were completed, the decision was made to turn around and head back to Cuba to turn in the valuables they had collected for Diego Velasquez and King Ferdinand, and divide the rest between the investors and themselves.

The amount of gold returned with this later delivery to Velasquez was equivalent to approximately four thousand dollars.

However, the axes that had been traded to the Spaniards, who thought they were made of low grade gold turned out to be copper, and had corroded. The men who had traded for the axes were roundly laughed at, and made fun of.

Chapter 4—Hernandez Cortes de Monroy and Bernal Diaz del Castillo

1518-1521

THE NEXT NAME of importance to that time period was don Hernan Cortes de Monroy, whose mother's last name was Pizarro, which made Cortes a second cousin to Francisco Pizarro, the later conqueror of Peru.

As a child, Cortes was sickly, and his parents sent him away to an uncle in Salamanca to learn Latin with the hopes of him becoming a lawyer. After two years, he returned to his parents' home, and since the legends and stories of the great wealth to be had in the "new world" were circulating, preparations were made that he join a family acquaintance and distant relative, Nicolas de Ovando, the newly appointed governor of Hispaniola, in sailing across the ocean.

However, Cortes suffered an injury preventing him from sailing with that group. He wandered around for two years before arranging passage on a ship commanded by Alonso Quintero in 1504, arriving in Hispaniola that same year. He became a citizen which entitled him to property and slaves, and within a short period of time was appointed notary in a nearby town.

In 1511, the young Cortes was an ambitious soldier who accompanied Velasquez, and after arriving in Cuba, took command of the troops and conquered the indigenous people there which led to an appointment of being clerk to the treasurer of Cuba, then called part of "New Spain."

With this position, he was responsible for assuring that the king of Spain received one fifth of all taxes collected from the assets of the island. As time wore on, Cortes worked his way upward in the political chain to where he became the magistrate of Santiago, and eventually strained relations between Velazquez and himself.

Stories of the riches to be found in the area we now call Mexico were quite numerous, enticing Velazquez to move toward the conquest of that area. Because of the successes of Grijalva, the men who were interested in becoming a part of this new expedition were much in favor of having Grijalva be the captain general again.

However, there were other men high in the politics of Cuba who made a pact with Cortes, and put pressure on Velasquez to appoint Cortes as captain general. They would supply money for the expedition in the name of Cortes, but would expect a large portion of his rewards from the trip on his return.

Velasquez appointed Cortes to head the expedition, not thinking that collecting six ships, three hundred fifty soldiers, and all of the supplies, could be accomplished as quickly as Cortes did in one month. In between all of the preparations, Cortes married the sister-in-law of Velazquez, which did nothing to make matters better. On the evening of April 7th, 1518, Cortes, and many of his important investors met with Velasquez, sharing many good wishes and embraces.

The following morning, after having attended Mass, the Cortes flotilla left port. As Velazquez moved to take the command away from Cortes, he ignored the orders and put out to sea with his group beginning the conquest of Mexico on April 8th, 1518.

The first port of call was Trinidad where a number of additional men joined the group, one of whom was Alonzo de Avila, a former captain of one of Grijalva's ships. More ships and people were added, as Cortes enlisted many well-to-do people from around that port. Also, horses were purchased at high prices, as they had been brought from Spain on past shipments. A ship owned by Juan Sedeno, a settler of Havana, laden with cassava bread and salt pork, landed near the ten ships already in Cortes's fleet, and Cortes bought the ship and its contents with credit, and Sedeno and his ship were added to the fleet.

After ten days in the port of Trinidad, during which time the blacksmiths made head pieces for protection from arrows, spears, or swords, the soldiers polished their armor and crossbowmen made arrows. All preparations had been made and sails were set to leave the harbor.

The next stop was Havana, where there were more men that were to join the group. However, the flagship ran aground on the way there, and had to lighten its load before floating clear, and the gear had to be reloaded, causing a delay in its arrival in Havana. The group was anxious for Cortes to join them and lead them to the riches for which they all had joined. He rejoined them six days after the main fleet had landed.

And it was there that Cortes assigned the captains and divided the horses among the ships so that his flagship and the lighter ships which could approach landings in shallow waters would have a horse aboard. A messenger had been sent to Havana by Velasquez, telling Cortes to relinquish his command, but the messenger was convinced by the many politically-connected people who had joined and sailed with Cortes, that they wanted Cortes to be their captain general.

The fleet left Havana after Cortes had instructed two of the vessels to sail north along the coast toward Cozumel, one containing seventy soldiers, while the other ship searched for more food, which would be needed later in the voyage. The ship containing the seventy soldiers ignored the orders of Cortes to wait for the fleet to assemble before landing at Cozumel.

Upon the ship and soldiers arriving there, they found all of the natives had seen them coming and had left the town. The soldiers entered the buildings in the deserted town, taking anything of worth with them. They followed a path to an adjacent town, again finding it deserted, with the exception of a woman and two men of the village hiding in the woods. They found fowls left behind by the retreating townspeople and brought them to the first town, and sat down for a feast.

Upon the arrival of Cortes, the captain and pilot of the ship that had ignored his order were put in chains, the items that had been taken from the buildings in both towns were set aside for return to the natives, and the interpreter, Melchior, requested that the two men and the woman contact the people of the two villages, asking them to come back to accept some of the beads, Spanish shirts, and other trinkets in exchange for gold.

Cortes had cautioned the entire garrison that the native people were not to be bothered in any way, and that all of the stolen goods would be returned to them, along with beads, little bells, and Spanish shirts to pay for the fowl eaten by the men of the ship that had arrived before the rest.

The following day, the people of the villages did arrive, moving among the sailors and soldiers as if they had known them for their entire lives. This was the first opportunity where Cortes was able to bring the natives and the members of his group together without fights breaking out.

After three days of being in Cozumel, Cortes took a complete inventory of all ships, men, all of the horses, guns, crossbows and arrows, the food and water supplies. There were five hundred eight soldiers, without the shipmasters, pilots, and sailors, eleven large and small ships, plus a small launch carrying supplies, and the people manning the ships numbered one hundred. There were thirty-two crossbowmen and thirteen musketeers, eight large brass cannons, plenty of balls and powder, four falconets, sixteen horses and mares, and the attack dogs, all fit for sport or chargers.

Because of talk among the group about the expected next landing, the shouts of the natives upon seeing the Grijalva group, "Castilans, Castilans" became a point the group puzzled about, with

Cortes telling Melchior to ask the native chiefs if they knew of any other Spaniards in the area. The chiefs admitted that a town two days inland from where they lived did have two Spaniards that had been captured in that previous landing, and were made slaves.

Cortes then sent out two of the native chiefs to the village to bargain for the release of the two Spaniards. Gifts of beads and bells were sent to pay for their release. One of the captured men was happy to return to his people, while the other man said that he was married with three children, had been tattooed on face, limbs, and body, had been appointed as a sub-chief in that town, and would not be accepted by the Spaniards if he were to return. He chose to remain in that town. The chiefs and the man who had been released by the chief he was serving as a slave returned to the place where Cortes and the group had landed, but by then the group had left, so the man who had chosen to return to Spanish life began his walk back toward the town in which he was a slave.

The fleet was ready to move on, and Cortes commissioned two of the captains to leave the anchorage early and proceed to the area of Campeche, but not to enter. On the way, one of the ships carrying the cassava bread began sinking. That ship was escorted back to Cozumel for repairs. That is also where they met the one Spaniard who wanted to rejoin Spanish life, his name being Aguilar. He had not gone too far toward his old town before he was found and brought back to Cortes.

As he approached the men of the fleet, he could not be recognized as a Spaniard because he had been exposed to the sun, browning his body, his hair had been cut similar to the natives of the area, and his speech had become slurred due to not having spoken Spanish for so long. He was happy to be accepted by the men of the fleet.

After repairs were done to the ship that had been sinking, the fleet sailed once more toward Campeche, but due to stormy weather, they anchored outside of Tabasco. Observing more than twelve thousand native warriors waiting on the shore for the

Spaniards to disembark from their ships, Cortes did not waver in his commitment to conquer the land and its people.

Canoes approached the ships, and although the interpreter, Melchior, told them that they had come in peace, the chiefs of many villages had convinced the chiefs of Tabasco and the surrounding towns to fight these people who came to take their land and lives from them. Canoes began to surround the ships closest to the entrance to the town, and showers of arrows were directed toward the men in the ships.

Cortes had sent a group of crossbowmen out during the night to a pathway leading from a palm grove to the town, and although it was a longer way to enter, that group eventually joined the larger group that had slipped into the water led by Cortes, advancing toward the shore step-by-step.

The noise from the guns fired by the Spaniards, the screaming and hollering, the drums, and shrill whistling of the natives seemed to shake the whole world as the two armies battled. With guns, crossbow arrows, and swords slashing at any and all natives as they retreated slowly, not turning their backs on the Spaniard soldiers, the town was gradually taken by the soldiers. There were many casualties on both sides, but when a great hall was taken with many idols inside, the natives ran from the town into the woods surrounding the town.

A halt was ordered as Cortes had attained the great hall which held the idols that these natives worshipped, and following the natives into unknown woods may have endangered his soldiers and used firepower that might be needed later. Cortes drew his sword and made three cuts into a large tree indicating that he had taken possession of that land in the name of His Majesty, the king, and would defend it against any attackers. All of the witnesses, soldiers, sailors, and men sent by the government to oversee such activities, as well as the priest, were present to see the act adding their approval.

Cortes, being a very capable statistician as well as an

accomplished commander of fighting and sailing forces, took an accounting of his fighting men, finding that fourteen Spanish soldiers had been wounded, and eighteen natives had been killed. The soldiers and the officers slept in the large community square of the village with guards and sentries on the alert.

The next morning, Cortes sent out Pedro de Alvarado in command of one hundred soldiers, fifteen with guns and crossbows, to examine the interior of the country, two leagues deep. He told Pedro to take Melchior with him, but Melchior had taken flight with the natives, leaving his Spanish clothes behind. Cortes also sent Francisco de Lugo with one hundred more soldiers, twelve with guns and crossbows, in a different direction with the same orders. As Francisco advanced with his troops, they were met by a great many native archers carrying lances and shields, raining showers of arrows into the Spanish soldiers.

The Spaniards were quickly surrounded, and attacked mercilessly. A certain Indian who had accompanied Francisco's troops ran back toward Cortes's campsite, asking for immediate help. Pedro's troops had come to a creek that presented a problem to crossing, and had taken a detour that led close to where he heard the gunfire of Francisco's troops, and the noise of the battle brought his troops running to help Francisco.

This additional firepower did offer Francisco's troops an orderly retreat along with Pedro's troops toward the campsite of Cortes, only to find that area being attacked as well. Having the entire group of soldiers fighting from that position, the battle turned toward the advantage of the Spaniards, and once again they put the natives to flight.

Taking another count, Cortes found that two of Francisco's soldiers were killed, and eight wounded. Pedro had three men wounded. There were fifteen natives killed and three captured, one being a chief. Aguilar, the Spaniard who had been the slave to one of the chiefs but had joined Cortes's group, was the interpreter in asking why the natives had attacked. He was told that Melchior, the traitor who had left the group and fled with the natives, had counselled the chiefs of the natives and told them to attack the Spaniards as they were few in number.

One of the captives was given some beads to take to the chiefs and bargain for their words of peace, but that captive never returned. Realizing that there would be more natives joining the group that would fight his soldiers, Cortes had the horses brought to shore, and readied for battle.

It took one day before horses had become used to dry land again, and all soldiers, healthy and injured, were armed and ready to defend themselves against the coming attack. The best horses and riders were paired, and formed a cavalry, with the horses outfitted with bells attached to their breastplates.

The cavalrymen were ordered to spear the attackers, aiming for their faces as they rode toward the native soldiers, with Cortes himself in the lead. Cortes ordered a captain by the name of Mesa to command the artillery, and a Diego de Ordas to command the foot soldiers, musketeers and bowmen.

After the entire Spanish force attended Mass, the army advanced toward the battlefield where Francisco's forces had been attacked. On the way, the horses were not able to cross a marshy area, and took a roundabout trail to the anticipated battlefield. As the foot-soldiers arrived, the native army had assembled and began their attack. They were so numerous that they surrounded the entire Spanish forces, showering them with arrows, javelins and stones, injuring over seventy men in their first rush.

Due to the good sword play by the foot-soldiers, the natives drew back to where their arrows, javelins and stones could damage the surrounded troops, but Mesa with cannons booming did much damage to the natives as they bunched together. It was suggested by Bernal Diaz to rush them as the swords had been the reason for their retreat, but just then Cortes and the horses entered the battle from the rear of the natives' troops, spearing and slashing them at will with their swords, riding through the great throng, and scaring them into a fast retreat.

The foot-soldiers attacked from the front, and the natives ran for their lives. They thought that the horse and rider were one animal, for they had never seen horses before. During that battle, two Spaniards were killed, and many were injured. Three horsemen were injured and five horses suffered small injuries.

From the fat of a dead native, the injuries to men and horses were seared and bound with cloths found in the town. Burying the two soldiers was the duty ordered by Cortes, and was carried out quickly by the sailors who had brought the horses in from the boats, and had remained on shore waiting to take the horses back to the boats. Checking the field of battle, there were eight hundred natives that had been killed, most by sword thrusts, some by cannon fire, musket fire, and crossbow arrows.

Five native prisoners were captured, two of them being chiefs. Returning to the town campsite, the men and horses were fed and given the rest they all had earned. Guards and sentries were posted, but the natives had enough fighting for the day and night, and the Spanish camp had a good rest.

The following day, Aguilar the interpreter spoke with the prisoners, and found the two captured chiefs to be fit persons to be released and sent as messengers to the other chiefs of the native towns that had joined the fight the day before.

He advised Cortes to release them and send them back with gifts of beads and bells, hoping that these men could sway the many natives to return to the Cortes encampment seeking friendship and peace. It was done as Aguilar had suggested, and as a result, fifteen slaves of the native chiefs brought fowls, baked fish, and maize cakes to the Spanish camp. Cortes greeted them graciously, but Aguilar berated them, telling them to return to their masters, and telling their masters to present themselves and bring gifts in return for the gifts the Spanish had sent to them.

They delivered the message to their chiefs and the next day thirty of the highest chiefs entered the camp bringing fowls, fish, fruit and maize cakes, and asked Cortes for permission to retrieve the bodies of their dead soldiers in order to burn and bury them. They added that otherwise the decaying flesh would stink, and burying them would protect the bodies from being eaten by mountain lions and jaguars.

Permission was granted and many natives who were waiting for their chiefs' orders began burning and burying their dead. The chiefs then asked to be excused as there were a great many other chiefs from other villages that were to meet at another place and talk over peace conditions between them and the Spanish.

They left in great haste, looking one more time toward the horses and cannons that were within the camp.

Cortes told the men standing around him...

> *The natives think that the horses are both animals and men. Bring the mare that dropped a foal near the stallion, so that the stallion smells the mare, and when the stallion gets excited and starts neighing, bring the two horses to me, and the natives will think that the horses are talking to me.*

The men began to bring the mare and the stallion near each other, and the two horses interacted just as Cortes had said. Also, Cortes had told Mesa, the captain of the artillery group, to load the largest cannon with a large ball and plenty of powder.

Later that day, forty of the top chiefs arrived at the camp, dressed in their best clothes, and through Aguilar, asked for forgiveness for making war upon the Spaniards. Cortes feigned anger toward them, asking them how many times he had asked for peace between them, and each time was rebuked by war.

This should have allowed the natives to be put to death, but since the Spaniards represented the great king of Spain, who was a believer in life and the great benevolent God, they would accept the meaningful words of the chiefs in their appeal for peace. Just then, the cannon was lit and the ball that emerged flew well over the hill outside the town, and the native chiefs cowered in fear.

Cortes told them it was okay, and that the cannon was angry, but through the discharge was temporarily appeased. Then the stallion was brought out to where it could smell the mare, and it reared-up, then pawed down, snorting and neighing as though angry, and again the chiefs cowered, while Cortes went to the animal, putting hands to its neck, and having the man in charge of the horses lead it away.

By that time the chiefs were anxious to go back to their people and tell them of the great power these Spaniards had over animals and weapons. Cortes spoke to them about how they must come again to discuss peace, and how the Spaniards might help the natives know of the true God that they represented. Before the chiefs left, thirty more natives brought food for the people of the camp, which was gratefully accepted by the men.

After the talks between Cortes and the chiefs ended, the chiefs returned to their people with the promise they would return the next day to work on the friendships leading to peace.

The following day, the chiefs and those of neighboring towns arrived, paid homage to all of the Spaniards, and brought gold of great value, quilted cloth, and twenty women, whom the men were very pleased by. One woman in particular was very beautiful and seemed to be very intelligent, for she was baptized, became a Christian, and was re-named Dona Marina.

Cortes was very happy to have seen what the chiefs had brought, taking them aside and speaking with them through Aguilar about the ideas he had for the town. He gave them thanks for the presents they brought, but there was one request that he wanted them to do, and that was to reoccupy the town with the men, women, and children that had lived there in the past.

This would indicate their acceptance of the friendship and peace he was offering them. He told them he wanted the people to return in two days, and that would be a sign of true peace. He also asked that they give up the idol worship and sacrifices they had been performing, and introduced a statue of Mother Mary holding baby Jesus, explaining their importance to the God they worshipped; that their religion was based on peace, and explaining that Jesus gave His life nailed to a wooden cross for all of the people who believed in Him.

The chiefs were so taken by the explanation they asked Cortes if they could keep the statue in their town. An altar was built on which the statue was placed, and overnight a large cross was built and erected next to the altar by one of the carpenters of the Spanish sailors.

Trees were cut and logs were arranged to form a shell around the altar and next to the cross, making it the first church building in that part of the world. A neighboring town asked for such a building and cross to be built for them, and the carpenters and other sailors helped to frame another building acting as a church with an altar.

As the injured regained their health, the horses were re-loaded onto the ships, the cannons restored to their places on the ships, and with the men going back to the ships they had been sailing on, it was time to move on. Sailing along the coastline heading west, the fleet passed by the towns that Grijalva had stopped at, and men who had been with Grijalva such as Bernal Diaz pointed them out to Cortes. Thus they passed by La Rambla, which the natives called Ayagualulco, Tonala which the Spaniards had named San Antonio, the entrance to the great river Coatzacoalcos, the lofty snow-capped mountains, and the Sierra of San Martin.

There were other locations that the soldiers who had sailed with Grijalva pointed out, such as Rio de Alvarado, where Pedro Alvarado's ship had entered, and Rio de Banderas, where trading had brought the Grijalva's expedition the sixteen thousand dollars' worth of gold.

Next were the Isla Blanca, Isla Verde, and the soldiers showed Cortes where the expedition found the Isla de Sacrificios at which they had found the altars and the remains of many victims of the native sacrificial ceremonies. But their goal was San Juan de Ulua which they approached just after mid-day on Holy Thursday, 1519.

One of the pilots who had sailed with Grijalva cautioned the heavier ships to anchor outside of the harbor as there were many rock formations just under the waterline that could damage the undersides of the ships.

After setting anchor, Cortes's flagship hoisted her royal standards and pennants, and shortly thereafter, two large canoes filled with Mexican natives rowed out to that ship, recognizing it was the ship of the leader of the expedition. As they approached the vessel several of the headmen requested permission to board, and since Dona Marina was aboard that ship and understood their language, they were permitted to board the ship.

They paid homage to Cortes, then announced that they were vassals of a great leader, Montezuma. Also, they had been sent to find out what kind of men the ships contained, what they wanted, and if they needed anything these native leaders could help them attain, they would help. Cortes welcomed them, telling them that he and his group offered no cause to worry, that they came to trade.

After offering them beads as presents, he also offered them food and wine, and speaking through the interpreters, Aguilar and Dona Marina, the chiefs were satisfied enough for them to depart the ship, rowing ashore and walking back into their town.

The following day, Good Friday, the men were sent ashore to set up a village of their own on the sand dunes, which overlooked the harbor. The cannons were provided areas from which they would have clear shots toward the native town, and the horses were provided a covered corral as the heat and sunlight were extreme.

Huts were constructed for the men, and an altar was set up for Masses each day. These arrangements were set up on Holy Saturday. On Easter morning, a procession of natives approached the Spanish village led by two well-dressed and seemingly important natives, followed by the chiefs who had been aboard Cortes's flagship, and many of the townspeople, men, women, and children.

All of the natives bowed toward Cortes, and then the men of his command, showing respect. All of them curiously looked at faces of the Spaniards, suddenly recognizing Dona Marina as a very important person in their eyes. They wondered aloud among themselves, "Why is she with these strangers?"

Cortes welcomed their entrance into the village of huts through the interpretation of Dona Marina, and asked they be seated while having the Mass be said for himself and his people. This was a strange but beautiful ceremony, with the priest garbed in colorful vestments, and the men and Dona Marina, standing, kneeling and sitting at various times on the sand in front of the table being used as an altar.

There appeared that no sacrifice was made, but the people appeared interested in what was being done and sung. After Mass had concluded, a dinner was prepared and shared by Spaniards and natives alike. Cortes and a few of his captains dined with the two native representatives of Montezuma, one named Tendile and the other Pitalpitoque, with Dona Marina interpreting for that group.

It was suggested by Cortes that Aguilar sit among the chiefs and other captains of the Spanish group, while the sailors, soldiers, and native people used signs as language between their two groups. The natives had brought food from their village, along with gifts of gold and cloth, which were given initially to Cortes, who in turn, gave the items to his captains for safekeeping, and handed out gifts to the natives, in order of importance—the two representatives of Montezuma first, the chiefs secondly, and the rest of the people lastly.

During the meal, Cortes explained to the two representatives of Montezuma that his group were Christians and vassals of the greatest lord on earth, who had many princes as his vassals and servants, and it was at his command that they came to this land, and mentioning that he had heard rumors about the country and the great prince who ruled it.

He went on to tell them that it was his intention to become friends with this prince, and tell him many things in the name of the lord that would greatly please Montezuma. He also told them of the advantages of trading with his people, and he hoped that Montezuma would suggest a place where they could meet and discuss important things.

One of the representatives, Tendile, told Cortes that his group had just arrived, and already requested a meeting with their prince, Montezuma. He presented a box to Cortes in the name of Montezuma, which, when opened, contained many articles of finely worked gold figures of animals. After Cortes had opened the box and seen the beautiful gifts it contained, Tendile called out to the chiefs standing nearby for them to bring to him ten loads of white cloth made of cotton and feathers, plus a large quantity of food. Cortes received the gifts in a gracious manner, and in return presented gifts of beads to the two representatives.

He then asked that they go to the surrounding villages and tell the people there to bring gold to trade for more beads as he had brought many beads from Spain, his homeland. The two representatives agreed to that request, whereupon Cortes ordered his men to bring an armchair, which was exquisitely carved and inlaid with stones of many intricate designs, a string of twisted glass beads packed in cotton scented with musk, and a crimson helmet with a golden medal of St. George on horseback, with lance in hand, slaying a dragon.

Cortes told the representatives to deliver the chair to prince Montezuma, so that he could be seated in it when he, Cortes, came to see and speak with him. Also, that Montezuma wear the helmet on his head, and that all of the gifts were from his lord, the king of Spain, as a sign of friendship. Cortes then asked that a day and place be named where he could meet with the great prince Montezuma. The two representatives agreed to take the gifts to Montezuma, ask him about a time and place for a meeting, and return with his reply.

The representatives had brought some artists with them when

they had arrived at the Spaniards' camp, and had begun painting pictures of Cortes, the captains, sailors, soldiers, horses, cannons, ships, Aguilar, and Dona Marina.

Even pictures of the two dogs were painted. The pictures showed the strengths of the manpower and weapons these strangers possessed. One of the artists noticed a soldier wearing a dented helmet which looked much like a helmet that was placed on one of their idols back in their capital, and brought it to the attention of the two representatives.

They asked Cortes if they could take the old helmet to Montezuma, and permission was granted. As another display of power, Cortes ordered the cannons be loaded with ball and extra powder in order to present the deafening roar when fired, and the horses and horsemen be prepared for an example of their ability to gallop on the shoreline so as not to get stuck in the sands of the sand dunes.

This demonstration was a huge success, amazing the natives with the speed and maneuverability of horses and riders. After the horses were taken away, Cortes called the natives to assemble near him and gave a wave of his hand as a signal to fire the cannon. The noise of the firing and the crashing of the ball landing among the trees beyond the sand dunes scared all of the natives, representatives, chiefs, and the serving people who had accompanied them.

These demonstrations left lasting memories for those who witnessed them and the many people who were told of them by those witnesses. Shortly after the demonstrations the natives left to return to their homes, or in the case of the representatives and artists, hurried with Tendile to report back to Montezuma, while Pitalpitoque stayed in the Spaniards' camp, ordering the people of the surrounding towns to prepare and bring food and trading goods to the camp.

This they did, although the food went to Cortes, his captains, Pitalpitoque, and Dona Marina, while the rest of the men traded beads and other items for food.

Tendile hurried to Montezuma carrying back the chair, helmet, and other gifts that had been given, and was received immediately, as there was much talk about these people from a far-off land. Upon seeing the helmet, Montezuma recalled the story passed on by his ancestors over many years that people wearing these head coverings would one day come to rule over his native people.

He received the gifts with great admiration, and yet, he was fearful of what was to come.

Several days later, Tendile re-entered the camp of the Spaniards, leading over one hundred men carrying gifts for Cortes, and a chief from another village, whose facial and bodily features greatly resembled Cortes. That chief's name was Quintalbar, and they looked so much alike that the Spaniards called Cortes "our Cortes" and Quintalbar "the other Cortes."

Upon the native group's arrival, they kissed the ground and used incense to fumigate Cortes, his captains, and all of the men around him, before giving great bows and honoring Cortes with many presents. As they sat down with Cortes and Dona Marina, Quintalbar and Tendile were the spokesmen for Montezuma.

After welcoming Cortes and his group to this part of their world, Quintalbar ordered the presents to be presented to Cortes, one at a time. The first present was a shield of gold, as large as a cart wheel, with pictures painted on it. After it was weighed a few days later, it was said to be worth more than ten thousand dollars. The second present was an even larger shield made of silver, with pictures painted on it.

It was very heavy for it was a representation of the full moon, and perhaps an acceptance of a change in all of their lives, natives and Spaniards. Next came the helmet being returned, filled with gold grains, just as it looks coming from the mines, and was worth at least three thousand dollars. That was the most important gift according to the men of the command as it showed that the mines there did contain gold.

Then came intricately carved golden animals, such as ducks, dogs, jaguars, mountain lions, and monkeys, ten beautiful golden collars, and several necklaces. Next were twelve arrows, a bow with string, two rods like staffs of justice, five-palms long, all in beautiful hollow work of fine gold. The presents kept on being presented including crests of gold, plumes of green feathers, other items of gold and silver, and then came thirty loads of beautiful cotton cloth decorated with brightly colored feathers, and many other gifts.

After all of the gifts had been presented, Quintalbar and Tendile requested Cortes to allow them to convey the words that Montezuma had told them to tell Cortes. After receiving his approval, they told him that Montezuma was pleased that such valiant men, as he had heard they were, should come to his country, for he knew all about what the Spanish had done at Tabasco.

He would very much like to see the Spanish great emperor who was such a mighty prince and whose fame was spread over so many lands, and that he would send him a present of precious stones. He urged Cortes and his troops to remain where they had built their town, with the natives of the surrounding towns continuing to bring food to the camp at the supervision of Pitalpitoque, the representative who stayed in the Spanish camp.

Although Cortes asked many times in different ways to be allowed to meet with Montezuma, Quintalbar and Tendile remained steadfast to the words of Montezuma, "But as to the interview, Cortes should not worry about it; there was no need for it," and Montezuma's advisors had cautioned him from meeting with Cortes. Cortes was disappointed, but showed no emotions toward the Tendile and Quintalbar.

He thanked them for the presents and encouraged them to return to Montezuma as his spokespersons, and tell Montezuma he and his men had traveled across many seas, and had journeyed from distant lands solely to speak with him in person. If he, Cortes, were to return without speaking with Montezuma, the great king of Spain and lord which Cortes and all of his men served, would be very angry with Cortes, and that wherever their prince Montezuma might be, Cortes and his men would surely go and see him and do whatever Montezuma might order them to do.

The two men agreed to go back to Montezuma and tell him the words of request by Cortes, but reminded him that the previous request was declined. Cortes gave each of the two men holland shirts, a cup of highly decorated Florentine ware engraved with trees and hunting scenes and gilt, plus a few other less valuable things.

The two men and their carriers left to return to their capital and to Montezuma, expecting that the request by Cortes would fall on deaf ears.

After the men departed, Cortes dispatched two ships to explore more of the coastline, looking for a better place to raise a settlement. The sand dunes were thick with mosquitos, and did not offer firm support for buildings. The two ships sailed to a place they called Rio Grande, but the winds and tide made sailing any further too difficult, so they turned around and returned to San Juan de Ulua.

Also, after the ambassador's group had left, Pitalpitoque, the native representative who stayed in the Spanish camp with the job of encouraging the native towns in the area to bring foods to the camp, began to slacken his effort to provide food for the camp, and fewer natives came to trade. The entire camp waited impatiently for the return of Tendile, who brought several natives with him.

After fumigating all of the Spaniards with incense, as was their custom, presents of fine rich feather cloth, some green stones much valued by the natives, and a few other gold items were given to Cortes. Then, after requesting permission from Cortes, Tendile and Pitalpitoque joined Cortes, Aguilar and Dona Marina, reporting that Montezuma was very pleased with the gifts Cortes had sent to him, but as to the face-to-face meeting, no more was to be said about it.

Cortes thanked the messengers, giving them presents. Just then, the bell rang for the Ave Maria, at which time all of the

Spaniards and Dona Marina who had converted to the Catholic Christian faith, fell to their knees before the large wooden cross that had been raised beside the altar.

The natives looked in wonder at all of these foreigners kneeling, and Tendile asked Cortes the meaning for the humbling of the people in front of a wooden tree cut that way. It gave Cortes and the Padre who was there next to him a perfect opportunity to try to explain the faith in which they had grown to men.

As he touched on many of the important parts of the Catholic faith, he mentioned that it was the king of Spain, his benefactor, who had sent them to this place to abolish human sacrifices and idolatry worship, counseling them to refrain from robbing each other, and all other things that the church considered as sins.

The men were quite intelligent, and understood much of what had been told them by Cortes. He asked them to return to their capital and begin placing crosses inside their temples, and gave them a statue of Mary, the mother of God holding the infant Jesus. They were very respectful of the proper way all of the Spaniards prayed to their God without any bloodshed. They did promise to take the statue with them, and bring the thoughts relayed to them by Cortes to the attention of Montezuma, and then they left.

As has been said, Pitalpitoque did not put any effort into supplying food for the group of Spaniards. The sailors went fishing daily and their catch was divided among all of the group.

In payment, the soldiers would trade with the few natives that would come and offer items of worth, which were then traded with the sailors for food. When the friends of Diego Velasquez saw that the men were trading for gold, they approached Cortes, saying that Diego was not sharing in the profits these men were making. Cortes told them to appoint one of their own to collect the tax, but then asked them where they would get food and with what it would be paid for.

A few days later, all of the natives disappeared from the campsite, having fled without a word of explanation. Later, it was found out that Montezuma had ordered that no more connections between the natives and the Spaniards was to be allowed, for he was devoted to the idols, one of which being the god of war called Huichilobos, the other the god of hell who was called Tezcatepuca. Montezuma sacrificed a youth per day to each of them, hoping to get an answer about what to do about the Spaniards.

He had formed a plan to get all of them under his power in order to raise a breed of them, and also to keep them for future sacrifices. As these thoughts and words became familiar through one native who came back to the camp seeking beads, lookouts were posted day and night, watching for a possible attack. One day, as two lookouts were observing from behind a large sand dune, five natives approached the pathway to the camp, and they were stopped by the two lookouts. They did not seem afraid, but rather told the men they were from a different town, and were afraid to come to the Spaniards' village as they were not friendly with the people of Montezuma's towns, in fact they were enemies, but woefully under-manned and had few weapons.

Bernal Diaz, who was one of the lookouts, walked these five natives into the camp and up to Cortes. They paid Cortes great homage, and called him prince and great lord. These men were heavily tattooed, with holes in their lower lips filled by colored stones, and their ears had earrings of gold.

Their speech was different than the people who had left the camp and the surrounding area. Aguilar and Dona Marina had trouble initially understanding them, but eventually were able to translate their stories to Cortes as two of the five could understand the language spoken by Montezuma's Mexicans.

What they told him was that they were enemies of Montezuma, but were afraid of him and his followers. Their chief had sent them to see what kind of men the visitors were, and that it would please him to be of service to such valiant and powerful men. They knew that Montezuma had issued warnings to the people of this region not to interact with Cortes nor any of his party. Through their talks, Cortes found out that Montezuma had opponents and enemies, which he was delighted to hear.

It was unexpected good news to Cortes, and he rewarded the five native men with beads, telling them that he would come to their town and visit with their chief, then sending them back to their homes.

A disagreement arose between Cortes and the men sent by Diego Velasquez. Diego's men had been sent to watch over and guide Cortes toward collecting the riches and returning to Cuba, where Diego and the king would get their shares, leaving for Cortes and his men only what was left over.

Cortes and his captains didn't think that was fair, because Cortes had formed the group to explore uncharted territories and establish a town—something many of the men had wanted. Cortes's men wanted to live a gentleman's life with land, a home, and slaves to work for them.

A great division formed with secret meetings of both groups seeking the upper hand. There were the sailors and soldiers who backed Cortes, and the group that were for Diego Velasquez and returning to Cuba.

Eventually, Cortes imprisoned those followers of Diego, placing them in irons aboard one of the ships. Over a short time, many of the followers of Diego changed sides as gold was placed in their hands, which made the change economically good judgement. Cortes stated that "this land is to be settled in the name of his majesty, and by Hernando Cortes in the name of his majesty. We await the opportunity to make it known to our lord the king of Spain."

Most of the men made known their choice for chief justice and captain general, and that was Cortes. The town was formed at a place the Spaniards called "Villa Rica de la Vera Cruz" because they arrived there on Holy Thursday of the last supper, April 21st, 1519, left the ships and gained dry land on "Holy Friday of the Cross," April 22nd, 1519, and "rich" because of what one of the men said to

Cortes, "Behold rich lands! May you know how to govern them well."

As soon as the town was founded, officials were appointed.

After the town was pretty much laid out and buildings began to rise, it was ordered that Pedro de Alvarado should explore inland as there was word that there were towns nearby. He took one hundred soldiers with him, among them fifteen crossbowmen and six musketeers. As he marched inland, he came to several small towns that had been vacated that same day.

He found bodies of men and boys who had been sacrificed, with the walls and altars stained with blood, and the hearts of the sacrificed placed before the idols. He also found the knives covered with blood which had been used to open the chests to withdraw the hearts, and many limbs of the sacrificed were missing.

Alvarado found the towns with much food left behind, but could only find two men to carry maize, and each soldier had to carry as much poultry and vegetables as he could on their return to their town. No damage was done to those towns they marched through, as Cortes was looking for natives that would help him in any future battles he might face. As time went on, all of the Diego Velasquez followers became Cortes followers, and good friends of the captain general.

The next movement made in the exploration of the area was to search for the town from which the five natives had visited when the Spaniards lived near the sand dunes. Although they entered many towns, only a very few had residents that would approach them as their fear of cannons and horses overcame good manners.

At one of the towns they met twelve native men who invited them to spend the night at their town, having prepared a place that would accommodate the entire group to sleep, and had maize cakes and vegetables for fresh food for the group to eat. However, the regular inhabitants were not in the town while the Spaniards were there.

The next morning the Spaniards returned to the pathway and

set out for a town called Cempoala. Word was sent ahead to the town by way of six of the twelve natives who had met them and seen to the needs of the group. As they approached Cempoala, they were met by several of the important people of the community, who explained that the chief was so fat that he could not walk to meet them, but was awaiting their arrival at his home.

As they walked into the entrance to the town all of the group noticed how the buildings had been recently washed as they shone brilliant white in the sunlight. The important people of the town led the group into the town and up to the chief's doorway. He struggled to his feet, helped by four men, one on each arm and two pushing from behind. He attempted a bow to Cortes, but it was a very feeble attempt to pay homage to him.

The two men began communicating with Dona Marina being the chief interpreter. Asking what was needed by the Spaniards, the chief ordered the people of the town to make available room for all of the group for sleeping, and brought maize cakes and plums for everyone to eat. This was considered a feast as food along the march was less than adequate.

The eating had taken place within the plaza, but after they had finished, guides began leading them through the town, and the men were amazed at the cleanliness, construction of the buildings, and the largeness of the town. It appeared as would a garden of beauty in Spain. They were made to feel comfortable in this town.

While talking continued between Cortes and the fat chief, it was made known to Cortes that the people of this town feared Montezuma, and paid large taxes, both in gold, food, and cloth, as well as having many young men and women taken by Montezuma's tax collectors for sacrifices in their capital city, Tenochtitlan. They certainly were not fond of Montezuma, his tax collectors, and the way they were being treated by their government.

Cortes promised to help them when they needed help, and that was to occur sooner rather than later. Cortes had found out that the town they were next going to approach was the fortified town known as Quiahuitztlan, which stood amid great rocks and lofty cliffs, a town with natural defenses. After climbing the hills leading to the town they entered the great plaza where they were met by fifteen men of that town all wearing ceremonial clothing.

They approached Cortes who was in the lead, fumigating him with incense and moving through the ranks of men doing the same to each man. Cortes displayed much friendship toward them, giving them some green beads and other small inexpensive items.

As Cortes was speaking with them through Aguilar and Dona Marina, one of the sentries interrupted and told the natives speaking with Cortes that five tax collectors from Montezuma's capital had entered their town expecting to speak with them and arrange to collect the taxes, including young people to be used as human sacrifices.

As these five men and their servants passed by the group of Spaniards, not one word of recognition was spoken between the groups. Following them closely were the chiefs of other towns in the area, and they did not leave the five men until they had been seated and fed. After eating their fill, the chiefs of the surrounding towns as well as the chief of Quiahuitztlan were called together and chastised for welcoming and entertaining the Spaniards into their towns and homes without the permission of their lord, Montezuma.

The chief of Quiahuitztlan was able to get back to Cortes and complained to Cortes that several of Montezuma's tax collectors had arrived in his town, and expected payment of valuables including his own daughter, who would be a sacrifice to the idols. He asked for Cortes's advice. Cortes had the chiefs gather together and told them that he and his men had been sent there by the greatest king of the world to chastise evil doers and he would permit neither sacrifice nor robbery.

He boldly suggested that these tax collectors be imprisoned immediately, and be held in custody until Montezuma was told the reason, namely that they had come to rob them of their wealth and carry off their wives and children to be made slaves and sacrificed.

The chiefs were dumb-struck by the idea, but with Cortes's assurances, the incarceration took place. Using long poles and collars the men were restrained, all except for one who tried to fight his way to freedom, but he was flogged until he could be collared.

All of the chiefs that had been called to this town to be chastised by these five tax collectors, after seeing what had been done, hurried back to their towns, spreading the word of what had taken place, and thinking more than ever to revolt against Montezuma and his terrible reign, if helped by the Spaniards' cannons, horses, guns, crossbowmen, and swordsmen. After a day of being imprisoned, Cortes arranged for two of the prisoners to be brought to him secretly, and he asked them what had happened, and why.

They told him the story that the natives of the surrounding towns had taken them by force and imprisoned them because they were doing their duty for Montezuma, their lord. Cortes said he knew nothing about their imprisonment, and allowed them to return to Montezuma to tell him that the Spaniards were willing to help him in any way he asked of them.

Feigning ignorance of the escape, Cortes asked that the three remaining prisoners be taken out to his ships, where he would be responsible for their imprisonment. This was done, and a day or two later, they were taken by ship to an area from where they could make their way back to Montezuma with the same story of the help provided by Cortes.

A few days later, word came from a town nearby that had been occupied by an army of Montezuma's soldiers who had torn up fields of vegetables, and threatened the people who lived there. The chiefs of the surrounding area asked that Cortes back up his words of protection, and he conceived an idea to thwart an actual fight between his forces and the forces of Montezuma.

He called for his oldest, ugliest, and orneriest musketeer, and ordered him to walk toward that town alone, telling the chiefs and people that that man would take care of everything for them. Slyly, he told that man to fire off his musket when he reached a river that ran between Quiahuitztlan and the town of Cingapacinga, where Montezuma's soldiers were doing damage, and he would send out a runner to recall him to Quiahuitztlan.

This was done, and the musketeer returned. Cortes then announced to the native chiefs that he and his entire army would proceed to Cingapacinga and expel Montezuma's soldiers. He ordered the native chiefs to supply one hundred carriers to transport the cannons, and the next day a force of four hundred men, fourteen horsemen, crossbowmen, and musketeers set out for battle.

Some of the men who had been under the influence of Diego Velasquez requested passage back to Cuba, saying they did not want to go to war, but Cortes prevailed upon them not to desert the effort to settle this great land, and they consented. The entire group as was formed began marching toward Cingapacinga.

The first night the group slept at Cempoala, and the next day two thousand native warriors that had joined the Spaniards were divided into four commands, ready to help evict the soldiers of Montezuma from the town of Cingapacinga.

However, before they left Cempoala, Cortes witnessed the sacrifice of a young boy, and before he could stop it, the deed took place. He was very angry, calling the chief and all of the important people of the village together, and demanding that the idols be torn down and destroyed.

The native people were trembling, not wanting to destroy the gods their ancestors had worshipped, but afraid of the might that the Spaniards had if the act was not done. They backed off, and Cortes himself struck down the first and largest idol, while his captains destroyed the rest. The high priests of the town came out of their homes, picked up the broken pieces and burned them.

When the deed had been done, Cortes brought the entire population of the town together and announced that now they could be considered as brothers, and would be protected as the Spaniards would protect any other natives that threw down and broke their idols, and become true believers in the Christian religion. Cortes presented the town with a statue of Mary and the child, Jesus, to whom they were instructed to pray.

He told them much about the Catholic faith, telling them of the Ten Commandments, emphasizing the ones that pertained to robbing and killing, and worshipping the only one true God. After completely washing the walls, the altars themselves, and the flooring, a Cross was set up behind the altar that had held the idols, and the statue of Mary and Jesus was placed on the altar.

After that was done, Mass was said, and the entire population watched the solemn ceremony, surprised to see the Spaniards kneel in humility before the altar at times during the Mass.

The high priests of the town were asked to come forward in white robes. Cortes sheared and combed their hair to an acceptable length, and they were told to take care of the altar, the statue, and remember to pray to the one true God represented by this new altar. Cortes also left one of the oldest soldiers, a Juan de Torres de Cordoba, who had become lame, to help the high priests keep the area clean and the altar cloths white, and teach the people of the town the main ideas and rules of the church. He read to them from the Bible each Sabbath.

Rather than proceeding further toward a confrontation with Montezuma's forces, Cortes decided to march back to the settlement of Villa Rica. Upon his arrival there, a ship from Cuba commanded by Francisco de Saucedo arrived in port.

Another arrival was Luis Marina and ten soldiers. Saucedo had brought a horse and Marin a mare, and they brought news that made the entire camp happy. A decree from Spain had reached Diego Velasquez that he had been given authority to trade and build settlements in New Spain, at which the men most aligned with Diego Velasquez were happy they had stayed with Cortes. Many of the soldiers were anxious to get back to their quest for gold, and to see what this Montezuma looked like, and how they wanted a chance to return to battle.

Before Cortes was ready to march again toward Cempoala, a determination was needed on what to do with the gold that had been given in trade to these men—Cortes, his captains, sailors and soldiers.

Some of the men who were aligned with Diego Velasquez wanted to give him the percentage he had demanded at the time of their leaving Cuba, others wanted to give everything to King Charles, but it was finally decided that letters would be written to the king, sending him some of the gold and requesting that he anoint Cortes as the captain general of the newest part of New Spain.

They also wanted to remain in the country which would be under Cortes's leadership, and that was signed by all of the men who were not of officers' rank. Another letter was written by the captains, and a final letter written by Cortes, although no one actually saw that letter. The men who were assigned to sail to Spain through the Bahama Islands left on their long voyage.

Four days later, a group of followers of Diego Velasquez met secretly, planning that they steal a ship and sail back to Cuba alerting Velasquez that he could catch and gain those letters which were designed to effectively relinquish the hold he had on Cortes and his expedition.

However, the night before that vessel was scheduled to leave, one of the men who signed on to go back to Cuba backed out, and the story got to Cortes before the ship could leave. He took justice into his hands and ordained that two of the men were to be hanged, another to have his two feet amputated, and the sailors to receive two hundred lashes each. Father Juan Diaz had also signed to sail to Cuba, but because of his position in the Catholic faith, he was chastised severely, scaring him into submission and confessing his sin of a planned desertion.

After the sentences were carried out, Cortes ordered two hundred soldiers and all of the horsemen to follow him back to Cempoala. Before leaving Villa Rica, it was suggested to Cortes that all ships be disabled, so that deserters could not steal a ship and return to Cuba. That was done to the satisfaction of Cortes and the many men who wanted to remain living in this part of New Spain.

He sent one of the ships' captains out to bring to land all of the anchors, cables, sails, and everything else on board that might prove useful, and then gave orders to destroy the ships and preserve nothing but the small boats. The sailing masters, pilots, and sailors who were too old and of no use for war were ordered to stay in the town of Villa Rica, and with the two nets they possessed should take up fishing, for fish were always in the harbor, but not really plentiful.

Led by Cortes, the sailors marched with the soldiers and other horsemen to Cempoala, with carriers transporting the cannons. From Cempoala, Cortes sent out a summons to all of the chiefs of towns in the area whom he counted on as opposing Montezuma, and told them how they must help the Spaniards left in Villa Rica to finish building the church, fortress, and houses.

Taking one of his captains by the hand before all of the chiefs, he told them that the captain was his brother and they were to obey his every command, and if they needed any protection from Montezuma's people they should call on him, and he would come to their assistance. Cortes prepared all of his troops for battle, telling them that now that the ships had been destroyed, there was only one thing that mattered to them, and that was to go forward and defeat the enemies of Spain.

He told them they had to rely on their comrades, the strength of their arms, and the steel blades of their swords. It was shortly thereafter, a runner from Villa Rica arrived bearing an urgent letter from the men left there. There had been a ship that passed by the harbor, and the men stationed there lit smoky fires trying to alert the shipmates of the town they were building, but the ship passed by.

One of the men tried to follow in one of the small boats to see where the ship would anchor, which he reported to be about three leagues away, and the men wanted to know what Cortes wanted them to do. Cortes turned command of the troops in Cempoala over to Pedro de Alvarado and Gonzalo de Sandoval, a young soldier who had shown great courage and intelligence. Then Cortes mounted his horse, ordered four other horsemen to accompany him and fifty soldiers to follow him as he rode back to Villa Rica.

The ship had been sent by the governor of Jamaica to the area in which Cortes had chosen for the settlement of Villa Rica; the intention being to claim all of Mexico for Jamaica as well as for Spain. The men of Cortes's army captured two of the crew from that ship, and they were the ones who told Cortes who the people were on the ship and their purpose for coming there. Cortes, accompanied by the four other horsemen, the fifty soldiers, and the men they had captured from the Jamaican ship, returned to Villa Rica, where they ate and rested for the night.

The captured men joined the army of Cortes, and all of the horsemen and soldiers went back to Cempoala where they prepared for the long march toward Montezuma's territory. After consulting with the chiefs of the surrounding towns, a route through friendly towns was chosen. These towns were known to consider Montezuma and his government as enemies, so the army was welcomed as saviors.

The march began on August 16th, 1519, and was very strenuous, as there were many changes in altitude ranging from 1,500 to 10,000 feet above sea level. The two hundred carriers of the cannons from the friendly towns and the soldiers walking had a hard time trying to keep up with the horses, whose riders would occasionally stop in order for the men to catch up. It took many days of up and down walking through passes and over mountains to get to Tlaxcala, and they crossed the frontier into that area on August 31st, 1519.

Before arriving there, the army approached a town they called Castilblanco, as it reminded many of the Spanish-born of the towns in Spain. It had a white gleam on the rooftops, the homes of the important people of the town were lofty and were covered by white plaster. Messengers were sent into the town, and the army was met at the entrance to the town by the chief and his other government officials.

The name of the chief was Olintecle, and he conducted Cortes and his officers to some lodging and fed them. The soldiers were also fed, but not as much food was offered them. After Cortes and his officers had eaten, Cortes began asking questions through Dona Marin about Montezuma. Chief Olintecle was very open in answering the questions, such as the great strength of Montezuma's warriors, which were kept scattered throughout his large territory, and then began to tell of the great fortress of Tenochtitlan.

He told of how houses were built in the water with bridges as the only way of passing from one to another, other than canoes. The buildings all had flat roofs with breastworks that could be raised when needed, which turned them into fortresses. He mentioned that the town could be entered from three directions with drawbridges that could be raised which would refuse entry to anyone not permitted to enter. Next he mentioned the great store of gold and silver, and the many other riches which Montezuma possessed, and he never ceased telling Cortes how great a lord Montezuma was.

Cortes finally replied when chief Olintecle took a bite of a plum followed by a swallow of the fine plum wine that had been served, that...

> *...he and his men had traveled a great distance at the command of the Spanish lord and king, who has many and great princes as his vassals. His command is that the great prince Montezuma cease from sacrificing men, women, or children to the idols, to cease robbing from the towns that serve him, and not to seize any more lands, but to give his fealty to the lord, the king. This is commanded of you and all of the chiefs' dominions, as well. You must stop all sacrifices to your idols, and no longer eat the flesh of your own*

> *people, and stop the other evil customs you practice.*

After the talking was finished and Cortes and his captains left the area to go to their quarters, the other chiefs that had been part of the meal and the discussions were left to talk over the meeting between Cortes and themselves.

The chiefs that had accompanied Cortes and his group answered some of the questions asked by chief Olintecle and the chiefs from his area about the weaponry and abilities of the Spanish soldiers. When asked about the artillery, the chief from Cempoala, who had witnessed the firing of the cannon, told the others of the balls that were fired traveling distances, killing many soldiers at one time.

When asked about the horses, he said they could outrun deer, and when an arrow hit the breastplate they wore, the arrow was deflected, never injuring the horse, and the rider wore protection that also repelled arrows and stones, and the slashing swords were used to slay opponents as they rode through the ranks opposing them.

The Spaniards had also brought a vicious dog called a lurcher, which barked all night long, and Chief Olintecle asked whether it was as lethal as a mountain lion or jaguar? The chief from Cempoala answered saying, "No, it is not a mountain lion or jaguar, but it is just as vicious, and they bring it with them to kill anyone or anything that annoys them." Having learned that it was these men who had captured Montezuma's tax collectors, had them incarcerated for a period of time, and warned them not to rob the many towns under the protection of Montezuma of gold, food, or people who would be used as slaves until they would be sacrificed to the idols, they began to be scared.

They had been told by the other chiefs that were accompanying Cortes of the defeats of the towns of Tabasco and Champoton, and the terrible loss of life of the native people during those battles. They also told of the presents their own prince Montezuma had presented to these men of Spain, and this village had given them nothing but sleeping quarters and food. That began a series of presents being offered to Cortes, rather small in worth, but there were some gold necklaces, bracelets, and cloth.

It was decided by Cortes and his captains to press on toward Tlaxcala, which was nearby, with a series of rocks providing a barrier between Castilblanco and Tlaxcala. Prior to leaving Castilblanco, Cortes demanded twenty warrior chiefs from chief Olintecle, which he readily surrendered. As they marched toward Tlaxcala, they first came to a town named Xalacingo, whose chief met the Spanish group, paying great homage to Cortes, and giving Cortes some gifts of a golden necklace, some cloth and two women. It was from there that Cortes sent two native messengers to Tlaxcala, asking that their town allow the Spaniards to enter the town peacefully, as the Spaniards wanted them as friends.

But the town had been aware of the victories by the Spaniards at Tabasco and Champoton, and the many friends they had made in towns that paid tribute to Montezuma that were now furnishing warriors to fight against the common enemy, Montezuma. The chiefs of Tlaxcala were afraid that this group of Spaniards and the added native warriors were coming to overthrow them and force them to come under the government of Montezuma. They decided to fight this invasion of their domain.

As the Spanish group pressed on, they came up to a concrete building. Demolishing it was hard to do, but eventually it was leveled. When asked what purpose it served, the native chiefs said that it was built to defend the town from advancing armies that had in the past entered their area, causing much damage to important places and the inhabitants.

It was normally defended by Tlaxcala soldiers, but they had kept many of their warriors closer to the town with the intention of setting a large ambush against the advancing troops. Cortes had sent out scouts, and they had spotted some of the scouts of Tlaxcala ahead of them. One Spanish scout went to Cortes telling him of the contact. Cortes sent four horsemen ahead with the scout, and as they moved forward, they were fallen upon by an ambush of three thousand or more Tlaxcalan soldiers.

The horsemen and horses suffered some wounds, but their swordplay did much damage to the native fighters, eventually killing five of them. Hearing the sounds of the swords hitting metal, the rest of the group entered the fight with the cannons firing and blasting away many lives with each firing. Muskets did wonders in turning the tide of battle, with the Tlaxcalans giving up ground with every discharge, the dogs going after native soldier after native soldier, and the swords slashing everything within each swing.

The crossbowmen did themselves proud as each arrow found its target. No tally was taken on killed native soldiers but there were four wounded Spanish soldiers, one of whom died a few days later. As the Tlaxcalans retreated, Cortes commanded a halt not to follow them, and an overnight camp was set up. They had camped near a stream, and with fresh water, and the fat taken from a dead native warrior, the wounds to men and horses were seared and covered. Guards and sentries were on alert all night, but everything was quiet.

The next day, as the Spanish troops marched toward Tlaxcala, another army of six thousand attacked with shouts, sounds of drums, trumpets, and shrill whistling, with arrows launched in salvos, acting like brave warriors. Halting the Spaniard's advance, Cortes released three prisoners that had been taken in the fighting the previous day, and told them to tell the native soldiers to stop making war on them as the Spaniards wished to treat them as brothers.

However, this just increased their propensity to strengthen their attack, and Cortes had to rally his counter-attack, which killed many of the Tlaxcalan soldiers including three of their captains. That army of six thousand retreated as a group, leading to ravines in which the cannons were useless, leaving the crossbowmen, musketeers, and swordsmen as the only defensive and offensive weapons to use against them.

This led the Spanish group into a larger ambush of forty thousand native warriors, which completely surrounded them. Fighting valiantly, and with the help of once more having cannons set up and firing, they pushed the enemy backward, but at the cost of one horse and almost the rider, Pedro de Moron.

As he urged his mount toward a very fierce troop of native fighters, he got too close and one of the natives grabbed the bridle, twisted it to the side and cleanly cut off the head of the horse, killing it immediately. Seeing the position Pedro was in, other riders moved in to rescue him before he would have been killed. As it was, he had been severely injured. Parts of the dead horse were carried off by some of the warriors, to be made as an offering to their idols later.

Shortly thereafter the Tlaxcalan army began to retreat, and again, Cortes called a halt to chasing the enemy. They had been fighting very close to the town of Tehuacingo, which after the battle had finished, the Spanish group entered. The town had much food, and they found a supply of poultry, little dogs, cakes, and vegetables. The group used this town in which to rest, bind up the many wounds they had suffered, and Cortes took this opportunity to convince two of the fifteen natives that had been captured during the battle, both of whom were among the head chiefs, to go to Xicotenga the elder, who was the captain and head chief of the province of Tlaxcala, with gifts to ask for free passage through the province in order to speak with Montezuma.

The reply was enough to scare each and every Spaniard, so much so that the priest and friar heard confessions from the Christians all night. The reply was that after they were defeated, the Tlaxcalans would delight in offering their bodies to the idols and then eating them. It was also spread among the group that there were more than fifty thousand troops waiting for their approach.

The following day, which was the fifth day of September in the year of our lord 1519, the troops were mustered, with Cortes cautioning each to “shoot your musket while the other would reload”, with similar directions to the crossbowmen.

All of the men, the healthy and the injured, reported for duty, as they realized this would be a fight they should always remember, if they survived. As they assembled for the march, the horsemen were up front, with musketeers next, then came the crossbowmen, followed by the swordsmen.

The cannons were near the front pointing in three forward positions and one behind. They marched that way, four hundred dedicated men facing as many as fifty thousand native Tlaxcalans defending their towns, families, as well as their own lives. The natives began their charge, hoping to overrun the Spaniards. The arrows and stones sent by bows and slings rained into the midst of the small army, but were met by cannon shots, musket-fire, arrows from the crossbows, the sweeping swords swung by the desperate men and the constant attacks by the lurchers.

Slowly but surely the Spaniards pushed back against the tremendous numbers of native soldiers. Later it was said that a division between two of the five native commanders led to a lessening of pressure on the Spanish troops, but desperate men do desperate things, and the battle began to swing toward the small army.

The will of the Tlaxcalan army seemed to suffer, and realizing the forces of the two native commanders were not going to help, they began giving up ground. One of their most important chiefs had been killed, and the native army fled in retreat.

The horsemen and lurchers followed the retreating army attacking the slowest fighters for a short distance as they knew that if they rested themselves or their horses, they would not have the strength nor courage to restart a battle. During this battle, one Spanish soldier was killed and at least sixty were injured. There were no counts of killed or injured Tlaxcalan fighters as they were picked up as they fell, and taken with the retreating army.

It was by the grace of God that the Spaniards had prevailed against overwhelming odds, and during a Mass held on the following morning, all of the group gave praise and thanked God for the protection he offered them.

Cortes held a discussion with not only his captains but with all of the men in attendance, asking advice on how to proceed. He had suggested sending two captured chiefs as messengers to the chiefs in the main town of Tlaxcala; the two chiefs were Mase Escasi and Xicotenga the elder, father of the commander of the Tlaxcalan armies.

Those leaders were sent, but were not convinced that this small army could defeat their large army, so they consulted the high priests in the temples which housed the idols. The high priests told the two chiefs that the Spaniards could only be defeated at night, as during darkness they lost their will to win.

They called Xicotenga, the son and head of the army, telling him to mount an attack at night, but the Spanish guards and sentries were alerted by the noises made by the advancing army, and woke up the camp.

The troops had been so weary, they were still wearing their fighting clothes, with their weapons close beside them. Although surrounded, the troop dispersed the attackers with the cannons firing, the muskets and crossbowmen hitting their targets, the dogs and horsemen driving such huge holes in the native ranks that they turned and ran, followed for a short way by the horsemen.

This battle seemed to change the minds of Mase Escasi and Xicotenga, the elder, and together they decided that the many offers of peace made by Cortes be considered, as after this night battle he again sent messengers requesting peace. These two wise men sent for the chiefs in all of their domain to come and listen to their decision.

At that meeting of all of the chiefs of the Tlaxcala province, the two men told the chiefs that...

> *Cortes, the leader of the Spaniards, has become friends of the people in the town of Cempoala, friends of ours. They have taken two of*

> *Montezuma's tax collectors as prisoners, and sent them back to Montezuma without any taxes, and the chiefs of the towns they have come through tell us they are enemies of Montezuma, our enemy. It is time to allow them to help us.*

After hearing the words of their greatest chiefs, the other town chiefs agreed that peace with the Spaniards would be sensible. After their meeting, Xicotenga, the elder, summoned his son and told him that the decision had been made for peace with the Spaniards, but the son was headstrong, and refused to accept his father's decision.

He insisted that he would lead the army of Tlaxcala to victory, and completely destroy the Spanish group. He gathered a large group of soldiers, informing them that they would again attack at night. He sent spies into the Spanish camp with food, and four old women, whom, through the words of the spies, he "could use as sacrifices, as they were no good to him."

After determining that these men were spies, Cortes ordered their hands to be cut-off and sent back to Xicotenga, the younger and head of the army, with the message that he and his men were ready to fight again. This had a definite effect on the young native leader, as well as one of his trusted captains who took his men from the army and went back to their town. Suddenly Xicotenga lost his bravery and courage.

The next day, the sentries who watched the roads leading into the camp came rushing up to Cortes telling him of many people carrying food and presents approaching the camp. Cortes was sure that it was a sign that peace had been accepted by the leaders of the province, and that the people should be welcomed as they entered. Cortes spoke to them through Dona Marina, telling them he "was sorry for all the deaths and pain they suffered because of the fighting," but it was their fault as he had come in peace, and did nothing more than defend himself and his group.

He assured them of his dedication to help them in any way he could, if they, in turn, would help him. He began telling them to stop all sacrifices to idols, and stop the robbing between towns. There were many days during which the dead were buried and the injured healed, both men and horses, before they were invited to enter the town of Tlaxcala, but that date was September 17th, 1519.

The fame of the battles between the native Tlaxcalan army and the Spanish expedition raced through the country, even as far away as Montezuma's city of Tenochtitlan. Upon hearing of the defeat of his sworn enemy, Tlaxcala, Montezuma sent five representatives to the Spanish camp, bringing presents such as gold, richly jeweled ornaments, and twenty loads of fine cotton cloth, and congratulations on the victory over so many warriors.

While Cortes was talking with Montezuma's representatives, a sentry came to tell him that a large group of Tlaxcalan chiefs, led by Xicotenga the younger, were approaching the site, all dressed in white and red robes, carrying their banner which floated in the breeze. Xicotenga, the commander of the Tlaxcalan warriors, was escorted to Cortes, and made several movements indicating an offer of showing respect, and was seated alongside Cortes.

Xicotenga began speaking, with Dona Marina interpreting, saying he had come on behalf of his father and Mase Escasi and other important chiefs of the commonwealth of Tlaxcala, to pray Cortes to admit them to friendship, and that he came to render obedience to the king of Spain and lord, and to ask pardon for having taken up arms against them. This had been done as they did not know who they were, what their intentions were, and had taken this path to war as they thought that they were part of their sworn enemy, Montezuma, and his Tenochtitlan people.

He went on to say that they were very poor people with no gold, no silver, no cotton cloth, not much food, because Montezuma gave them no opportunity to go out and search for it. He said they were kept busy defending themselves because of constant attacks by Montezuma's armies.

Cortes accepted the words of Xicotenga, thanking him very

courteously and flatteringly, and told him that he, his soldiers, his king and his lord would accept his and his people's friendship, and offered to help them in any way he could. Xicotenga then begged Cortes and his group to enter their town as all of the chiefs and important people looked forward to meeting them.

Cortes politely told him that he was in negotiations with five of Montezuma's representatives, and would enter Tlaxcala soon after the talks would end. He told Xicotenga to return to the town, make certain the peace would endure without any change, or he and his men would destroy the town and kill all of the people.

When Xicotenga, and all of the important men who had accompanied him from Tlaxcala had heard and understood his words, they left to return to their homes.

While this discussion had taken place, the representatives of Montezuma had been listening and began to understand that their purpose of coming to congratulate and find out the intentions of Cortes had been detailed by Cortes and Xicotenga.

The representatives requested that Cortes wait six days before entering and befriending the people of Tlaxcala in order for them to consult with Montezuma to find out his orders on what they were to do. Cortes agreed to the six-day delay as he was suffering from fever, and although he doubted the sincerity of the representatives' words, he knew that there was a small chance they would return with an offer of peace rather than war.

Six days passed as the Spaniards rested and regained their health, always being mindful of the possibility of surprise attacks, but none came. The representatives of Montezuma returned, along with slaves carrying gold jewels worked into various shapes, two hundred pieces of cloth, and all richly decorated with feathers.

Cortes received the presents with delight, thanked them, and told them he would repay their lord Montezuma with good works. Montezuma's representatives then warned Cortes that the Tlaxcalan were devious, and that they would turn on his friendship, and imprison him and all of his people if he trusted them too much.

Cortes asked them to stay at his camp for three days after he entered Tlaxcala, just to see what would happen.

They agreed to his request, and at that moment one of the sentries alerted Cortes of a great many townspeople walking to their camp. Some people were being carried in hammocks, some on peoples' backs, and among them were Mase Escasi and Xicotenga, the elder. As they approached Cortes they showed great respect and Xicotenga, the elder, began speaking saying...

> *We have sent many times to implore you to pardon us for having attacked you and to state our excuse that we did it to protect ourselves from the hostility of Montezuma and his powerful forces, for we believed that you belonged to his party and were allied with him.*

He went on to say that they begged of him to enter their town with them so that they might give them whatever they possessed, and they would serve them with people and property.

Cortes told them that he would have entered earlier, but he had no carriers for the cannons. He also told them the reason for the representatives of Montezuma being with him was that he was trying to arrange peace with them, but they would leave within three days of his entry into Tlaxcala. After the chiefs had left and returned to their homes, five hundred carriers were sent to the camp for transporting the cannons. The following morning Cortes, his men, horses, all of the supplies, weapons, and the representatives of Montezuma began the walk into Tlaxcala.

Entering the city of Tlaxcala on September 23rd, 1519, Cortes was accompanied by the two representatives of Montezuma as well as the Spanish soldiers and the other native chiefs that had joined the Spanish cause. Montezuma's representatives had requested accommodations within the same quarters given to Cortes as they feared that the people of Tlaxcala would attack and kill them for past wars their two armies had fought.

Preparations had been made to welcome Cortes and all of his soldiers and native friends, providing food and comfortable rooms in which to heal and rest, although weapons were always available close by if needed.

Over the next twenty days much discussion and planning took place as Cortes, his captains and soldiers, and the native chiefs who knew of the terrain, detailed the make-up of the area in and around Montezuma's stronghold, the city built within a lake, the approaches, drawbridges, battlement stations, and the defenses of the capital, Tenochtitlan.

The strengths of Montezuma's army were discussed, with as many as one hundred fifty thousand or more soldiers under his command. Cortes learned that the waterways could be used by canoeing from small islands to others; he learned of the depth of the waterways; and that all of the houses and other buildings were flat-roofed.

The farmers lived on the outskirts of the city, with the level of importance of the farmer's family granting the family more centralized locations. Of course, the homes of Montezuma were in the center of the city, protected by moats.

Also, masses were held daily, with the Tlaxcalan people becoming accustomed to seeing the Catholic followers kneeling humbly during the services, and receiving small pieces of bread and sips of wine from the priest near the end of each service. The small wooden table acted as an altar, with the cross and Jesus nailed to it behind it, the statue of the beautiful lady with infant son clutched to her breast beside it, and the priest presiding, most often Juan Diaz, because Padre de la Merced was ill and feeble. This form of sacrifice and worship was certainly foreign to their ways.

Those days were advantageous to the tired soldiers who had overcome great odds in defeating the huge armies sent against them. It took all of those days to heal their bodies and rebuild their minds to their strengths, with the future battle against Montezuma's huge armies for Tenochtitlan looming just ahead.

During those twenty days, the Tlaxcalan people presented many gifts to Cortes, his chiefs, and soldiers. Five of the most attractive young women were presented to Cortes, who in turn presented them to his chiefs, as he was married, and they were not.

The most beautiful was the daughter of Xicotenga, the elder, who was given to Pedro de Alvarado, who had a son and daughter by her later in life. It was she whom the Tlaxcalan people showed reverence to, presenting her with many gifts.

One last duty to be performed was to climb an active volcano near the city of Huexotzingo, and that duty was assigned to Diego de Ordas, and two of his soldiers, accompanied by two chiefs of that city. As no Spaniard had ever seen a volcano before, fears were heightened by the words of the two chieftains when they told Diego that the shaking was so severe as they climbed up the side of the mountain that they would be unable to remain climbing, and that the fiery stones, tongues of flame, and ash it emitted would certainly burn through their bodies.

However, Diego and his two soldiers did climb to the top rim, and were able to see the great city of Tenochtitlan in the distance. The summit was within twelve or thirteen leagues of that capital, and upon his return to Tlaxcala, the people considered his feat of climbing to the top of the volcano a very daring and dangerous accomplishment.

There was but one more city under the control of Montezuma between Tlaxcala and Tenochtitlan, that being Cholula. Cortes sent representatives to that city, asking why their chieftains had not come to invite his Spaniards to their city, which was nearby to Tlaxcala, but the reply given to the representatives was to send gifts by way of four unimportant residents of that city to Cortes, representing a mockery of his request.

Again, Cortes requested that the chieftains come to visit with him in Tlaxcala within three days, or he would consider their city's residents as rebels and that he and his armies of Spaniards and

Tlaxcalans would do things that would anger and displease them.

The answer came back that since Cortes included their ancient enemies, the Tlaxcalans, the city of Cholula would not agree to send its chieftains to Tlaxcala, but would welcome the entrance of the army of Spaniards. Since that was a reasonable excuse, Cortes ordered that only two thousand Tlaxcalan soldiers accompany his army, along with the carriers for the cannons, to the city of Cholula. Cortes and his army did enter Cholula, and were given food and shelter, while the Tlaxcalan soldiers set up camp outside the city.

During this stay, representatives of Montezuma entered the city, advising the chieftains of Cholula to trap the Spaniards, bind them and send them to Tenochtitlan as prisoners to be sacrificed to the idols there, but keeping twenty in Cholula to be sacrificed there.

There were two high priests of the city who were not happy with the planned subversion, and came to Cortes with the outline of the plan. A wife of an older chieftain also came to support the high priests' story of subversion after being coerced by Dona Marina; the wife had requested that Dona Marina leave her Spanish husband and marry the woman's son. Dona Marina convinced the old woman that she would comply with the old woman's request, but turned the woman over to Cortes for questioning.

After hearing the story of treachery from both sources, Cortes requested and received assurances from all three people that the plans they had told him were true, and that they were not to tell anyone else that they had given the information to him. The old woman was placed under guard and not allowed to return to her family.

Calling his chiefs and soldiers together, Cortes told them of the plans disclosed by the high priests and the old woman, and through discussion, decided that they would allow the Cholulan warriors to enter the area that had been set aside for the Spaniards' shelters, but then sealed off the exits after a large number had entered.

Cortes, astride his horse, and the soldiers, musketeers, crossbowmen and sword-wielding shielded soldiers waded into the throng of Cholulan warriors, downing a large number before the Tlaxcalan warriors entered the fray, killing many of the Cholulan warriors outside the compound where the Spaniards were dispatching many lives of the warriors inside the compound.

Those chieftains who were spared their lives insisted that it was not their idea to war upon Cortes and his men, but that the representatives of Montezuma had insisted they defeat and capture the Spaniards before they could advance on Tenochtitlan. After the fighting ended, the Cholulan people who had been captured by the Tlaxcalan soldiers were released according to the demands of Cortes, and the entire city of Cholula was examined, with the prisons containing the young men and women held for sacrifice opened and all were released to their families. This did much to relieve tensions among the citizens of Cholula and Tlaxcala, uniting them as friends rather than enemies.

As many warriors had been sent to lie in wait for the Spaniards to exit Cholula on their way toward Tenochtitlan, after hearing of the outcome of the fighting within Cholula, the warriors hurried back to Tenochtitlan, carrying the news of the defeat and resignation of the city to the Spaniards and Tlaxcalans.

The news preceded their reports as the representatives of Montezuma left Cholula as the fighting began to favor the Spaniards. This news greatly troubled Montezuma and he began to talk with his high priests and offer more human sacrifices to the idols. From the high priests who determined the results from the idols, he was told to allow the Spaniards into Tenochtitlan, where they could be killed at his leisure by the many soldiers quartered there.

This did nothing to assure him of his remaining as powerful as he had been throughout his reign, so once again he sent representatives laden with gold, silver, and valuable other presents to Cortes, asking that he not enter the city, but again, Cortes told the representatives that he and his men had been sent by his king, and that his God protected and directed him to meet with Montezuma, to introduce him to both the benevolent king and the

God of his people.

Cortes had been warned by people of the surrounding area that after leaving Cholula he would come to a fork in the road ahead, with one clean road leading toward Chalco, where many of Montezuma's soldiers waited in ambush. The other was blocked by felled trees which led to another city called Tlamanalco.

Both cities were subject to Montezuma. Cortes requested men from Cholula to clear the road toward Tlamanalco of the felled trees, and as that was accomplished, they followed that road to the city. The road led to high, cold, snow- covered mountains, but Cortes led his group of soldiers and native helpers to the gates of Tlamanalco.

They were greeted by the chiefs and residents of Tlamanalco, and many other people who came from the surrounding area. There was much food available there as the fields were rich with corn and other growing foods.

Presents of varied worth were presented to Cortes, and friendships were accepted by the people of the many cities represented by those people from near and far. A new recognition of cooperation was born between the people of the cities through which Cortes and his people had traveled.

No longer were they considered to be foes, but rather, united in the great hope and trust that could rescue them from the abuse they suffered under Montezuma. However, they cautioned Cortes not to enter Tenochtitlan as Montezuma had overwhelming forces that might conquer the small army that Cortes would lead into the island-city.

Yet, he had promised himself, his army and all of the native people that he would free them from Montezuma, his tax collectors, and the robbery they inflicted on these cities, towns and villages. The chiefs of many of the cities asked Cortes to stay in the area where they could help defend him against Montezuma's huge army, but Cortes told them that he and his army were not afraid of Montezuma, as they were fighting for their freedom, and bringing the words of the one true God to them and all of the people of

Mexico.

This endeavor would protect them and help assure them of victory.

More expensive presents were brought to Cortes by representatives of Montezuma, all with the request that Cortes not enter Tenochtitlan, and Cortes informed them that the chiefs of the cities he had had to fight had blamed Montezuma for ordering them to resist his entry.

The representatives were told by Cortes that he still did not believe the chiefs, as he considered Montezuma a friend through all of the gifts he had sent. He still wanted to meet Montezuma face-to-face in friendship.

Another four representatives of Montezuma entered Tlamanalco, bringing presents of gold, silver, and finely woven cotton cloth, again telling Cortes that Montezuma would furnish more gold and other forms of wealth for the king of Spain and Cortes, but Cortes replied that it was his duty to accommodate the king's wishes, and to bring the words of the one true God to all of the people of Mexico.

Following their meeting, the representatives of Montezuma were dispatched back to Tenochtitlan and Montezuma, and the small army of Cortes began preparations to march toward Tenochtitlan.

As the area between Tlamanalco and Tenochtitlan was heavily populated, shorter marches were undertaken. Approaching the city of Iztapalatengo, they found that city was half built on water, the rest on land. It was to that city that Montezuma, who had heard from his representatives the words of Cortes, decided to send his nephew, Cacamatzin, the lord of Texcoco, to welcome Cortes to Tenochtitlan, and to assist him, and his people to their quarters within the capital city. Cacamatzin arrived with great pageantry on a throne atop a litter carried by eight of the chiefs of other important cities.

Alighting from the litter, Cacamatzin walked along the walkway which was swept clean by the eight litter-carriers right up to the area in front of where Cortes stood. Cacamatzin informed Cortes that he would offer any help requested on the way to the quarters that Cortes and his party would occupy within Tenochtitlan. Cacamatzin also begged forgiveness for his uncle, Montezuma, who was suffering from an illness, or he would have come to greet him himself.

Cortes warmly embraced Cacamatzin, and gave him some stones called margaritas which display several colors when provided sunlight, while giving less valuable gifts of beads to the chiefs. The men of Cortes's party were stunned by the pomp and pageantry that accompanied the Cacamatzin arrival, wondering that if this was only Montezuma's nephew, how would Montezuma present himself when they were to witness the meeting?

After the exchange of presents, Cortes and the group with him were escorted along the road to another city named Iztapalapa, which, like Iztapalatengo, was built half in water and half on dry land.

All of the buildings were built of masonry. Entering the city and being guided to the palaces within which Cortes, his soldiers, and the many people attached to the group, were lodged, was something unexpected in a land so far away from what the Spaniards knew as civilization.

After looking at the beautiful, spacious, and well-built rooms, the men went into the gardens just outside the places they were quartered, seeing and smelling the beautiful flowers and trees, and watching and listening to the birds flying about and fish swimming in the waters surrounding the tall buildings. It appeared as a fairyland to the Spaniards, and many of the natives who accompanied Cortes's group had never seen these sights either.

The following morning Cortes, his Spanish soldiers, the group of chiefs following him from various other cities, and the group which accompanied Cacamatzin left Iztapalapa marching along the causeway, with large masonry buildings rising from the land on one side and with equally tall and well-built masonry buildings rising from the waters on the other.

Canoes were paddled in and around the waterways, under bridges and along the many canals. Stopping after having just entered the streets of Tenochtitlan, the entourage waited for a great procession of important chiefs to approach Cortes, his soldiers, and the many people with him. Behind the approaching chiefs, a large, beautifully decorated litter carrying Montezuma himself approached the area immediately in front of Cortes.

Cortes dismounted from his horse as Montezuma's litter approached. The litter was lowered and prince Montezuma stepped down, aided by four of his nephews. All of the people around Montezuma had their eyes lowered in very deep respect.

Montezuma welcomed Cortes and Cortes first offered his hand to Montezuma, but the men stationed around Montezuma brushed the hand away. Cortes then brought out a stunning necklace of gold with many margarita stones flashing in the brilliant sunlight, placing it gently around the neck of the great Montezuma.

Both men appeared comfortable talking with each other through the translation of Dona Marina, and Cortes told Montezuma that now his heart rejoiced in having met him in person, having done the bidding of his king in Spain, of whom he was a mere vassal.

A few more pleasantries were exchanged between the two men, and then Montezuma was escorted back to his litter, which was picked up by the eight carriers, and he left the area with orders for Cacamatzin and his group of followers to escort the Cortes party to their lodging.

As Montezuma departed, all of the people who had been part of his group began following him, all with downcast eyes, until they passed out of sight.

Chapter 5—The Conquering of Tenochtitlan in Mexico

1519-1521

CACAMATZIN RETURNED TO the throne on his litter and the eight carriers lifted it onto their shoulders, leading Cortes and his group into the city where they were taken to the palaces containing the huge rooms in which they were to be lodged. Upon entering the palace, Cortes was met by Montezuma, who waited as Cortes approached, presenting and putting around the neck of Cortes a beautiful gold necklace.

After the thank you had been expressed, Montezuma left for his own rooms in the palace, not far from those of Cortes's group. The placement of the company of Spanish soldiers was done with the artillery group facing in outward directions, the cavalry, crossbowmen, musketeers, and swordsmen were assigned to rooms where, if attacked, they would be of most use in defending themselves and the groups with them.

The rooms provided comfortable beds for everyone, and food was brought for their dinners. This all took place on November 8th, 1519.

Actually, the capital of Tenochtitlan was founded by a group of Aztecs looking to find a place in which they could build a city offering protection from people who would approach from the east, defeat and enslave them, according to legends and myths passed down through generations. One of their idols, said to be Huichilobos their god of war, told them to look for a place where an eagle would be seen, resting on the arm of a saguaro cactus, with a snake between its jaws.

While searching for such a place, in 1324, in the midst of a swampy area of a lake called Chalco, they indeed saw an eagle perched on an arm of a saguaro cactus with a snake clasped sideways in its mouth. After draining some of the swamp, many islands appeared on which masonry buildings were erected.

The city of Tenochtitlan was once comprised of two separate cities, Tenochtitlan and Tlaltelolco, which grew side-by-side until 1473, when Axayacatl, a powerful chief of Tenochtitlan, conquered the forces of Tlaltelolco and united the two cities as Tenochtitlan. It has been said that as many as two hundred thousand residents lived within the city when Cortes and his group arrived there in 1519.

After four days of resting, eating, sleeping and visiting with Montezuma in both men's quarters, Cortes made arrangements by sending two of his captains to Montezuma, asking that he and his captains and five soldiers be permitted to visit the temple in which their idols were contained. Although Montezuma was not in favor of allowing it, he arranged for a number of his chiefs and soldiers to accompany himself and the group to the temple which was the highest-level building within the city.

After walking to the very top, the entire group saw the wide, blood-covered platform in the middle of the top floor, and the recent happenings occurring at that place gave all of the Spaniards deep feelings of sorrow for those unfortunate enough to have been sacrificed there. Looking out over the sides, they saw the magnificence of the cities, towns, and villages that provided food, clothing and other necessities for this large city. The mountains that surrounded them were beautiful in the brilliant sunshine, and there could be seen the forests of trees growing almost to the summits.

This was both a beautiful and terrible sight to behold. Cortes then asked Montezuma for permission to enter the rooms in which their idols were housed, and, after consulting with the high priests of that temple, Montezuma led Cortes and his party inside a room in which two altars stood.

On the first altar stood a huge statue of a giant, fat, wide-faced monster, with terribly large eyes and many gold and pearl jewels displayed all over its body. There were also gold and other precious stones in the form of snakes entwined around its body, and with one hand it held a golden bow and the other golden arrows. When asked for its significance by Cortes, he was told by the chief priest that it was Huichilobos, their god of war. Next to that statue stood a smaller one, holding a lance and shield richly covered by gold and silver. Another tall statue of the same height as Huichilobos was on the other side of the room.

This statue had the face of a bear, with eyes shining brightly as they were made from mirrors reflected as the door remained open. The stench of death swept over the group as they looked upon the walls covered by the blood of the many who had been sacrificed there. Cortes was told that that statue was to their god of hell, Tezcatepuca by name, and that the hearts of five young Tenochtitlan people had been sacrificed that day after they had been killed, and had their hearts cut from their chests.

After witnessing the rooms in which their two greatest idols were contained, the Spaniards were filled with disdain for the religion of death these people practiced, and Cortes and his group returned to the quarters in which they were housed. That is when they received a secret message delivered by two men from the city of Tlaxcala that the men he had left behind at Villa Rica had been attacked by men of Montezuma's command.

After the group that had accompanied Cortes to the temple had a night to contemplate the situation they were in, being a bit confined to their rooms, not knowing if and when an attack by the many warriors within the city and under the orders of Montezuma would come, some of them approached Cortes advising him to take Montezuma captive, and hold him within the rooms they were occupying.

At first, he demurred, but after the captains offered plans on how to take Montezuma captive and escort him to their quarters, all the while threatening him with painful death, he accepted the idea. Asking for permission for his usual group which visited Montezuma regularly, and grudgingly receiving it, the men went to Montezuma's palace and presented their demand. He offered to have members of his family go in his place, but Cortes demanded it be him that they wanted to take. Finally, Montezuma agreed to accompany them to their quarters, and remained there for several days. He explained to his chiefs and family that he had done this on his own, and wanted to remain with his friends and benefactors. He was treated with the best of intentions, eating the best foods, engaging in talks with his advisors, while his tax collectors continued to bring in that which they collected.

However, the word of the attack on the men of Villa Rica had enraged the captains of Cortes and their soldiers. Cortes was told to have Montezuma request the return to the city those captains that had killed the men at Villa Rica, and they were returned and placed in irons. Cortes rendered a death sentence by fire to each of them, and while that sentence was carried out, Montezuma was also placed in irons. Following that event, Cortes offered to release Montezuma, but told him that he valued him closer than a brother, and would hate to see him leave his protection.

There had been words leaked from Montezuma's confidants that a new leader might be announced, and that Montezuma would no longer be the leader of all Mexico. Fearing for his life if released, with his young nephew Cacamatzin most mentioned as the leader of the rebels bent on overthrowing his uncle, Montezuma decided to remain in the custody of Cortes. Cortes convinced Montezuma that Cacamatzin was a person who must be dealt with immediately, and that he should order Cacamatzin to come to visit his uncle in

Tenochtitlan.

This was done, and Cacamatzin was captured by some of the captains who were loyal to Montezuma in the city of Texcoco, the place in which Cacamatzin ruled in a despotic way. He was brought to Montezuma, who turned him over to Cortes. Cortes then appointed the brother of Cacamatzin as king of Texcoco, replacing his brother, with Montezuma calling together the principal chieftains of that province, informing them of the change, and even changing the new king's name to Don Carlos, king and lord of Texcoco.

While this was going on, another threat appeared in the form of a huge army of over one thousand four hundred Spanish soldiers, outfitted with twenty cannons, much powder, stones and balls, two gunners, eighty horses and horsemen, ninety crossbowmen, and seventy musketeers, arriving in nineteen ships, financed and sent by Diego Velasquez, the governor of Cuba.

The leader of this great force was Panfilo Narvaez, a man for whom some of his captains had no love. He had been engaged to find and kill the Cortes group, and return the riches which that group had accumulated. Word of the wealth accumulated by the Cortes group had spread throughout Spain as Cortes had sent some gold and precious items to King Charles V, who had replaced King Ferdinand upon the latter's death in 1516.

Three Spaniards who had been sent by Cortes to mine for gold wandered into the camp of Narvaez, who had landed at San Juan de Ulua, a mere eight leagues from Villa Rica, where captain Gonzalo de Sandoval was still in command of the seventy soldiers left behind by Cortes. The three men were happy to be able to eat and drink wine for the first time in over a year, imbibing more than should have been consumed at one time, suggesting that a force should be dispatched to Villa Rica and take over the town.

Upon the arrival of the ships and the many soldiers, word was taken to Montezuma by chiefs of the villages near San Juan de Ulua, but Cortes was not told until Montezuma, himself, told him about the landing. At that time, Cortes decided to release to his men some of the fortune in gold and precious stones that he had kept for himself, which were really the wealth he had withheld from them in the first place. Requesting that they remain as part of his army in exchange for the "gifts" he kept his group together.

Sandoval called his soldiers together upon learning of the landing at San Juan de Ulua. Expecting an attack on his small outpost, he told them not to surrender the town to anyone, to which they agreed. He sent two men to watch the roads leading from the landing place to the small outpost, and they reported to him the approach of six men, one being a priest whose name was Padre Guevara. Padre Guevara became the spokesman after entering Sandoval's living quarters, stating that Diego Velasquez had spent much money on the fleet, and that Cortes and his group had been traitors, as the percentage that had been agreed upon of any wealth the group would receive was never sent to Velasquez. Hearing the words of the padre, Sandoval admonished him saying that all Spaniards were to better serve his majesty, King Charles V, not Velasquez.

Hearing the harsh voices coming from Sandoval's living quarters, a number of the native people working at the outpost rushed into his quarters, trussing up the six men in hammock-like vines, carrying them off toward Tenochtitlan by a number of relay carriers.

As they were carried through the large cities on their way to Cortes, the six men were amazed at the size and quality of construction, and the beauty of the animals, birds, and gardens they saw along the way. Cortes had advance warning of the arrival of the six men, and upon their arrival in front of the palace entrance, he met them and had them released from their bonds.

When those men became aware of the opulence of the city, the other cities within the large lake, the soldiers under the command of Cortes, and his good treatment of them, they were amazed, and after two days, upon their dispatch back to Narvaez, they had offered their fealty to Cortes. Upon their arrival back at the camp of

Narvaez, they began to tell some of the captains what they had heard and seen, how Cortes had treated them with courtesy, and awarded them with gold and other precious items.

They also gave some of those precious gifts to the captains who showed interest in revolting against Narvaez. This became the start of the downfall of Narvaez.

Cortes had sent one of his most loyal captains, Juan Velasquez with an orderly named Juan del Rio, both adorned with heavy gold necklaces, long enough to be wound twice around their waists. Also, stealthily hidden in the clothing they wore were additional smaller items of gold to be given to captains known to be acquaintances of Cortes. Upon the arrival of Juan Velasquez at the camp of Narvaez, the captains and soldiers of Narvaez noted the riches the two men were wearing, not speaking of them while surrounded by the other men of Narvaez. By Cortes's request, Juan Velasquez told Narvaez that Cortes would surrender to Narvaez when and if the representative of King Charles V would produce a signed decree that Cortes should be taken as a prisoner and returned to Spain.

Of course, no such signed decree existed, but only one signed by Diego Velasquez, governor of Cuba, Cortes's own cousin. After dinner had been eaten, Juan Velasquez had time enough to steal away and deliver the presents of gold to the captains Cortes had mentioned, returning shortly thereafter.

After harsh words were spoken by a nephew of the governor, whose name was also Diego Velasquez, toward Juan, Narvaez rushed Juan and del Rio from the camp before any bloodshed took place. Many of the captains had seen the confrontation, with the responses by Juan to Diego's outbursts making sense to them. However, the warnings of Cortes's approach alerted the Narvaez group to post guards and spies in the areas that would afford pathways that could be used by Cortes's troops.

Cortes, after sending Juan Velasquez and del Rio to Narvaez's camp, ordered Pedro de Alvarado, his most favored captain to become his representative in charge of the city of Tenochtitlan, and telling him in no uncertain terms that Montezuma was to be guarded and kept in captivity until Cortes would return.

After that, Cortes brought his troops, all two hundred sixty-six of them together, and began a long and pointed talk about the task they were facing, that being to defeat troops that outnumbered them six to one. Their faith, loyalty to Cortes, and self-preservation were what he talked about most, but cautioned them to silence as they approached the enemy.

Upon the arrival of Juan Velasquez and del Rio back to the camp of Cortes, he learned from them the plans of defense by Narvaez's forces, and, because of rains that were falling heavily in the area, many of Narvaez's captains, and even Narvaez himself, returned to their quarters to stay dry and comfortable.

The most important information that was brought back was the location of Narvaez's quarters, the nephew Diego Velasquez, and other important men of Narvaez's army. Stealthily, Cortes's army crossed a stream that led to Narvaez's camp, capturing one of the guards across the stream and near to the camp. Another guard saw what was happening, and called out toward the camp, "To arms! To Arms! Cortes is coming."

This warning came a bit late, for the soldiers of Cortes were able to rush through the artillery, losing but three soldiers by cannon fire, and Juan Velasquez's command rushed the steps behind which Narvaez was sleeping until the shouts woke him. He was protected by guards for a short few seconds before a soldier was able to fight through and wound Narvaez.

He called out in fright, "Holy Mary, they have killed me and destroyed my eye!" Narvaez was wounded, but survived. The nephew Diego Velasquez was taken prisoner, as were others who were not mentioned among the Narvaez captains and troops. All were treated with honor by Cortes, but remained in custody until they promised fealty to Cortes.

Following this crushing victory, Cortes ordered that the ships by which Narvaez's forces had arrived be disabled, and the sailors eighty crossbowmen, as many musketeers, and two thousand Tlaxcalan warriors carrying the heavy cannons and following that meaningful army. As they passed through cities they had gone through before, no chiefs and very few of the residents were seen in the streets, preferring to stay out of range of any attempts on their lives in retribution for what the people of Tenochtitlan had brought upon themselves.

Upon reaching Tenochtitlan, there were few people seen around the palace. Cortes was met in the courtyard by Montezuma who congratulated him on his great victory, but Cortes brushed him aside, which hurt the pride of the prince, who went back to his quarters depressed. After Cortes and his soldiers were assigned to their quarters with the men of Narvaez's command being offered other accommodations, Cortes found de Alvarado alive and unhurt.

In telling Cortes of the revolt, it was said that the high priests had inspired captains in the city to fight to rescue Montezuma from the clutches of the Spaniards, and remove the cross and statue of Mary and baby Jesus that had been placed in one of the rooms inside the temple.

When the warriors tried to remove the cross and statue they were unable to do so, and some said that it was a miracle and abandoned the effort. As word came to Montezuma of the defeat of Narvaez, he calmed the outbreak, and stopped all attacks on the palace and de Alvarado's troops, but did not ask his followers for food for himself or the soldiers inside the palace.

As these explanations were told to Cortes, he lost his temper, not only as these deeds by de Alvarado and his men were not as he would have done, but he was upset by the fact that the chiefs of many cities they passed during their forced march did not come out to honor him as he thought they would, and none brought gifts for him, nor his men.

Shortly after hearing all of the stories told by de Alvarado and his men, a man from Tacuba, a city in which Cortes had placed several young women given to him by chiefs of cities, and even the

daughter of Montezuma, came stu
speak with Cortes immediately.

Brought to Cortes, the man
warriors attacked his city, carryin
been left there to be cared for until

Cortes ordered one of his ca
among them horsemen, crossbowr
out this issue, but as his group r
palace, a large army of warriors
rocks from their slings, slashin
launching javelins, from the fror
Many soldiers were wounded, som
men tried to fight their way bac
been surrounded and made slight
the palace.

Another huge force of warr
directions, wounding at least for
while cannons, crossbowmen a
warriors from overrunning the tr
long the attacks kept coming, fi
inside the rooms they fought to
soldiers smothering them with dir

There were times that the s
such fury, the warriors withdrew
soldiers, trying to cut off the
comparative safety of the mason
the shrill whistles, the constant
and words calling the soldiers
encourage the soldiers any mor
Plans were made to fight from w
soldiers acting as large wooden
day to push the closely-lined war
more damage, but as the warrior
backs to the soldiers.

Rathe
drawbridge
within the
drawbridge
warriors ju
struck by th
This a
they fought
temple and
of Mary an
the cross ar
been remov
and preserv
his soldiers,
room in wh
kept, and up
burned.
Having
Cortes, who
the idols had
soldiers had
the way of
accompanyin
During
plans to hav
attacks and
After reques
the announ
Padre de la
his help, to f
When
recognized b
began to spe
broke in sayi

and their captains be brought to Cortes. Upon their arrival, they were sent to different areas of the country to establish cities, towns or villages, with many of Cortes's men interspersed with those sailors, while all of Narvaez's soldiers joined Cortes after he offered them riches.

Among the men that had accompanied Narvaez was a black Moorish man who had become ill with smallpox on the journey, and as he spread the disease many of the natives were stricken and died. The native people had never been exposed to such a terrible disease, and had no immunity.

Also, word was brought to Cortes that revolt had occurred in Tenochtitlan, and that Pedro de Alvarado was attacked in the palace, fires being set to drive him out, with seven of his soldiers being killed. This first report was delivered by runners from Tlaxcala, which was followed by an urgent request from de Alvarado. Preparations for an immediate departure were made, and forced marches were ordered by Cortes.

During the first day of marching, four representatives of Montezuma met the army, stating to Cortes that de Alvarado had left the palace with all of his men and fell upon unsuspecting residents of Tenochtitlan. This had occurred as the residents were celebrating a feast in honor of their idols, Huichilobos and Tezcatepuca, the gods of war and hell.

De Alvarado's forces killed many of the residents but suffered the deaths of the seven soldiers, as he retreated inside the palace. By that time, news of the victory by Cortes over the army of Narvaez had traveled to many parts of Mexico, and with Cortes already on his way back to Tenochtitlan, Montezuma was furious. As the forced marches reached Tlaxcala, they were informed that Montezuma had stopped his forces from attacking de Alvarado, but Cortes and his troops were battle weary, hungry, and thirsty, as no provisions were ordered by Montezuma.

The forced march continued with a total of one thousand three hundred soldiers under the command of Cortes, ninety-six horses, eighty crossbowmen, as many musketeers, and two thousand Tlaxcalan warriors carrying the heavy cannons and following that meaningful army. As they passed through cities they had gone through before, no chiefs and very few of the residents were seen in the streets, preferring to stay out of range of any attempts on their lives in retribution for what the people of Tenochtitlan had brought upon themselves.

Upon reaching Tenochtitlan, there were few people seen around the palace. Cortes was met in the courtyard by Montezuma who congratulated him on his great victory, but Cortes brushed him aside, which hurt the pride of the prince, who went back to his quarters depressed. After Cortes and his soldiers were assigned to their quarters with the men of Narvaez's command being offered other accommodations, Cortes found de Alvarado alive and unhurt.

In telling Cortes of the revolt, it was said that the high priests had inspired captains in the city to fight to rescue Montezuma from the clutches of the Spaniards, and remove the cross and statue of Mary and baby Jesus that had been placed in one of the rooms inside the temple.

When the warriors tried to remove the cross and statue they were unable to do so, and some said that it was a miracle and abandoned the effort. As word came to Montezuma of the defeat of Narvaez, he calmed the outbreak, and stopped all attacks on the palace and de Alvarado's troops, but did not ask his followers for food for himself or the soldiers inside the palace.

As these explanations were told to Cortes, he lost his temper, not only as these deeds by de Alvarado and his men were not as he would have done, but he was upset by the fact that the chiefs of many cities they passed during their forced march did not come out to honor him as he thought they would, and none brought gifts for him, nor his men.

Shortly after hearing all of the stories told by de Alvarado and his men, a man from Tacuba, a city in which Cortes had placed several young women given to him by chiefs of cities, and even the daughter of Montezuma, came stumbling into the palace asking to speak with Cortes immediately.

Brought to Cortes, the man told him that a force of many warriors attacked his city, carrying off the young women who had been left there to be cared for until Cortes's return.

Cortes ordered one of his captains to take four hundred men, among them horsemen, crossbowmen and musketeers, to straighten out this issue, but as his group reached the street in front of the palace, a large army of warriors blocked their way, firing arrows, rocks from their slings, slashing with swords and knives, and launching javelins, from the front and from the rooftops above. Many soldiers were wounded, some were killed. The captain and his men tried to fight their way back inside the palace, but they had been surrounded and made slight progress toward returning inside the palace.

Another huge force of warriors attacked the palace from all directions, wounding at least forty-seven in the first few minutes, while cannons, crossbowmen and musketeers barely kept the warriors from overrunning the troops fighting from within. All day long the attacks kept coming, fires were started by the attackers inside the rooms they fought to enter, and were put out by the soldiers smothering them with dirt and clothing.

There were times that the soldiers attacked the warriors with such fury, the warriors withdrew a short way, then swept behind the soldiers, trying to cut off the retreat to the palace and the comparative safety of the masonry walls. The banging of the drums, the shrill whistles, the constant trumpet blaring, the many shouts and words calling the soldiers cowards or worse, did nothing to encourage the soldiers any more than their struggle to stay alive. Plans were made to fight from within defenses built by some of the soldiers acting as large wooden shields, which helped the following day to push the closely-lined warriors back to where the cannons did more damage, but as the warriors retreated never did they turn their backs to the soldiers.

Rather, they would retreat to the bridges which had drawbridges over open water between the many buildings and cities within the huge Lake Chalco. Before they entered the area of drawbridges, which protected the interior of the city, many of the warriors jumped from the causeway into the water to avoid being struck by the swords of the soldiers.

This all happened as the warriors gave way to the soldiers as they fought their way to the main temple, intending to enter the temple and destroy the idols, and make sure that the cross and statue of Mary and Jesus were not damaged. Approaching the area where the cross and statue had been placed, the soldiers found that it had been removed, later finding out that Montezuma had had it removed and preserved in safekeeping. It became most important to Cortes, his soldiers, and the warriors from Tlaxcala to fight their way to the room in which the two idols, Huichilobos and Tezcatepuc, were kept, and upon attaining that room, the two idols were smashed and burned.

Having accomplished the mission of destroying the idols, Cortes, who led the push into the temple and to the room in which the idols had been, led his troops back to the palace where he and his soldiers had been quartered, although many warriors tried to block the way of the soldiers and brave warriors of Tlaxcala who were accompanying the Spaniards.

During the next several hours, Cortes and his captains made plans to have Montezuma make a plea to the warriors to cease the attacks and allow the Spaniards and Tlaxcalans to depart in peace. After requesting Montezuma to climb to the top parapet and make the announcement, Montezuma refused. It took words from the Padre de la Merced, who spoke with much reverence in requesting his help, to finally persuade Montezuma to make the plea.

When he appeared at the parapet, he was immediately recognized by his subjects, and the noise was muted temporarily. He began to speak, but one of the high priests among the crowd below broke in saying that Montezuma had been replaced by another as the lord, whose name was Cuitlahuac, and the war must go on as they had promised their idols to kill each and every Spaniard, and those who had chosen to help them.

Then the bombardment of stones attacked the men on the parapet; three stones struck Montezuma, one on the head, one on the arm, and the final one on his leg. The stone which hit his head killed him, and the Spaniards who had gotten to know him were in tears, as he had become dear to them.

After informing the crowd below that Montezuma was dead at their own hands, the attacks resumed, and new plans had to be made. Since many bridges had been badly damaged, it was decided that a long, wide, wooden covering would be constructed that could be transported by carriers and laid to span the openings.

The soldiers would cross over it, and then the temporary bridge would be carried on to the next opening. This movement from the palace to the outskirts of the city would be done at night in the hopes that the warriors would need sleep, and not be as quick with their weapons.

As the plan was being carried out, the leading group including the horsemen led by Cortes were able to cross the safe bridges and the wooden covering, facing many squadrons of warriors after the call went out that the escape was underway. The Tlaxcalan warriors were behind the horsemen, followed by the musketeers, who at night, were not able to reload after firing one shot as they were running for their lives.

The crossbowmen were faced with the same issue, not being able to nock arrows as they were running too. The swordsmen were slashing along the sides of the causeway as they ran, and did most of the damage to those warriors who attacked from the canoes alongside the causeway. By the grace of God, some of the Spaniards and Tlaxcalans made it to the city of Tacuba where they waited for whoever of the men who had managed to escape from Tenochtitlan.

Many horses, riders, and other soldiers were killed during the escape, and most of those who survived were injured in some way.

Cortes's army and the Tlaxcalans sought protection in a building within Tacuba, where they found Dona Marina, Dona Luisa, the daughter of Xicotenga, and Maria de Estrada, a Spanish woman who had accompanied Narvaez, and who was the only Spanish woman in New Spain.

While there were many attacks made by the Tenochtitlan warriors, there were a few counter-attacks made by the soldiers. The Tlaxcalan warriors knew of a side trail that led to their city, and the entire group followed them to a building that the group used as a fort. The warriors of Tenochtitlan followed them to that building which was defended during the next day. The following evening, the Tlaxcalans again led the group toward their city using every precaution. The scouts who preceded Cortes's small army led by the Tlaxcalans reported that the fields through which they were leading the group were filled with Tenochtitlan warriors, and that the only way through them was to send some horsemen ahead along the path which they were using, with the rest of the group following closely behind.

The horsemen used their lances, aimed at the warriors' faces, in clearing narrow, short spaces for the group to advance, with the swordsmen slashing at the bodies of warriors who came too close to them. The lurchers fought well, running alongside the soldiers attacking the arms and legs of the warriors that came before them. On and on they plodded, forcing their way through the waves of chiefs and warriors, looking for the open spot where they might find rest.

Ahead, they saw the banners of the captain general, many chiefs of various cities, and they were outfitted in rich golden armor, all wearing plumes indicating their degree of importance. Knowing that trampling these leaders would scatter their warriors, dishearten their resolve to kill the small army, and perhaps lead to perhaps a temporary peaceful solution to this war, the horsemen led the rest of the group toward the Tenochtitlan army's leaders.

Orders were passed through the ranks that the men with

plumes on their helmets were to be killed as quickly as possible.

With Cortes and the other horsemen in the lead, and the rest of the group following closely behind, the attack on the leaders led straight to the captain general, whose banner was knocked from the hands of that leader, but it was another horseman, a rider whose name was Salamanca, who made the thrust that killed the captain general, after which the warriors lost much of their bravado.

This battle had taken place at Otumba, still a distance from Tlaxcala, but with the partial victory over the huge army of Tenochtitlan warriors, the Tlaxcalan troops became much more engaged in the protection of the Spanish soldiers and kept the rest of the Tenochtitlan warriors away from the weary and wounded soldiers.

As the small army approached Tlaxcala, many of the chiefs of the surrounding area came toward the approaching army expecting to meet the conquering Tenochtitlan warriors, and were surprised to meet the victorious Spanish forces. These chiefs wore much gold, their colorful plumes and banners, and were accompanied by their captains. Finding a building that accommodated all of the soldiers and Tlaxcalan fighters, wounds were seared and bound, and much-needed rest was allowed, while the defenses against the fewer following Tenochtitlan warriors was undertaken by guards on a rotating basis.

Another day of marching brought the group closer to Tlaxcala, another night of healing and resting, and fewer warriors of the Tenochtitlan army following. The next morning, as they attained the crest of a hill, they saw the tops of the homes inside Tlaxcala, a place they hoped to find food, rest, and comfort.

As they drew closer to Tlaxcala, the chiefs, Mase Escasi, Xicotenga, the elder, and many other chieftains of that area arrived, banners flying, golden necklaces sparkling in the brilliant sunlight, and shouts of welcome greeted the group of just over four hundred spared souls.

The Tlaxcalans were very happy to see that Dona Marina and

Dona Luisa had survived unhurt throughout the struggle. The group was led triumphantly into Tlaxcala, although many of the bodies were still healing from the many injuries they suffered. Four soldiers died during the period of rest at Tlaxcala, but the respite improved the health of most of the rest. There was much pain and sorrow over the large number of soldiers and Tlaxcalan warriors that had died in the escape from Tenochtitlan, brothers, husbands, and sons of the residents.

Thoughts of the people who were ordered to remain in Villa Rica circulated among the men, and it was not long before Cortes sent word to Villa Rica that no ships were to be allowed to leave that harbor, that they remove the sailors from the two ships owned by Narvaez and then destroy those ships. All weapons found on those ships were to be brought by those sailors, who numbered seven, for use by his soldiers, and the sailors duly arrived with the additional weapons.

During the twenty-two days the Spaniards spent in Tlaxcala, Xicotenga the younger began contacting friends of his who had been captains and warriors under his command, urging them to join him in killing all of the Spaniards and retaking the city. Word was leaked to Mase Escasi and other chieftains including his father, Xicotenga, the elder, of the plot.

Knowing that the city and surrounding area had been enriched by the Spaniards' entry, and that the army had defeated a much larger force, they ordered Xicotenga to be brought before them and severely chastised. As he stood before them, he told them that they were not his leader. His own father threw him down the steps leading to the riser on which the chieftains sat. He was restrained along with his revolutionary friends and imprisoned.

Nearing the three weeks of rest and recuperation, Cortes gathered his captains together announcing a plan of going to the province of Tepeaca, which was nearby. When word spread to the soldiers, the men who had arrived with Narvaez were against any more fighting, asking permission to return to Cuba.

Cortes informed them there were no ships to transport them, and promised riches in settling this land. A requisition for their return to Cuba was drawn up by a king's notary, presented to Cortes, but ignored by him.

The time that had elapsed from the escape from Tenochtitlan, July 10th, 1520 to the battle at Otumba, July 15th, the two additional days to reach Tlaxcala, and the twenty-two days spent in that city, brought the date to August 8th, 1520, the day that Cortes began his war of retribution against Tenochtitlan.

A Spanish army of approximately four hundred twenty men, armed with but sixteen crossbows and arrows, the rest with swords and shields, led by seventeen horsemen, and accompanied by two thousand Tlaxcalan warriors armed with blowguns, bows and arrows, darts, and stones to be released from slings, left Tlaxcala marching toward Tepeaca.

The battle with the warriors of that city was fought in the maize fields and plain outside their city, and was a rout after the horsemen and lurchers waded into the enemy's ranks, what with the swordsmanship of the horsemen, and the fierce lurchers tearing at the warriors. Meanwhile the Spaniards with the crossbows sent volley after volley into the ranks of the men of Tepeaca, and the fierce way the Tlaxcalans fought in defeating the warriors of Tepeaca was breathtaking.

Few lives were lost, although two horses were injured during the fight. Word of the defeat of the men of Tepeaca spread across the areas controlled by the new ruler of Tenochtitlan, as the man who succeeded Montezuma had died of smallpox. This newest leader was named Guatemoc, a nephew of Montezuma.

He immediately sent out orders to stop Cortes before Cortes and his armies could take over any more areas that recognized Guatemoc as their lord and ruler. Giving gold and jewels to the chieftains in the areas leading toward Tenochtitlan, in order to buy their support, he expected them to stop and kill Cortes before Cortes could reach Tenochtitlan.

During this time, two ships arrived at Villa Rica separately, one with a good friend of Cortes, Pedro Barba by name, along with thirteen soldiers, a horse and mare. Pedro Barba had brought a letter addressed to Narvaez which requested that Cortes be brought back to Cuba in chains if he was still alive, to be transported to Castile, Spain by the command of the bishop of Burgos.

After going ashore, the men of Villa Rica advised Barba of the location of the Cortes forces. On arrival at Tepeaca, Barba was met by the entire garrison with great honors bestowed on him by Cortes. The second ship transported a gentleman by the name of Rodrigo Morejon de Lobera, who brought with him eight soldiers, six crossbows, much twine for making bowstrings, and a mare. All of these horses and weapons were happily greeted by the soldiers.

Guatemoc sent two armies to two different locations, one being to Guacachula and the other to Izucar. These armies began taking advantage of the people of these cities, so much so that the chieftains took offense at these men who took the daughters and wives from their homes, raping and defiling them in many indecent ways, and who stole food, clothing and possessions from the houses.

Secretly, four chiefs of Guacachula came to Cortes, asking him and his armies to stop these soldiers from committing these heinous crimes against their people, promising help in informing of the placement of these Tenochtitlan troops, the weapons they carried and other important information that could be used against them.

This valuable information was passed on to the man who Cortes chose to head up the group to set the city of Guacachula free from the ties to Guatemoc and his rowdy warriors. Cortes selected Cristobal de Olid to command the horsemen, crossbowmen, and a large number of Tlaxcalan warriors sent to Guacachula.

Most of the best horses and horsemen were among Cristobal's command. As that command approached the area, some of the chieftains came out to meet Cristobal, detailing where and how the Mexican troops of Culua were aligned inside the city, and it took but an hour to put them to flight under the hooves, the arrows of the crossbowmen, and the weapons wielded by the Tlaxcalans.

There were casualties during that fight with two horses being killed and eight more wounded, and some of the soldiers were injured. Cristobal did not wait for further orders but immediately led the troops under his command, and some of the warriors of Guacachula joining with them, to the city of Izucar, where his army defeated the squadrons of Tenochtitlan troops in quick order. Then, Cristobal returned to Cortes's new headquarters at Tepeaca.

During this time, more ships arrived at Villa Rica, after having stopped at a harbor called Panuca, where Francisco de Garay, the governor of Jamaica, had earlier sent a group to form a city under his rule. Unfortunately, that settlement had been attacked and defeated, with no one left alive to tell of the fate of the settlers.

Upon viewing the carnage, the ships looked for the settlement Cortes had founded. These ships brought more soldiers, horses, cannons, muskets, powder, balls, crossbowmen, arrows, and twine for restringing the crossbows. As these men and supplies were directed from Villa Rica to Cortes, they were greeted warmly by Cortes and his group.

With the addition of the soldiers, their supplies, and weapons, Cortes began sending groups of soldiers to areas in which the warriors of Guatemoc were committing many crimes against the people of those communities and defeating and scattering the warriors they deposed. Cortes's men found that items worn by horses and soldiers had been placed by the people of those communities in their temples in front of their idols, and so they took women and children from those communities to be branded on their bodies as slaves.

The cruelty of the branding was horrible to behold. After the branding, the women and children were divided among Cortes, his captains, and the Spanish soldiers, with the prettiest women being taken and hidden away by Cortes and his captains. After much commotion, Cortes announced that an auction for the remaining women would take place.

Reports were brought to Cortes of additional crimes being committed by Guatemoc's warriors at other cities controlled by Guatemoc. Cortes dispatched other captains and armies of his soldiers and the Tlaxcalan warriors to take these areas and place them under his rule. Cortes led a large well-equipped army of Spaniards, as well as over ten thousand Tlaxcalan warriors toward the large city of Texcoco, defeating a group of Tenochtitlan and Texcocoan soldiers in a large ravine outside the city.

Just before entering the city, ten chieftains from that city met them with the head chief carrying a golden banner, bowing humbly before Cortes, giving the banner to Cortes, and asking him to spare the city from damage, offering food, shelter, and any other reasonable requirements the army would need.

After hearing their words of peace, Cortes conferred with his captains and a few of his soldiers, who cautioned him to be aware of entrapment within the city, and Cortes finally agreed to accept the words of the chiefs and enter the city. Cortes also demanded that the Tlaxcalan warriors not take items from the homes nor people of the city. As many of the residents had fled the city, even the head chieftain, Cortes found the city nearly empty of women and children.

The accommodations were found to be adequate, and food was brought to them. In the rooms they found idols of worship which were destroyed by the troops. When Cortes spoke to the chiefs who were left in Texcoco, he heard that the head chief was not truly the man most qualified for the position, and that a younger man was chosen to replace him, and he requested to become a Christian. Cortes became his godfather, and changed his name to Don Hernando Cortes.

He was a very good and understanding lord and king of Texcoco. It was explained to him that Cortes would have two ships built within his city as the great Lake Chalco would afford an avenue of attack on the many cities that were contained in it and supported by Guatemoc's armies.

The new lord and king, Don Hernando Cortes, understood and offered help in building the ships and in any other projects that needed to be done. After twelve days of living in Texcoco, the Tlaxcalan soldiers had run out of provisions and requested Cortes to allow them to advance further into the areas where Guatemoc had power.

Cortes led the forces which left Texcoco, advancing toward the city of Itzapalapa, but this effort was doomed to fail, as many of the defenses of that city extended into the waters of Lake Chalco, which were places that provided for ambush by the warriors of Guatemoc. As Cortes and his army advanced along the causeways gaining entrance into some of the cities built into the lake, water cascaded into the areas in which the soldiers and Tlaxcalan warriors had sought sleeping quarters for the night, as dams released huge amounts of water flooding many of those small islands, and drowning two Tlaxcalans who were not familiar with swimming.

Cortes and his troops retreated all the way back to Texcoco, leaving behind many weapons and powder drenched and useless until dried. The defeat did much to bolster the spirits and resolve of the Tenochtitlan lord and king, Guatemoc, and his warriors.

Reaching the safety of Texcoco, Cortes and his army healed and resupplied, with the return to Itzapalapa with retribution uppermost in their minds. Also, there were a few cities that were still under the powers of Guatemoc that came to Cortes, asking for peace and forgiveness for killing Spanish soldiers and warriors of Tlaxcala during the retreat from Tenochtitlan.

Cortes was pleased in the requests and the fealty offered by these cities, but was informed that the warriors of Guatemoc were advancing toward the four communities closest to Tenochtitlan. The main purpose of approaching those areas was that they had supplied maize for Tenochtitlan and the many areas controlled by that city in the past, and they were sent to collect the crop for the season.

Being requested by those four chieftains from those cities led Cortes to send out a group of ten horsemen, one hundred soldiers, some crossbowmen and a few musketeers to protect the people gathering the maize, and beat back the attacking warriors. This occurred more than once with the Guatemoc warriors retreating back to their canoes, leaving fifteen of their warriors lying dead on the field of combat, while five were captured and brought to Cortes.

The following day, more of the chiefs of the surrounding towns came to the camp of Cortes, honoring him greatly, and offering their services in return for protection against the armies of Guatemoc. Cortes was perplexed as some of his soldiers were healing from injuries and many of the Tlaxcalan warriors had accumulated gold and other precious items and were asking to return to Tlaxcala as men of wealth.

He decided to attack Chalco first and then to proceed to Tlamanalco, cities in which Tenochtitlan garrisons held positions. He sent Gonzalo de Sandoval and Francisco de Lugo with fifteen horsemen, two hundred soldiers, musketeers and crossbowmen, and the remaining Tlaxcalan warriors on this mission.

They were to defeat and scatter the warriors defending Chalco, and proceed to Tlamanalco, which would help clear the road to Tlaxcala, allowing safe passage through Tlaxcala to Villa Rica. That safe passage would ensure the timber that was being cut for the boats to be built at Texcoco could be transported safely. Sandoval and Lugo engaged and defeated the soldiers at Chalco and again at Tlamanalco, although many of the horses were injured in the battle, some crossbowmen and musketeers were injured, and there were casualties among the Tlaxcalan warriors.

Sandoval and Lugo returned to Texcoco and were greeted warmly by Cortes. Chiefs of both of those cities accompanied the returning combatants, and thanked Cortes for freeing their cities from the Tenochtitlan rule.

The next mission in importance was to have the timber for the boats brought from Tlaxcala, where it was being cut, to Texcoco; so Cortes ordered Sandoval, and an army of two hundred soldiers, fifteen horsemen, twenty crossbowmen and musketeers, a large company of Tlaxcalans, and twenty chieftains from Texcoco, along with some elders and youths from Chalco to be safely taken back to their city.

That large group set off marching toward Chalco, intending to go through one of the smaller cities that was under the protection of Chalco, but had been fierce in fighting the Spaniards as they fled Tenochtitlan, and they had taken many prisoners, sacrificing them to their idols.

As they entered that smaller city, the residents fled and Sandoval's soldiers followed and killed four of them before Sandoval halted the army, feeling sorry for the people who had fled. Upon entering the temple where the idols were worshipped, they found many Spanish suits of armor, helmets, and even faces of sacrificed soldiers, their beards still on their faces.

A message had been scrawled on the wall of the room in which the men had been imprisoned saying that Juan Yuste, a soldier who arrived with Narvaez, and some of his mates, were imprisoned, and gave their souls to God, as they were sure to die. Apparently they were sacrificed, and since the deed had been done during the recent past, nothing more could be done about it by Sandoval.

There were women who were captured by his army, but feeling sorry for them, he released them with orders to bring the rest of the residents back to their city, which they did, giving much honor to Sandoval, and promising fealty to Sandoval and the god he worshipped.

Sandoval then began his march toward Tlaxcala, but was met along the way by eight thousand Tlaxcalans carrying the sawn timber toward Texcoco, being led by Martin Lopez, the master carpenter in charge of building the boats.

The army was aligned to protect the group as they marched through a part of the land that was controlled by the forces of Guatemoc, but they were not attacked, entering Texcoco two days later. The building of the ships was undertaken immediately, with the construction near Lake Chalco.

Thirteen ships were built with the aid of eight thousand Tlaxcalan citizens, and the builders were attacked three times when Guatemoc's warriors tried to set the ships afire, but they were defeated and fifteen were taken prisoner during those attacks.

The chieftain of the Tlaxcalans requested permission from Cortes to lead his fifteen thousand soldiers from Texcoco to fight the enemies of Cortes, and asked in which direction Cortes would like him to go. Cortes told him that he wanted to lead an attack on a city named Saltocan, a city a short distance from Texcoco which had a land-based entryway into the city, and would be happy to have the Tlaxcalans join his army. Marching up to where the entry road had been, the soldiers of Guatemoc attacked the Spanish army and the Tlaxcalans with furious volleys of arrows and rocks from bowmen and slings, doing much harm to the foot-soldiers and horses. The horses and horsemen could not follow the attackers into the brush, trees and water in order to get close enough for the horsemen to swing their great swords. Also, the swordsmen could not get close enough to do any damage.

Two warriors from a nearby town told Cortes they had watched the men of Saltocan destroy the entrance road, but they had left another approach further beyond this entrance. Cortes led his army to the other entrance and ordered them to cross and enter the city, although he and the horsemen became the rear guard so that they would not be attacked by warriors sent by Guatemoc as reinforcements.

When the foot-soldiers and Tlaxcalan warriors attained level ground they were able to dispatch many of the Tenochtitlan warriors with deft sword-play and the weapons used by the Tlaxcalans. As the Tenochtitlan warriors saw victory slipping from their grasp, they entered canoes and swiftly left the battle scene. After that victory, Cortes led that army to several other cities around the perimeter of Lake Chalco, always advancing toward Tenochtitlan.

As the advancing army moved ahead, the cities in which Cortes had expected to wage war had been abandoned and their wealth taken with the former residents. The warriors of Guatemoc had been told to make a stand at a city called Tacuba, where during the flight from Tenochtitlan, the Spaniards had stopped to gather themselves together before retreating further.

It was at Tacuba that Cortes and his army were attacked by thousands of warriors from Guatemoc's armies. They fought so close together the horsemen were hard-pressed to force their way through the ranks, striking at all warriors who stood in their way. The soldiers with their crossbows and those with muskets had no problem in hitting a warrior with their arrows and balls, but the time in between for reloading was filled with slashing knives and falling stones from slings.

This would have been a great time for cannons, but they had not brought any with them. Tacuba was a city which had bridges between the islands containing homes, and these bridges had drawbridges. Guatemoc's army had instructions to draw Cortes and his army beyond one of the bridges with a drawbridge, and then raise the drawbridge trapping Cortes and his men where they could be surrounded and defeated.

However, by the grace of God and good fortune, Cortes and some of his men escaped the trap and returned to Texcoco. The experience of falling for a plan of entrapment made Cortes think more cautiously. He needed some time to recuperate in Texcoco. The Spanish had, in the past, helped defend several cities in the area from attacks being waged by Guatemoc's squadrons, and once again the cities requested help. Cortes ordered Sandoval to assemble an army of twenty horsemen, two hundred soldiers, twelve crossbowmen, ten musketeers, and the few Tlaxcalan warriors who had not gone to their homes in Tlaxcala carrying with them whatever wealth they had earned or stolen.

Sandoval was offered warriors of Chalco, which he happily accepted. As they approached the city of Chimaluacan, the army of Guatemoc sent three squadrons attacking Sandoval from three sides, mostly from uneven ground, making it difficult for the horsemen to be effective in breaking up the ranks of the squadrons, leaving much of the battle between the foot-soldiers and warriors.

As the army of Sandoval moved forward, the squadrons were forced to retreat, and Sandoval's horsemen gained the upper hand chasing the warriors, and inflicting many injuries to them. Reining in, the horsemen returned to a camp which had been set up by the foot-soldiers at Oaxtepec, and began to take food and rest. The guards surrounding the camp came in shouting, "To arms, to arms, they are attacking!"

As is normal, the men had their weapons next to them when eating or resting, and were able to meet the attackers, and the horsemen were able to break up the assault by riding through their ranks, striking blows from their swords on the way through and attacking again from their rear, and the crossbowmen and musketeers kept up their barrage, the swordsmen slashing their way forward, setting the Tenochtitlan warriors to flight, after a long and fierce battle.

Sandoval then sent word to the city of Yecapixtla where a large army of Guatemoc's warriors were supposedly garrisoned, waiting for the Spaniards to enter that city. His message asked that the chieftains realize what happened to the garrisons in Oaxtepec, and requested that they expel the garrisons from their territory, but they sent no answer.

The chiefs and warriors from Chalco warned Sandoval that if he left to return to Texcoco, the warriors waiting in Yecapixtla would attack their city of Chalco, leaving no one alive. The men of Sandoval's command that had arrived with Narvaez requested that they return to Texcoco, and from there be allowed to return to Cuba. Only the Tlaxcalan warriors were anxious to advance to Yecapixtla, hoping to find there more riches to take back to their homes.

Sandoval reluctantly agreed to advance on Yecapixtla, hoping that the Tenochtitlan warriors had left, but that was not to be. As his group approached the city, the Tenochtitlan warriors met them, sending volleys of arrows and stones at the advancing troops without them being able to return fire from their muskets and crossbows because of distance.

Noticing that the Chalco warriors who had joined his war party were not participating in the fray, he shouted to them to begin fighting with his men and they replied they could not for they feared reprisals if the Tenochtitlan warriors won the battle.

But, as the battle began to swing toward Sandoval's army, the warriors of Chalco joined in, seeking the plunder of good-looking women, and anything else of worth they could steal from that city. Putting the Tenochtitlan warriors to flight, Sandoval and his army returned to Texcoco to report.

Sandoval found an unappreciative commander, Cortes, who thought that because of an error of judgement, many men had been lost in the battles. While this meeting was taking place between Cortes and Sandoval, captains from the city of Chalco came, requesting immediate help from Cortes as there were two thousand canoes headed to Chalco carrying twenty thousand Tenochtitlan warriors with orders to burn down the city.

Cortes was so angry at Sandoval, he commanded that he turn around with what was left of his army and hurry off to help the people of Chalco. In the meantime, the other chieftains of Chalco had hurried to their neighbors of Huexotzingo, who extended help of up to twenty thousand warriors to add to the warriors of Chalco, and between the two armies, defeated the warriors Guatemoc had sent to burn Chalco. There were many captives taken by the Chalco and Huexotzingo armies, among them fifteen chiefs and captains of the Tenochtitlan squadrons.

This defeat at the hands of people whom he had considered to be under his control did much to anger Guatemoc, and embarrass the Tenochtitlan army. Sandoval, upon his arrival at Chalco, was pleased that his army would not need to fight so soon after the fighting at Yecapixtla, then marching to Texcoco, and then to

Chalco. He and his troops rested there for several days, then took the captives along with him back to Texcoco.

Not wanting to anger Cortes, he sent one of his captains to report to Cortes, and he and Cortes mended their differences to become good friends once again. The captives were branded as slaves, and after the fifth were set aside for the king of Spain, and a fifth for Cortes, the rest were distributed to the other Spaniards at Texcoco.

Another ship arrived carrying a king's treasurer named Julian de Alderete, and many supplies of arms and powder, which were badly needed by Cortes and his army. Also, at that time, Cortes saw that the building of the ships had been completed, and recognized the need for his Spanish troops to defeat the remaining kingdom of Mexico.

Ordering an army formed by thirty horsemen, twenty crossbowmen, fifteen musketeers, and three hundred swordsmen, he began marching toward Tlamanalco, whereupon reaching that city a good night's sleep was enjoyed by the entire group. The following day the army marched on to Chalco, where Cortes called for all of the chieftains from that area to come listen to what he would tell them.

After they arrived, Cortes told them of his plans, and asked them to provide additional warriors to join with the soldiers and warriors from other locations that had already joined his army. The following day the additional warriors swelled the ranks of Cortes's army to the largest number of fighting men ever seen by the Spanish soldiers. Having heard through the words of spies Cortes had sent out that Guatemoc had warriors stationed in the plains waiting to attack his army, Cortes ordered the huge army to advance toward the waiting warriors, hoping to fight them on the plain, not having to climb into the fortresses built into the mountains.

However, the squadrons had taken to the hills, from which volleys of arrows and stones fell into the ranks of soldiers and warriors, injuring many and killing some. Climbing toward the top, from where the Tenochtitlan warriors commanded the view, many of the soldiers were crushed by the huge boulders the warriors rolled down the hillsides.

Horsemen were sent around the hills searching for better avenues of attack, but finding none better than the one they were already using, they renewed with vigor their climbing, looking for alcoves that might protect them on their way up.

The difficulties became evident to Cortes, who had waited below, guarding against an attack from the plains, for he could see the great boulders injuring his soldiers trying to climb the hills. He called for a retreat for the climbers, and none too soon, as squadrons of Tenochtitlan warriors arrived attempting to mount an attack from the rear.

As the horsemen broke through their ranks, and the men returned to level ground from the hillsides, the Tenochtitlan warriors were put into retreat to other hills, from which they were able to stave off immediate defeat. There had been women and children hiding on the top of those hills who hooted and hollered at the large Spanish army and their local allies as they passed by to confront the Tenochtitlan warriors on the hillsides beyond.

However, from nearby hills, the musketeers and crossbowmen were able to wound and kill some of the Tenochtitlan warriors. Also, the Tenochtitlan warriors had fled to hills that held no water, and after constant fighting, those warriors pleaded for peace.

As the Tenochtitlan warriors, women and children came down from the hills they all gave fealty to Spain and Cortes, and were allowed water after walking to Oaxtepec, where water was abundant. After resting there overnight in a garden, Cortes, his captains, and even Julian de Alderete, the king's treasurer, said there was not such a beautiful garden in all of Spain.

The army then set off toward many other cities which were under the influence of Guatemoc. At the first city, called Yautepec, the army met and put the warriors of that city to flight. The horsemen pursued them to another large pueblo called Tepostlan, which had been abandoned by its chieftains prior to the entrance of Cortes's army.

However the residents did not have time to flee, and the soldiers found many good-looking women and children in that city, and much wealth that had not been taken away. Cortes sent word to those chieftains to return to the city or he would burn it to the ground. Since none of the chieftains returned until they saw some of the homes going up in flames, some homes were destroyed.

While waiting for the chieftains to return, the chieftains of Yautepec came to Tepostlan to pledge their fealty to Cortes and the king of Spain. The following day, Cortes and his army left Tepostlan, following a route to many cities leading to Tenochtitlan. Coadlabaca, a large city built on an island which could be entered by crossing two bridges, and mostly surrounded by deep waters of forty-eight feet or more, was the next target.

The two bridges had been destroyed in preparation for the defense of the city. Upon reaching the destroyed bridges, the army of Cortes found no way to enter the city initially, while the warriors of Tenochtitlan and the warriors of Coadlabaca fired salvo after salvo of arrows, lances, and stones from their bows and slings. Eventually a number of trees were discovered that had branches spanning the water between the island and the surrounding land. Some of the soldiers and Tlaxcalan warriors swung from the trees to the island, attacking the flanks of the defenders.

Also, one of the scouts brought back to Cortes information that there was another bridge beyond the two that had been destroyed, and it could be crossed by the horses. Cortes led the horsemen down to the other bridge, and attacked the defenders from the rear. In a short time the defenders had been defeated, running for their lives from the foot-soldiers and horsemen.

Shortly thereafter, twenty chieftains of Coadlabaca approached the camp Cortes had ordered to be set up, paying great homage to Cortes, and saying they would pay fealty to him, his army, the king of Spain, and the god that the Spaniards worshipped.

They also explained that the lord of Mexico, Guatemoc, had demanded that the garrisons destroy the entrances to the city and repel the advancing Spanish soldiers and the warriors that had joined them. Furthermore, they said that from what they had seen and heard, there was no place, however strong the defenses were, that Cortes's army could not and would not attack and defeat those defenders.

Cortes had the army on the march the following day. They had chosen a route that took them through arid areas where no water flowed, and all of the soldiers, warriors, and horses became very thirsty. Two men died of thirst, but Cortes sent two horsemen ahead looking for water. One soldier, Bernal Diaz Castillo, and a Tlaxcalan warrior who always fought at his side, followed behind the horsemen, not allowing themselves to be seen.

One of the horsemen looked back, and upon seeing them, told them to return to the place where Cortes and his army had stopped. Bernal requested that the two men continue behind the horsemen, as they were sure to find water soon.

Upon finding water near a row of farmhouses, all of them filled their canteens, and one of the farmers brought a large pitcher filled with cold water from his home, and that was carried back to Cortes by Bernal. Cortes moved his troops near the row of farmhouses and camped there overnight, resuming their march toward the large city of Xochimilco where many of the homes were built in a fresh water lake.

A great battle took place there as Guatemoc had sent many thousands of his warriors to prevent Cortes's army from entering that city, breaking down the bridges before meeting them outside the city. The plain in front of the village was filled with Guatemoc's warriors, with many more inside the city.

The fighting was fierce with the overwhelming number of warriors holding their tight line of defense as the horsemen wielded their swords, the crossbowmen shot their arrows, the musketeers fired and quickly reloaded their weapons, and the foot-soldiers pressed forward with swords flashing in the sunlight as they tried to carve their way through the warrior's ranks.

Attaining the bridge area, the soldiers and Tlaxcalan warriors waded their way forward, finally attaining solid ground on the island. Following the defending warriors who backed away from the swinging swords, the soldiers on the streets of the city kept advancing. The horsemen were guided in another direction, as more than ten thousand more warriors sent by Guatemoc as reinforcements arrived, and the horsemen waded into battle against them.

The horse that Cortes was riding broke down during that battle, and Cortes was pulled to the ground. He was being surrounded by the Tenochtitlan warriors when some Tlaxcalan warriors and a horseman named Cristobal de Olea came into that fray, swinging their swords and knives, clearing the way for Cortes to remount and continue battling.

Realizing that Cortes was in trouble, the foot-soldiers, both Spaniards and the warriors of Tlaxcala, moved over to help shield and help the horsemen attacking the Tenochtitlan warriors, pushing them back with swords slashing.

After the Tenochtitlan warriors had retreated behind barricades and drawbridges, Cortes ordered a halt in an area behind a barricade that offered time to sear the open wounds of the soldiers, Tlaxcalan warriors and the horses which had been cut. Screams, shouts, drums drumming, loud trumpets, and whistling were continuous, as the Tenochtitlan troops rained arrows, lances and stones over the walls of the barricades, but did not attack the entryway while the mending of bodies took place.

Some of the men of Cortes climbed the steps of the temple within that area, and reported seeing twenty canoes filled with Guatemoc's reinforcements headed toward the city, ordered to attack the Spaniards' position during nighttime hours, but this did not happen. Being told of those canoes approaching the city, Cortes ordered the crossbowmen and musketeers to block them from entering the city at the areas where they might have disembarked.

Other sentries were posted on the tops of walls next to the deep waters from where the warriors inside the canoes might try to scale, and as they heard or saw the canoes approaching, met them by heaving heavy rocks crashing into and through some of the canoes.

This was enough to turn the canoes away from the bombardment of rocks, and they paddled off to where the warriors joined with those who were waiting to attack across the causeways by land.

The following morning, the thousands of Tenochtitlan warriors began storming the barricaded area that had protected the Spaniards and Tlaxcalan warriors overnight, but all were aware and readied for the attack, with the horsemen assigned to fight from the area most firm of ground, with the crossbowmen and musketeers on both flanks of the barricaded doorways, and the sword-wielding foot-soldiers and Tlaxcalan warriors assembled tightly in ranks, so as to not allow the Tenochtitlans to infiltrate the ranks.

This method of defense was extremely effective, allowing the troops of Cortes to control the entryway, and take several chieftains of the Tenochtitlan warriors as prisoners. Learning from those prisoners the plans of Guatemoc was helpful in defending the position until another force of ten thousand more Mexican troops arrived, and attacked the small army of Cortes.

It was at that time that Cortes organized a retreat from the city, and a hoped-for route back to Texcoco. They marched through many deserted cities along that route before being met by the Spaniards who had been left by Cortes to guard the area of Texcoco, some new arrivals from Cuba and Spain, and the dignitaries of Texcoco, all of whom had been alerted to the arrival of Cortes's army.

Celebrating the return of Cortes, but lamenting the loss of many soldiers and warriors of his group, the badly-needed rest and binding-up of wounds took place in Texcoco. Also, there was a diabolical scheme set up by the new arrivals from Cuba and Spain that would have killed Cortes while eating at a table of celebration had it come to pass. Fortunately, one of the soldiers who became aware of the plot went to Cortes and informed him of how it was to occur, and he alerted his captains of the plot.

They went to the quarters of the man who was to do the deed, captured him, and hanged him from the window of the room in which he had quartered. The rest of the many important men who had signed onto the plot were not imprisoned, nor disciplined in any way, but after that, Cortes was surrounded by a group of guards, protecting his person day and night.

He then assembled all of the soldiers that had accompanied him in the various campaigns he had led, asking them to watch for other plots against his life, and begged them to alert him to any of those plots.

There had been many prisoners taken during the most recent battles, and those men, women and children were branded and sold at auction to the Spaniards and Tlaxcalan people as slaves.

The treasures, gold and other things of worth, were kept by the soldiers and warriors that had taken them from the various cities and persons as they could acquire them. Once again, one fifth went to King Charles, another fifth to Cortes, some of the best-looking women were given to Cortes's captains, and the rest went for auction among the soldiers and Tlaxcalan people.

Cortes found that all of the thirteen ships that had been assembled by Martin Lopez, the master carpenter in charge of that great effort, were ready to be employed once rigging, sails and oars had been added.

Next, Cortes sent samples of arrows with copper points to many of the cities that had pledged support to the effort of bringing down Tenochtitlan with instructions to make and bring to Texcoco eight thousand arrows from each city. Waiting for these items to be made available, alerting Xicotenga, the elder, and his son to make available thousands of warriors from their city, as well as requesting thousands more from other cities, Cortes made plans for the attack of Tenochtitlan.

While the plans were being made, Cortes assembled the many men under his command to present a review of the troops he would use in the invasion of that city. Eighty-four horsemen, six hundred fifty foot-soldiers carrying lances, swords and shields, one hundred ninety-four crossbowmen and musketeers with large quantities of arrows, powder and balls, marched in a parade in the great court of Texcoco.

Crews for the thirteen ships were picked from that array of soldiers, with twelve crossbowmen and musketeers, twelve rowers, six to a side, a captain and artillery man on each ship. Small cannons were affixed to each ship with plenty of powder and balls beside the mountings.

The ranks of the horsemen, foot-soldiers, and the many additional warriors from the cities would be aligned when they began the march of attack. There were many orders that were given by Cortes to all of the Spaniards, then passed to the native warriors, that were demanded of all participants.

Among them that no one was allowed to blaspheme against god, the church, or the saints; no abuse of the warriors who accompanied and fought alongside the Spaniards would be tolerated; no one aware of the methods and time of the attack were permitted to leave the immediate area, and all forms of protection to their bodies, armor covering as much of their bodies including their necks and helmets for their heads must be worn. Also, there was to be no gambling over horses, arms or provisions.

Finding that there were not enough men to man the oars for all thirteen ships, he ordered that sailors from all ships that had landed in Villa Rica or other landings in the area, and anyone who could reasonably help row the ships be conscripted to a ship for that purpose. After naming and assigning a banner for each ship, a captain was chosen to command the ship and crew. Preparations had already been made and carried out to deepen and widen the channel leading to Tenochtitlan.

As the warriors from Tlaxcala, led by Chichimecatecle, Xicotenga, the younger, and two of his brothers, approached Texcoco, followed by warriors from Cholula and Huexotzingo, Cortes went out with several of his captains to greet and welcome them with much respect, embracing their captains one by one.

This great army of natives had banners carrying their individual city's colors, all with a white bird, such as an eagle, displayed prominently on each banner. The warriors carried various weapons with which to kill the warriors of Tenochtitlan.

Some carried bows and arrows, two-handed swords, javelins; there were spear throwers; others carried small and large lances, slings and rocks to propel toward their adversaries, and blowguns and darts.

Captains of the squadrons were appointed by Cortes, the first headed by Pedro de Alvarado, who was assigned one hundred fifty sword and shield foot-soldiers, some with lances, thirty horsemen, eighteen musketeers and crossbowmen. Along with those troops, three other under-captains were assigned fifty additional crossbowmen and musketeers to be equally distributed between the three to be used as required.

Eight thousand Tlaxcalan and other friendly warriors and their leaders were also assigned to the command of Pedro de Alvarado, who led his squadrons from the front of the horsemen. Another squadron was led by Cristobal de Olid, with three under-captains to his command. The squadron had thirty horsemen, one hundred seventy-five sword and lance-wielding foot-soldiers, twenty crossbowmen and musketeers, and another eight thousand friendly warriors.

Another squadron was led by Gonzalo de Sandoval, with another three under captains, twenty-four horsemen, fourteen crossbowmen and musketeers, one hundred fifty sword, lance, and shield carrying foot-soldiers, with more than eight thousand friendly warriors of Chalco and Huexotzingo in his command.

The following day, May 22nd, the march began. The men of

Tlaxcala discovered that Xicotenga had disappeared and had returned to his city with the intention of overthrowing Chichimecatecle, who had become the high chief of Tlaxcala after Mase Escasi had died. One of the Tlaxcalan warriors came to Cortes's side to tell him of the defection of Xicotenga, and five Texcocoan chieftains were dispatched to try to sweet-talk him to return to the army he headed.

Unfortunately, that was not successful, and Xicotenga, the younger, was hanged for his treason in a town subject to Texcoco. It was said later that Xicotenga, the elder, father of the younger, even wrote to Cortes, suggesting that they kill his son as he knew him to be a person who could not be trusted.

After the march was restarted, the squadrons led by Pedro de Alvarado and Cristobal de Olid used the same route toward Tenochtitlan, both pausing to sleep overnight in a city subject to Texcoco. A disagreement between the two leaders led to bad feelings between them, but Cortes chastised the squadrons, and an uneasy peace was restored.

Marching through various towns that owed allegiance to Guatemoc, sleeping in the ones the squadrons reached before dark, their commands entered a deserted city of Tacuba. Many canoes manned by Guatemoc's warriors approached the city via the channels of water, and more arrived over the causeways, but stayed outside the city, calling out and shouting abuse toward the soldiers and the friendly warriors.

But tempers were cooled as the soldiers and warriors knew that night fighting was not all that effective. Guatemoc had ordered his warriors to protect the water lines running into the city of Chapultepec, an important city on the way to Tenochtitlan.

As the squadrons of Alvarado and Olid approached the conduits through which the water flowed, large groups of Tenochtitlan warriors blocked the causeway, and engaging the troops with volleys of arrows, javelins and stones from their slings, wounded three soldiers, but they retreated as the Tlaxcalan warriors began chasing them. The conduits were broken, cutting off their supply of fresh water to Chapultepec.

Advancing by way of the causeway, a huge force of Tenochtitlan warriors fell back allowing the Spanish troops to attain the first bridge, where again, they were attacked by huge numbers of Tenochtitlan soldiers who had been waiting in ambush for an attack at that very location.

Many arrows, lances and stones launched toward the Spaniards and their Tlaxcalan warriors had fallen on the causeway, and the fact that the Tlaxcalan warriors had followed closely behind the Spanish troops made the retreat dangerous. Stumbling on or over the fallen weapons was a huge problem, and as many as eight Spanish soldiers were killed, and over fifty were injured.

As the Tenochtitlan warriors were threatened on the causeway by the horsemen, they jumped into the water, being protected by the warriors in their canoes, who kept on firing their weapons at the retreating Spaniards. The Tlaxcalans gradually gave way to the retreating Spaniards, and when the Spanish soldiers reached solid ground, they were very thankful for their lives.

During the following four or five days the army of Pedro de Alvarado and the Tlaxcalan warriors under his command mended and rested having returned to their campsite. Cristobal de Olid took his forces off to Coyoacan, where Cortes had directed him, thus exposing Pedro's army to constant attacks, although none were catastrophic.

While the two squadrons were separated, smoke signals were spotted coming from hilltops around the huge valley. It was a signal that the Tenochtitlans had spotted that the Spanish sailing vessels had left Texcoco, and were headed toward Tenochtitlan.

The ships came to a halt as the canoes of the Tenochtitlans filled the channel ahead. Just then, a wind which favored the Spanish ships began, pushing them forward toward the canoes so swiftly, the ships sailed into the midst of the canoes, allowing the crossbowmen and musketeers to overcome the efforts of the Tenochtitlans within the canoes to paddle fast enough to stay ahead of the Spanish ships. Many canoes were overturned, and many Tenochtitlan fighters were killed or drowned.

The ships continued sailing right into the ports as they neared Tenochtitlan, where the Spanish soldiers of Pedro and Cristobal resumed their attacks along the causeway, causing many deaths to the Tenochtitlan warriors.

Also, the ship carrying Cortes docked at a causeway which led to a temple which housed idols worshipped by its residents, and while defeating the Tenochtitlan warriors sent to defend that area, he and his soldiers recaptured three large cannons that had been left behind when he and his army had retreated earlier from Tenochtitlan.

Those cannons were used along the causeway the following day when the huge number of Tenochtitlan fighters were stationed on the causeway ahead of the Spaniards, others lining the sides of the causeway from the canoes in the water, and still more from the island homes of a city called Acachinango. Upon seeing Cortes and his small army of soldiers being attacked, Cristobal de Olid hurried his army that was at Coyoacan to reinforce Cortes and his men, following the causeway, fighting through many Tenochtitlan warriors.

The fighting was fierce with the numbers of Tenochtitlan warriors seeming to grow, even as many were killed on the causeway and in the canoes. Because many of the canoes had rowed to the side of the causeway away from the Spanish ships, Cortes's men broke down the barriers of the causeway allowing the ships to sail through to the other side and chase the canoes from the causeway, forcing them to hide behind the island homes.

The ships followed the canoes where the depth and areas not sabotaged by stakes set up to poke holes in the ships allowed. Many canoes were captured and burned, their fighter-occupants dying by arrows, drowning, fire, gunfire, or swords.

A small accident occurred when a cannoneer blew up the

remaining powder that had been brought to that location, but Cortes sent an order to another captain, Sandoval, to have all of the available powder he had within his command brought to Cortes, and he should come to reinforce Cortes's efforts.

All this while Cortes kept attacking the causeway ahead with the cannons, horses, foot-soldiers, and the faithful friendly warriors. As Sandoval and his troops arrived, they dismounted from horses, and side-by-side, fought the many Tenochtitlan warriors, killing many with their deadly swords.

As they moved steadily ahead along the causeway, they came to many places where the Tenochtitlan warriors had destroyed the bridges, but Cortes put the ships to service by spanning the broken parts with the ships and allowing the soldiers to rush across the decks and renew their chasing of the retreating warriors.

For six days the two opposing armies were at close combat war, with the ships burning all of the island homes they could reach with crossbows firing arrows with fiery tips. Advancing ever closer to Tenochtitlan, the Spanish soldiers, firing the cannons into the ranks of the warriors they were chasing, entered an area of great temples, with many staircases giving access to the rooms in which the idols were housed.

They were penetrated and climbed, and in doing so, the chieftains and chief priests were killed, although they fought valiantly. There was a huge area that contained many Tenochtitlan warriors which the Spaniards were unable to breach, but they fought hard, hand-to-hand, before being driven back.

Just then two horsemen entered the area, and the Tenochtitlan warriors thought there were more of them and relented their attack. The horsemen struck ahead, using their swords relentlessly, temporarily pushing back the crushing bodies of the warriors.

More reinforcements came to the rescue of the Tenochtitlan warriors, and gradually by sheer numbers they pushed back the advancement of the Spanish soldiers. In that push the Spaniards left behind a cannon, but reached the safety of their prior night's campsite.

A number of days followed providing mending, rest, and time to scout for new approaches to the capital city of Tenochtitlan. Alvarado had found an area on the other side of the city where the residents went on about their business without fear of war. Finding a way to attack and take over that area became an alternative route to enter the city.

Cortes had two hundred Spanish foot-soldiers, twenty-five crossbowmen and musketeers, many friendly warriors, and two hundred fifty men in the ships able to sail along and protect both sides of the causeway, and an advance was ordered by him. Ten horsemen protected the rear by stationing themselves at the beginning of the causeway, with the men at Coyoacan and ten thousand friendly warriors watching there for any attacks from the rear.

Reaching an area defended by many Tenochtitlan warriors, the fighting commenced. The attack by the Spaniards did not falter, as they pushed on ahead to a barricade defended by a large number of Tenochtitlan warriors. The men on the ships fired with crossbows and muskets, routing the defenders and scattering the ones they had not killed.

Climbing up to the raised barrier, they lowered it, allowing Cortes's army to cross over without having to fight their way across. The Spaniards and friendly warriors rushed ahead, claiming the large area next to the large plaza and main buildings of the city. The unexpected push into the great city surprised the Tenochtitlan population and their warriors, who had rushed into the plaza and were stationary targets within the large circle.

Cannons were used and many people were killed, but the Tenochtitlan warriors would not surrender. Rather than surrendering they mounted a counter-attack against the foot-soldiers, and had it not been for the horsemen may have decimated the Spanish forces. Back and forth the horsemen rode, inflicting much damage to the Tenochtitlan soldiers, but they still advanced against the retreating Spanish troops.

The Tenochtitlans had built barricades to slow the Spanish advance, but they had been breached by the Spaniards. Now Cortes ordered them to be repaired, thus allowing the Spanish an orderly retreat back to the campsite.

As the ships were of great help in guarding the safety of the camp, three ships were dispatched to the camps of Alvarado and Sandoval, who were ordered to approach and defeat any Tenochtitlan warriors they would meet. This was very good planning as both captains captured many warriors and canoes. On Sunday, June 16th, 1521, Cortes and his Spaniards participated in Mass before readying themselves for another attack on Tenochtitlan. He left the camp with twenty horsemen, three hundred Spanish foot-soldiers, and a huge number of allied warriors from Tlaxcala, Texcoco, Xochimilco, and other friendly cities. As the Tenochtitlan people had three days to prepare for the coming assault, they had broken the breaches and raised the barricades that had been repaired prior to the retreat during the past attack.

This time the ships' sailors and soldiers fired their crossbows and muskets, then jumped from their ships to the barricades and breaches, repairing them so the soldiers could follow the retreating Tenochtitlan warriors. Arriving in the area of the great plaza, there was little fighting that took place. There were some small skirmishes, but nothing of major consequence occurred.

After returning to his encampment, many of the chiefs of the cities within Lake Chalco, having witnessed the fighting and realizing that Guatemoc's forces had been defeated, came to beg for peace, offering great fealty to Cortes, the Spanish King Charles V, and the god which the Spaniards worship. Cortes met those chieftains with greetings of friendship, assuring them that the war was not with them, but the people of the city of Tenochtitlan.

Cortes asked them to place their canoes at the Spaniards' use, and that their builders and carpenters build homes for the Spaniards alongside the causeways leading to Tenochtitlan. Both requests were acted upon immediately by the people whom these chieftains represented. The houses were built on both sides of the towers on the causeway, and so many were built they extended beyond the distance of four crossbow shots, with wide pathways that allowed foot-soldiers and horsemen to pass freely.

During the following week, Cortes led many small groups into the city as far as the great plaza before meeting any resistance, but advanced no further. On Sunday, June 23rd, 1521, Cortes had amassed over one hundred thousand Spanish and friendly native warriors in his camp. He began giving orders to his captains, sending four ships accompanied by one thousand five hundred canoes to go in one direction around the huge center of the city, while sending three other ships with another one thousand five hundred canoes around the other side, all filled with soldiers and friendly warriors ordered to burn and destroy everything they could.

Cortes ordered Pedro de Alvarado to proceed along a street that followed the same direction as the causeway. Pedro had with him seventy Spaniard crossbowmen and musketeers, with twelve thousand of the warrior allies, and six horsemen to guard the rear. Gonzalo de Sandoval was ordered to advance on another street with the same numbers of fighters in his group.

Cortes led a similar group on the causeway. There was great joy when the three captains were able to pass freely through the streets. However, complete victory with the surrender of the city and Guatemoc had not been achieved.

On June 30th, 1521, Cortes had been convinced by many of his captains and soldiers to capture the market place, where the people of the city came to buy food and water. He had turned down that idea until the king's treasurer, Julian de Alderete, convinced him that all of the camps were insistent on that plan of action.

After hearing Mass, Cortes began deploying his troops, sending out seven ships and more than three thousand canoes manned by friendly warriors of many different cities; Cortes himself led his army of twenty-five horsemen and all of the foot-soldiers and friendly warriors along the causeway. At the entrance to Tenochtitlan, Cortes divided up the soldiers and warriors into three squadrons again.

From that position there were three streets leading to the marketplace. Julian de Alderete led the troops comprised of seventy soldiers carrying crossbows, muskets, lances and swords, and twenty thousand allied warriors along the principal street. As a rear guard eight horsemen were assigned to him.

Some of the warriors carried barricades to fill bridge openings, others carried pickaxes to fashion the openings. The other two streets led from the Tacuba Street to the marketplace. Those two streets were narrower, and the causeway had bridges and canals. The broadest street was under the command of Pedro de Alvarado and Gonzalo de Sandoval, who advanced with eighty soldiers and more than ten thousand ally warriors.

At the narrower Tacuba Street, Cortes mounted two large cannons with eight horsemen to guard them. He then led eight horsemen, one hundred foot-soldiers including twenty-five crossbowmen and musketeers, and many allied warriors toward the marketplace.

He dismounted from his horse and ordered the horsemen to wait for further orders as he, the foot-soldiers, and the warriors rushed forward to a barricade at the end of a bridge, which was dismantled by the crossbowmen and musketeers and carried out of the way. The allied warriors had not waited for Cortes to lead them, and surged ahead to confront any Tenochtitlan warriors they could find.

Advancing beyond that point, Cortes and his men saw that the allied warriors had come under attack and were surrounded. Attacking the Tenochtitlan warriors from the back, the tide of battle swung toward the allied warriors, and they rallied against the Tenochtitlan army.

Another concern for Cortes was that the two other captains had advanced their troops so far and so fast, there was a possibility that the Tenochtitlans would allow the advancement and mount an attack from the rear.

However, the Tenochtitlan attack came at the force commanded by Cortes on the narrow causeway, and it was a brutal attack, killing a large number of his crossbowmen and musketeers, and some of the sword-wielding foot-soldiers, and those who were killed or taken captive became sacrifices to the idols. Cortes, himself, was put into grave danger during this attack, and escaped only through the deaths of many of his protectors, among them a servant of his named Cristobal de Guzman, who brought a horse to Cortes to mount, but while handing the reins to Cortes, was killed by a lance through his neck.

After Cortes safely exited the battle zone, he made it back to the staging area where he had designed the three squadrons' attack routes. Having his squadron counter-attacked and overcome by the warriors of Tenochtitlan, Cortes sent word to his two other squadrons to return to the staging area, but not by turning their backs to their foes. Their orderly retreat to the staging area was undertaken with no lives lost.

The warriors of Guatemoc were ecstatic at their victory, and from the tops of the walls and barricades the people threw down the helmeted heads of Spaniards they had captured, killed, and had offered to their idols. They also burned incense and fumigated the streets which had been used in the advance of the three squadrons.

However, when the Tenochtitlan warriors attempted to enter the staging area, the cannon fire stopped them from entering, blunting their attack. Upon gathering at the staging area, Cortes took account of the losses during the previous attack. There were forty Spaniards unaccounted for, and over a thousand allied warriors that had been lost.

Also lost were one small cannon, many crossbows, muskets, lances, and swords. The forces of Guatemoc kept attacking the camp day and night, with canoes attacking the ships that tried to keep the canoes' warriors from landing.

After witnessing the helmeted heads of some Spanish soldiers being thrown down from walls near them, many of the allied warriors left the area and rushed back to their cities, thinking that after the annihilation of the Spaniards, their villages would be attacked, and their families killed.

The few that remained offered good advice, one suggestion being that since the Spaniards controlled the entrance to the city, no food nor water would be brought to the residents nor warriors, thus starving the population into submission. This had been a serious loss which made Cortes wary of his next move. Combining his soldiers into one squadron would constrict their movement, dividing into two or three groups advancing down the same routes would divide up the Tenochtitlan warriors, but with the defecting warriors diminishing his fighters, his progress was stopped.

Defending his position was of the utmost importance. As sacrifices of the captured Spaniards took days for the Tenochtitlans to complete, with the idols promising a victory to the forces of Guatemoc day-by-day, and their not getting any closer to victory, the chieftain of Texcoco sent word to his city to send all possible warriors to return and help the Spaniards in their efforts to set them free of Tenochtitlan rule.

An army of two thousand warriors came from Texcoco to raise the count of fighters, and renew the wills of Cortes, his soldiers, and the allied warriors that had remained and fought with Cortes's army. Many other warriors from the cities that had furnished warriors to Cortes returned, swelling the confidence of the Spaniards.

Having these reinforcements available, Cortes ordered the advance of all three squadrons along the same streets leading to the marketplace. As they advanced to the area where broken bridges had been before, and after crossing them, they made certain the Tenochtitlan people would not be able to use the brackish water to drink.

The few Tenochtitlan warriors who had been guarding that opening were put into a wild retreat. Since much of the three routes had been leveled during the previous Spanish attack, the progress to the marketplace was mostly unimpeded. Having attained the area in which the idols were located in the temples, furious fighting took place with the troops of Guatemoc defending the idols.

The Spaniards cut deeply into their ranks, finally setting fire to the temples after destroying the idols, wrestling them to the floors, then hacking them to pieces, all the while fighting the enemies. After retreating from those temples, the Spanish army and its allies retreated to their campsite.

They found that many injuries to their comrades had healed enough for them to rejoin the effort of defeating the forces of Guatemoc. Two Tenochtitlan residents were seized by the guards, and when brought before Cortes, told him of the great hunger and thirst suffered by the residents of that city, and how many of them had died for want of those necessities. They were given food, then imprisoned to be branded as slaves at a later date. The canoes of the Tenochtitlans now held fishermen who were desperate to supply food to the people of the city.

But they were being attacked by the ships, overturned, and many of the men who manned the canoes were killed. For days, advances were made, and each day an intentional retreat was made with the hope that some careless group of Tenochtitlan warriors would attempt to follow, with groups of allied warriors waiting in ambush to kill all who attempted the foolish move.

More and more allied warriors returned, swelling the ranks. Bringing food and water, they were welcomed warmly.

On July 25th, the attack by the squadrons of Cortes, Pedro de Alvarado and Sandoval overran the temples and the home of Guatemoc, setting fires to each of them. The following day the advances were to the last small water line defended by Tenochtitlan warriors, who were felled by the slashing swords of the Spanish foot-soldiers, and the lances and knives of the allied warriors. When Pedro de Alvarado entered the battleground, the Tenochtitlan warriors fled in terror.

As the last bridge that had been destroyed by the Tenochtitlans was being filled, Cortes ordered his troops to advance no further. He, accompanied by a few other horsemen, rode forward into and around the marketplace plaza, aware of the many defeated warriors lining the tops of the walls around him.

Seeing the freedom of movement by the horsemen, the Tenochtitlan people could understand the legends of the past, which were orally passed down by their leaders which told of people arriving from the east to become their masters.

Establishing a campsite near the entrance to the marketplace plaza, several days of rest were taken by the Spanish forces. But on the fifth day, they became aware of many women and children filling the marketplace plaza, looking for any scraps of food, be it bark of trees or worms of the ground.

After offering those women and children peace terms, they fled the plaza, and were replaced by a multitude of warriors bent on the annihilation of the Spaniards and the allied warriors of their own country.

The Spaniards and allies fought so bravely that as the Tenochtitlan warriors fled the battleground, more than twelve thousand Tenochtitlan warriors' souls met god that day. Following that battle, Cortes had an offer of peace delivered to Guatemoc along with food and drink.

Four chieftains brought Guatemoc's reply of agreement to peace, with an offer to meet with Cortes at a specific place, but that was a deceit which the warrior chieftains had counselled.

An attack by the remaining Tenochtitlan warriors was made against the three squadrons, seemingly just beginning the war against the Spaniards and their allies. The Tenochtitlan warriors fought well, inflicting many more injuries to already hurting bodies, but once again, the Spaniards and allies weathered the attack and dished out more suffering to the attackers.

After the battle had subsided, each army attended to its injuries, and there was a lull of several rest days. Several offers of a peaceful solution were offered by Cortes to Guatemoc, but he had taken refuge in a home that could be reached only by water. After realizing that attacks by land would not bring closure to the conflict, Cortes ordered Gonzalo de Sandoval to command all twelve of the remaining ships and invade the area of the city in which Guatemoc had taken refuge.

Furthermore, he instructed him to restrain from killing or injuring any people of Tenochtitlan unless they attacked them. Sandoval set sail to the island homes in which Guatemoc was said to be hiding, and when his guards saw the ships approaching, they rushed Guatemoc into one of fifty canoes that began to be rowed into the lake in different directions.

Upon seeing the fleeing canoes, Sandoval directed a close friend of his, Garcia Holguin, a captain of the fastest ship, and a good sailor, to overtake the canoe carrying Guatemoc, the jewels, and important people who were fleeing with him.

Catching the overloaded canoe was not difficult, but when Holguin demanded the canoe stop, the rowers kept on rowing. As Holguin's ship drew abreast of the canoe, muskets were raised as if to shoot Guatemoc, and he surrendered. His words of surrender were...

> *Do not shoot—I am the king of this city and they call me Guatemoc. What I ask of you is not to disturb my things that I am taking with me nor my wife nor my relations, but carry me to Cortes.*

Prior to seating him aboard his ship along with the people who were within the canoe, Holguin embraced him with much respect, then gave them all food to eat, but touched nothing within the canoe.

Sandoval, upon hearing that Holguin had captured Guatemoc, hurried to shore where he met Holguin, and Guatemoc's party of important people of Tenochtitlan. The two Spaniards argued as to whom belonged the honor of capturing Guatemoc, but that was settled later by Cortes.

While being brought to Cortes, Guatemoc was bound between Sandoval and Holguin, and after being presented to Cortes, pleaded to be murdered by the knives of the Spaniards in attendance.

Cortes treated Guatemoc with much respect, telling him that he could remain as king of his people, and asking about his wife and other important people who fled with him.

On being told they remained aboard Holguin's ship, they were brought to Cortes and were greeted by the captains and him with great respect, fed and offered drink after being made comfortable. After finishing eating, Guatemoc and his people were taken to Cortes's camp where they were offered comfortable temporary living quarters, while new homes were being built for them.

The date of Guatemoc's capture and surrender of the city of Tenochtitlan, was August 13th. 1521.

Chapter 6—The Magnificent Adventures of Alvar Nunez Cabeza de Vaca

1521-1536

AS READERS MAY recall, the honorary title given to Martin Alhajo, the sheep herder who directed the Spanish soldiers to a pass that led to the headquarters camp of the Moorish army, was Cabeza de Vaca, which is translated as "the head of a cow."

He had fastened a cow skull at the uppermost entrance to a valley, surrounding it with rocks so that it would remain stationary. Then he sent word of the location to King Sancho of Navarre, and the army descended on the camp, defeating the Moorish army, which essentially ended Moorish control of southern Spain.

The Moors had ruled southern Spain from 744 AD until the battle of Las Navas de Tolosa, fought in the Sierra Morenas, and won by the Spaniards on July 16th, 1212. King Sancho of Navarre conferred on Martin the honorary title of Cabeza de Vaca, "head of a cow," which his family carried on for centuries.

Around 1490, a fourth-born son was born to a family in which the grandfather was Pedro de Vera, the sadistic conqueror of the Canary Islands. His baptismal name was Alvar Nunez. The father's name has been forgotten through history, but he was from the area of Vera, and his mother's name was Dona Teresa Cabeza de Vaca, and he adopted the Cabeza de Vaca as his own.

He grew up near the port city of Cadiz, but closer to the lesser-known port of San Lucar de Barrameda, the port from which Magellan sailed in 1519. Cabeza de Vaca was about ten years of age when Christopher Columbus was returned to Cadiz from his third voyage in chains. He may have witnessed that scene, just as he would suffer the same injustice at the age of fifty-three.

Cabeza de Vaca turned to the exciting world of soldiering during his teen years. At twenty-one he marched in the army which King Ferdinand sent to aid Pope Julius II in 1511, and saw action at the battle of Ravenna on April 11th, 1512.

He spent the next several years in the service of Spain, up to the warfare against the French in Navarre.

Having earned distinction in battle, he was awarded a royal appointment of second-in-command in the Pamfilo de Narvaez expedition for the conquest of Florida in 1527. Narvaez, as could be seen from the accounts of the Cortes conquest of Mexico, was a bungler, much apt to act for his own benefit than to the king of Spain, his benefactor.

Narvaez was a difficult man to work with, as he sent his men on orders that would imperil them and make him look good when they performed well and accomplished the feat for which he had sent them. He, himself, would remain in the rear of any attack, fearing for his life, until victory, then scooping up any possessions of worth for himself.

The large armada of five ships left the port of San Lucar de Barrameda on June 17th, 1527. On board were six hundred men, and five officers including Cabeza de Vaca, treasurer and mayor; Alonso Enriquez, comptroller; Alonso de Solis, quartermaster; and Juan Suarez, a Franciscan friar.

All were led by Narvaez, who had himself proclaimed as governor. They arrived at the island of Santo Domingo on approximately September 17th, there to gather provisions and round up horses for use upon reaching Florida. While there, the local women seduced one hundred forty men to desert the command by promises and proposals.

The next port of call was Santiago on the island of Cuba, where Narvaez recruited provisions, men, horses, and weapons. While there, the Spanish governor of Jamaica, Vasco Porcallo, offered some additional provisions if Narvaez would come to Jamaica and pick them up. Narvaez purchased another ship at the port of Santo Domingo, assigning a captain Juan Pantoja to pilot that ship.

Upon reaching Cabo de Santa Cruz, which was half-way to Trinidad, Narvaez put into port, sending his ship with Pantoja, and another ship with de Vaca aboard to oversee the transfer of provisions to the ship owned by Narvaez. After docking in the port of Jamaica, Pantoja left his ship, and was transported to governor Porcallo's home. De Vaca was invited to join Porcallo and Pantoja, but felt his duty was to remain with the ships. After being invited several times over the next few days, he relented and went ashore as the seas rose in great waves.

During dinner, a huge storm blew in, uprooting trees, blowing down homes, and nearly picking up the guests even though they locked arms while trying to find a safe shelter from the hurricane. The ships were lost in the storm, with timbers washing ashore days later, and battered bodies were returned by the swells of waves that battered the beaches for days after the winds abated.

Only one small boat was found—in the treetops about a mile from the port. Sixty men and twenty horses had been lost during that hurricane. Many days were spent in Jamaica assisting Porcallo in rebuilding his home and the cities in the nearby vicinity, as there was no transportation to rejoin the Narvaez fleet.

On November 5th, 1527, Narvaez arrived with four of his ships, which had sought shelter when the hurricane blew into the area near Cabo de Santa Cruz.

The sailors on board the four ships were very scared by that strong storm, and begged Narvaez to spend the winter in Cuba, which they did. The ships were put in the care of de Vaca over the winter, and did not leave port until February 20th, 1528. On that day, Narvaez arrived aboard a brig he had purchased in Trinidad, with a captain Miruelo, who had told Narvaez he had been to the River of Palms, and knew the whole northern coast. Narvaez had also purchased another ship beached at Havana with forty men and twelve horses aboard.

On February 22nd, 1528 the expedition set sail under the direction of Captain Alvaro de la Cerda, with a total of four hundred men and eighty horses aboard four ships and a brig. Steering the expedition toward the west, the captain ran the vessels aground among the keys of western Cuba.

Stranded there for fifteen days, a storm came up raising the seas enough to release the boats so they could resume their voyage toward Havana. As the ships neared Havana, a south wind rose and blew the ships toward Florida.

As the wind subsided, land was sighted on April 12th, 1528 as the ships sailed northward along the west coast of Florida. The following day, the ships were anchored in the mouth of a bay, from where some houses inhabited by natives were seen. On April 14th, Alonso Enriquez ventured to an island in the bay where he was met by some of the inhabitants who traded fish and venison for trinkets.

The following day, Narvaez and as many men he could fit into the small boats rowed their way ashore, but when entering the village and homes, they found them empty. The next day, April 16th, 1528, Narvaez raised flags and took possession of the country in the name of King Charles V of Spain.

Following that ceremony, he ordered the men who had remained on the ships to disembark and to lead to land the forty-two horses that had survived the stormy seas. The natives returned to their homes, but made gestures toward the Spaniards to leave the same way as they had arrived, by sea. Narvaez was curious to explore inland, so he designated Fray Suarez, Solis and de Vaca to join with him, along with forty men and six horsemen.

They walked northward for several hours, coming to a huge

bay, possibly what is now known as Tampa Bay. Narvaez then ordered the brigantine to sail northward in search of the bay he and his group had found, but Miruelo could not find it. Narvaez had further ordered Miruelo if he were not to find the bay, he was to return to Havana and bring the ship commanded by Alvaro de la Cerda with all of the provisions they could load aboard both ships and return to this bay.

More exploration inland brought four natives who were captured, and after showing them corn which was among the food provisions brought on the ships, they showed Narvaez small cobs, which offered little to nothing as food.

Ordering the captives to lead the expedition to areas that would have ripened corn or other foods, they were led to a village of fifteen huts. Finding crates filled with dead bodies covered by deerskins, Fray Suarez ordered them burned, as the stench of the dead surrounded the area.

There were other things of worth found within that village, including a few gold nuggets, parrot feathers of several colors, and some linen cloth. When the natives were asked from where these items had come, by sign language (as no translation between the languages had been established), the indicated answer was that the gold had come from far to the north of this, their home site. Their reply sounded like "Apalache," probably meaning the area now called Apalachee Bay in northwestern Florida.

The four natives became the guides for the small exploratory party as they searched further into the interior, finding a cornfield that contained corn ripened and ready for picking. The stated intentions of Narvaez were to explore further inland, leaving the ships sailing northward along the coastline, looking for the entrance to the River of Palms.

The group to undertake the additional exploration was increased to three hundred soldiers, two hundred sixty foot-soldiers and forty on horseback. Having been issued rations of two pounds of biscuits and a half pound of bacon per man for the expedition, and without finding additional food along the way other than palmettos, the group was near starvation when they approached a river. Swimming and rafting across the river became dangerous because of the swift current, and took almost a full day for everyone to cross.

On the other side, the group met a tribe of two hundred natives to whom Narvaez offered greetings, but they made threatening gestures for the Spaniards to leave. The Spaniards fell upon the tribe capturing six of them, who led the group to their homes.

Thankfully, the group found ripe corn which they plucked satisfying their hunger, and a good place to rest their weary bodies and minds. After three days of rest, collecting and eating the corn, Enriquez, Solis, and de Vaca petitioned Narvaez to send out a search party to find a port in which the ships could anchor, so Narvaez ordered de Vaca, with forty foot-soldiers commanded by Captain Alonso del Castillo, to search for such a harbor.

Finding a sandy patch much like a sandy beach, the small group followed the sand into a marsh, which deepened as they marched to thigh deep waters, their feet cut by sharp seashells, and before long they found themselves down river from the point where they had crossed that same river several days before.

Returning to the camp of Narvaez, and after giving him their report, Narvaez sent out another party led by Captain Valenzuela of sixty foot-soldiers and eight horsemen to re-cross the river and follow its course to the sea. Finding that the harbor was shallow, with no place to anchor, he and his group returned to Narvaez with the bad news.

Determined to find where the gold might be found, Narvaez ordered the resumption of the search for "Apalache," led by the six captured natives, although they still had no idea of where Narvaez wanted to go, and for what purpose.

Their next contact with people came when they met a native dressed in a painted deerskin, being carried on the back of another native, with flute players walking in front of the two men, and many other natives following, some pounding out rhythm on drums. Again, using signs, Narvaez informed the natives that he was seeking the "Apalache." The chief signed that the "Apalache" were his enemies, and offered to join the army of Narvaez if they were going to fight.

Not agreeing, nor disagreeing with the native chief, Narvaez and his group began following the natives. They were led to a great river where the water level was deep and the current very swift. Realizing that the river was too wild to raft across, canoes were built, and those carried the groups to the other side.

It took a few days to build the canoes, and one horseman tried to cross the river, but the current unseated him. He and the horse were found a mile down river. Camp was made for the night alongside the river, and for dinner the camp feasted on horsemeat. Having crossed the river, a soldier who had taken a walk along the river bank was shot by a native bowman, and overnight the natives abandoned the camp.

A few days later, after Narvaez ordered resuming the expedition, the natives began following the small squadron, which prompted Narvaez to set a trap of ambush by a few cavalrymen, which netted four of the natives who were pressed into service as guides for the group. Many days later, having marched through beautiful forests of tall trees, the group came into sight of Apalachen, a village, although from a distance.

As an approach to Apalachen was made, Narvaez ordered an attack led by de Vaca and Solis, followed by nine cavalry and fifty infantrymen. There was no opposition from the village as there were only women and children inside at the time of entry.

As the men returned, some arrows were fired at the Spaniards, but only one horse was killed before the native men fled into the thick forests. There was bountiful ripened corn and other foods in the village fields, but it was not what the Spaniards had expected as far as riches were concerned.

Upon taking over the village, Narvaez captured the chieftain of the village, although releasing all of the women and children they had first encountered. The men of the village returned, and seeing their women were not being held, but their leader was incarcerated, they began burning down the houses in which the Spaniards had taken refuge.

Upon being chased by the Spaniards after they set fire to a home or two, they dashed into the swamps and woods, running between and around the shielding trunks of the trees, and disappearing without a trace, only to return again to duplicate the deed. Another band of natives from across the lake attacked the Spaniards, and one of the slaves brought along by Juan Suarez, the Franciscan friar, was killed in that attack.

After twenty-five days at that village, having taken efforts of reconnaissance in three directions, it was decided to head toward a village called Aute, which was in the direction of the sea. The second day during the march, the group was walking through a deep swamp, filled with huge logs impeding progress.

Behind some of the logs were natives shooting arrows at the soldiers and horses, wounding a large number of men and horses, and even capturing the guide. Narvaez ordered the horsemen to dismount and charge at these Indians, who were scattered, but hiding behind other logs as they retreated. Returning to their horses, the horsemen re-mounted, and the route became free of the native fighters.

Having expended most of their arrows in that skirmish, there was little danger from native attacks until the group entered another band's territory. Narvaez, because of hearing of the Columbus expeditions calling the natives Indians, began using that term for the natives. Noticing tracks ahead of the advancing soldiers, plans were made to ward off Indian ambushes before they happened, so those became mostly non-events.

After traveling nine days from Apalachen, the group arrived at the deserted village of Aute, which had been mostly burned to the ground. However, the fields of corn, beans, and squash were very near ripening, and much was plucked and used for feeding the group. The second day the group remained in Aute, Narvaez ordered de Vaca, Juan Suarez, Captain Castillo, and a fellow named Dorantes, seven horsemen, and fifty foot-soldiers to locate the sea.

They walked through most of the day, finding an inlet that led to the sea. Many oysters were found there, for which these men were very thankful, as growing foods had a way of draining their strength, whereas seafood strengthened them. Watchful overnight, de Vaca sent twenty men to explore the coast.

The evening of the second day de Vaca's small group rested there, awaiting the men's return. The men returned, stating that the inlets and bays were huge, and the inlets extended so far inland, it would take much time and effort to follow them. They also reported that the open sea was much further away than had been previously believed.

Upon reporting that information back to Narvaez at Aute, de Vaca found that the men in that village had been attacked, and because many of the soldiers in the camp of Narvaez were sickened, they had all they could handle in beating back the Indian attackers. It was on August 3rd, 1528 that the army of Narvaez left the village of Aute, marching to the inlet found by de Vaca and his small detachment.

There were not enough horses to carry the sick, and those who were sick continued to become sicker. Upon reaching the inlet, disruption between the men emerged, with the horsemen wanting to desert, but advising Narvaez, their leader, of their plans. He persuaded them to stay, asking each well man in his command for their ideas of survival.

The most popular idea was to build rafts, or a ship that might transport them to the harbor by the open sea, but no one among the group knew how ships were built, nor how rigging or sails were constructed, and there were no tools among them. The following morning, one of the sailors who had been a member of Captain Castillo's crew, admitted he knew how to make wooden pipes and deerskin bellows. That encouraged the men to begin making nails, and forming saws, axes, and other tools from crossbows, spurs, stirrups, and other equipment made of iron.

Food was supplied by the horsemen returning to Aute every fourth day to pick the corn, beans, and squash, bringing back to the inlet all they could transport. Oysters were another food available, but meat came from a horse being killed every third day. Palmettos were twisted and used to make oakum, while a Greek sailor made pitch from pine resins.

Within forty-five days, without a real carpenter within the group, five barges (thirty to thirty-two feet long, caulked with palmetto oakum and tarred with pine-pitch) were finished. Everything in the possession of the group was available if it would help in the construction. From palmetto husks and horse tails and manes, ropes were braided; from shirts, sails were tied together; and from trees, oars were cut.

Large stones were used for ballast and anchors. During this time of construction, there were several men killed in attacks, even near to the camp. The Indian archers were accurate, and their bows sent the arrows very powerfully, as those men who were killed wore the heavy cotton armor that normally would repel lesser weapons.

Before embarking from that spot at the inlet, forty men had been killed in combat or had died from the terrible sickness or hunger. All but one of the horses had been consumed by September 22nd, the day the last horse had been consumed. The first barge held Narvaez and forty-nine men, the second had Alonso Enriquez, the comptroller, also with forty-nine men.

The third barge was in charge of Captain Alonso de Castillo and Andres Dorantes with forty-eight men, the fourth was under the Captains Tellez and Penalosa with forty-seven men aboard followed by the fifth barge with de Vaca and Solis in charge of the forty-nine men aboard. After boarding the barges, the edges were barely a foot above the waterline.

Seven days of sailing toward the open sea brought the group in sight of an island, from where canoes of Indians came within bow and arrow distance, but they abandoned the canoes as the barges approached. Some of the barges stopped at the island picking up any food they could find, as that was becoming very scarce. Passing through the strait, the group beached the barges on the coastline of the open sea, but moved on toward the west, searching for the River of Palms.

According to Narvaez and the sea captains, it would be easier and faster to find that river than to locate the ships which had transported them to this place called Florida.

Continuing to sail along the shoreline of the western part of Florida, they stopped at various places searching for food and water, not finding either at those many stops. Hunger and thirst forced many of the men to drink salt water.

A large storm arrived, with huge waves breaking over the sides of the barges, and so the small fleet put out to sea rather than having the boats crash into the huge rocks within the inlet. At night, as the storm still raged, the sound of canoe paddles passing by near the barges were heard, and although shouting by men inside the barges were heard between thunder claps and lightning flashes, the men in the barges saw a large canoe pass by without acknowledging the shouts calling for help.

It disappeared as it kept going at a brisk pace, and as the captains of the barges knew that the people in the canoe were on their way to safety, the barges were turned to the direction in which the canoe had disappeared. A cove which sheltered the barges from the high winds and rough seas was sailed into, giving protection to the hungry and thirsty men. The men were soaked through and through, and because of the raw and cold winds from the storm, many of the men were nearing death.

As the storm subsided, canoes filled with big, well-built unarmed Indians rowed out toward the barges, attempting to speak with the men in the barges, but since no common language was known, they led the barges to their village at the water's edge.

Happily stepping ashore, the Indians led the men to their chieftain's home. In front of their homes were large clay jars, filled with fresh water, still cold from the storm's rains.

And there were great quantities of cooked fish lying on slabs near the center of the village. The chieftain offered the fish and water to Narvaez and the men who were with him. There were other men too sick to be transported to the chief's home. In fact, during the time while sailing in the barges, a number of men died from the sickness, and others from the salt water they drank and the hunger they could not overcome.

However, during the middle of the night, the Indians attacked Narvaez and all of the men in his command, even the sick people lying on the beach. Narvaez was hit in the face with a rock, and although some of the men near Narvaez went to his defense, they were overcome by sheer numbers. Breaking away from the Indians who had held them, Narvaez and the other Spaniards rushed back to the barges, fighting off the charges of the Indians as they ran.

All but fifty men were able to scramble aboard the barges, but the barges were not pushed off from land. The fifty men who did not climb into the barges repelled more than three attacks during the night, and were successful in a counter-attack which put the Indians into retreat. Early the next morning, thirty of the Indian canoes were set afire to help warm the Spaniard's bodies, as another storm rolled in with the cold wind blowing down hard for several hours before blowing itself out.

When the storm and winds subsided, the barges began sailing out of the cove into the sea, remaining close to the shoreline. A distance away, the barges were turned into another cove, and twenty canoes manned by Indians came into contact with the lead barge in which Narvaez was riding.

Narvaez asked for drinking water, but the Indians indicated the water was in their village, and someone would have to go to retrieve it. The Greek, Don Teodoro, who had been the man who assembled the barges, offered to go along taking with him a Moorish slave he had with him.

They left the barge in which they were riding, and two Indians were taken as hostages by Narvaez. That evening, the chieftain and his warriors returned to the barges without the water and without Don Teodoro and his slave. As the canoe approached the barge of Narvaez, its occupants spoke to the two Indian hostages who tried diving from the barge. They were restrained by the soldiers, and the canoes paddled away.

The next morning a fleet of twenty canoes rowed up to the sides of the barges indicating to the Spaniards they were to follow them to their village, where they had Don Teodoro and his slave, water and food.

Other canoes appeared which blocked the waterway toward the open sea. Narvaez decided to attempt to break through the blockade, with the barges and canoes floating side-by-side, with the Indians demanding the return of the two hostages, and Narvaez refusing to give them up.

As a wind blew into the area, the canoes made for land, and their village. The barges resumed their sailing, following the curvature of land toward the west. Reaching what now is the Mississippi River, the barge which had taken the lead, and in which de Vaca was riding, found a small island, at which he anchored, waiting for the other barges to catch up.

When the barge in which Narvaez was riding arrived, he decided to enter the river to find another island to claim. The other barges joined him and they all found fresh water spilling from the river, headed to the sea. Unfortunately, the flow of water spilling from the river was so strong that the efforts to attain an island went for nil, as even with rowing the barges could not attain land.

The river water pushed the barges out into the sea, and only three could be spotted, one far out into the sea. The other two were the barge of Narvaez and the one with de Vaca. Shouting between the two vessels, de Vaca asked Narvaez if they should follow the third vessel and try to stay together, but Narvaez told de Vaca, "go to your oars and make for land," but the rowers of Narvaez were stronger than those on de Vaca's barge which was pushed out into the sea following the third barge captained by Penalosa and Tellez.

The two barges stayed together as well as possible for two days, until a storm ripped them apart and the barge of Captains Penalosa and Tellez was lost to the bottom of the sea. All men on board were also lost.

It was winter, and bitterly cold from the heavy clouds blotting out a warming sun to the cold winds rippling up the waves around the barge.

All hope had been given up as men fell on top of each other because of hunger and thirst. All lost consciousness during the night. As the sun rose in the eastern sky, the sound of breakers could be heard, and, peering over the side of the barge, de Vaca saw land. A large wave swept over the barge, drenching the men who had been so close to death during the night, awakening them with a cold, water bath.

Waiting until full daybreak, they rowed their way up to the shore with renewed optimism. The day of that landing was November 6th, 1528. That morning, de Vaca sent Lope de Oviedo, the biggest, strongest among the men aboard his barge to climb a high tree to check the surrounding area.

Oviedo could see they were on an island, and that animals had trampled the ground not far from where he was peering from near the top of the tall tree. After descending the tree, he followed the tracks to a series of empty huts, and upon entering one, found an earthen water pot, a little dog, and a few mullets. He returned to the area in which de Vaca was sitting, not being aware of the three Indians following him with bows and arrows.

After becoming aware of them, he waved them on to follow him, and as he reached the small group of men surrounding de Vaca, the Indians sat on their haunches waiting to see what would happen. Shortly thereafter, a hundred or more Indian bowmen joined the three men who were still waiting for some recognition from the

Spaniards. De Vaca and Solis rose, and approached the archers, stretching out their arms toward the Indians in apparent greetings and friendship.

Slowly the two men approached the group of bowmen, offering colored beads and small bells, and in return the bowmen gave the two men an arrow as a pledge of friendship. The Indians indicated by way of sign language they would return the following day with food and water. This tribe became known to the Spaniards as the Capoque tribe.

The following morning the Indians did bring fish and fresh water, and again that evening. For several days the Indians kept the men alive, actually rebuilding their strength, courage, and wills.

Days later, de Vaca and Solis decided to return to the sea and try to find others of their group, but the barge was partly buried in sand. So, stripping off their clothes, they dug the barge from the sand and placed in it their clothes and some food and water.

As they pushed out to sea, the barge was overturned by a large wave, and the men waded back to land, with the exception of Solis and two other men who held fast to the side of the ship with the loose oars hitting their heads, knocking them unconscious, and drowning them. After the barge was overturned, all was lost, clothing, food and water.

That evening when the Indians returned with fish and water, they looked upon the Spaniards unclothed, and they looked different. The Indians appeared scared. They also stared at two dead bodies of the men who had drowned, washed ashore by the pounding waves crashing into the shore.

It was a shock for the Spaniards to see the tears in the eyes of the Indians when they had realized what had happened. The loud chants, cries, and moans coming from the Indian mouths made the Spaniards think it was they that had lost their own people. After the grief of the Indians and Spaniards subsided, through signs, the naked Spaniards asked for shelter, as well as food and water.

Realizing their needs, some of the Indians collected wood, then built four fires along the path to their village homes, aiding the weakest of the men to the warmth while the few that had the strength to walk, struggled to follow them. Arriving at the Indian village, they saw a large hut having been recently constructed, and they were led to it.

There were warming fires within the hut, and food and water were brought to them. The Indians held a dance of celebration all that night, not allowing the Spaniards much time for sleep, or even relaxation, but the care which had been displayed allayed much of their fear.

Upon the food and water being brought to them, de Vaca noticed a trinket worn by one of the Indians was not one they had given to them during their first meeting. Asking by sign language from whom and where it had been obtained, the Indian explained that there were other men who arrived in another area of the island that had given him the beaded necklace.

De Vaca requested he be taken to the area in which the other men were camping, and along the path leading to the other men's camp, he and his guides met men coming from their camp toward the village in which they were now living. The other group were from the barge captained by Andres Dorantes and Alonso del Castillo. They had been blown ashore during the storm, and all forty-eight men of their command were saved.

This group had landed among another tribe called the Han tribe. In meeting, the two captains expressed sorrow at the appearances of de Vaca's men, but as they had no clothes other than what they wore, could not help in clothing them. Plans were made to repair the barge in which Captains Dorantes and Alonzo de Castillo had arrived, but it was beyond repair. A suggestion was made that four of the fittest Spaniard soldiers accompanied by an Indian guide search for the city of Panuco, which was thought to be close.

Then extremely cold weather arrived, during which the Indians were unable to feed themselves with roots they pulled from the ground, and fish were not caught in their traps. There had been five Spaniards from the barge of Dorantes and Alonzo who were sent to live along the coastline, watching for ships passing the island, but during this cold winter, with nothing to eat nor drink, the men died off, one at a time.

The remaining men turned to cannibalism as a last resort until the last one died all alone. The Indians were horrified by this action, and would certainly have killed the other Spaniards had they been aware, but fifteen of the eighty of the other members who lived inland survived.

Then, half of the Indian population died, presumably of the bowel disease that had stricken the Spaniards. Realizing that the disease had been brought to them by the Spaniards, they went to the Spaniards' huts with the idea of killing all of them. As the Indians entered the huts to kill them, the Spaniards individually asked that their lives be spared, but only the lives of de Vaca and a very few of his command were saved.

Living among the Indian tribe called Capoques was a lesson in understanding. Almost all of their methods of living were foreign to the Spaniards. The only weapons known to them was the bow and arrows. The bodies of the men carried cane stuck through their nipples and through their lower lips.

Their families meant everything to them, and when losing a son or daughter, the family went into mourning, not leaving their homes for an entire year, subsisting on food brought by friends within the village.

When visiting other Indian families, they were welcomed warmly, being invited to take anything from the family or home. The women worked incessantly, doing the work of men as well as their own. Funeral rites took place a year after death, and after the ceremony, all walls, altars, and floors were completely washed clean. The dead were buried, except for the medicine men who were cremated.

During cremations, dancing and merriment were performed by

the people of the village, and a year later, the ashes were combined with water and given to the family to drink. The deaths of the elderly were not mourned as their age bespoke of their good lives lived. As you can see, de Vaca had to adjust to many strange customs while living among these people.

He became the only known survivor of his group, and considered himself lucky to be alive. The Dorantes and Alonso de Castillo group were not threatened, but the four men who had been sent out to find the city of Panuco had not returned. Their original group had been found by another Indian tribe called Han, and they remained friends of that group.

Seeking a way to make the Spaniards a part of their civilization, the Capoques expected de Vaca to become a healer, or medicine man. Their medicine men used supposed magic in trying to heal their sick. Their methods of cure were to blow breath or laying of hands onto the area of the body that hurt, supposedly casting out the infirmity from the body.

Occasionally there would be a medicine man who would make incisions to the area of hurt, suck blood from the wound, cover it with leaves to cauterize the wound, and pronounce the hurt cured. The chief of the tribe insisted that de Vaca should do the same, but at first, he refused.

Denying him food and water over many days changed his mind, and he began to be taken to sick people and be expected to cure them. He applied some of their methods as they expected, but added a prayer and the sign of the cross, asking for divine help for the patient before pronouncing him or her as cured. Following a few successful cures had been ordained, the tribe considered him as a very important medicine man.

De Vaca himself became ill, and word was passed on to the group of Dorantes and Alonso de Castillo, who, along with other members of their group came to visit him. There was a total of fifteen Spaniards left from the ninety-eight men who rode in the two barges that landed on this island, presumably the island of Galveston, now in Texas. After the visit ended, the tribe that had kept de Vaca alive kept him with them for over an entire year. He slowly recovered from the sickness, and the treatment of him changed from being a respected medicine man to that of a harshly treated slave.

He sought to escape the Capoques tribe and seek the other group of Spaniards among the Han Indian tribe, hoping for better treatment. He escaped from the Capoques tribe, becoming a trader of goods between the tribes living on the island, being asked by one tribe to bring goods from another, giving what was given him to trade for the requested goods. In this way he was able to eat and get water to drink.

The fact was that the Indian tribes were not accepted in other tribes' villages, but a neutral trader was accepted and welcomed in all areas. His items most widely traded were seashell cones and other pieces of sea-snail, conches for cutting, sea-beads, and a mesquite-like bean used as a medicine and for a ritual beverage in dances and festivities.

It has been suggested that his travels took him all the way to Oklahoma from Galveston. De Vaca plied his trade from early winter in 1528 until early winter, 1532, or four years. The ability for him to move freely in any which direction he chose, the fact that he was not required to do any manual labor that was not helpful or necessary to him, and that he still sought out the whereabouts of other Spaniards, made this the perfect occupation for him. Finding Lope de Oviedo among the tribes with whom he traded, he tried to convince

Lope to join him, but it took until November, 1532 before he would accompany de Vaca across four wide streams, which became a huge effort, for Lope could not swim. After crossing the last of the four streams, the two men met another tribe who spoke of seeing three more men held captive as slaves in a tribe that would soon come to the area in which they were to collect pecan nuts.

Waiting for that tribe to arrive, the tribe that had told de Vaca and Lope about the three others, turned on them, threatening death.

Lope became very scared, running from the tribe toward a group of women who were walking toward the stream. He was never heard from again.

Two days after Lope had departed, the tribe which held Alonso del Castillo and Andres Dorantes arrived to collect and eat the pecan nuts. Actually, their women and slaves ground the nuts into fine powder which they ate during the two months they camped there. Prior to their arrival, an Indian approached de Vaca, asking him why he was there.

He was able to partially understand the man's dialect and replied that he had been told that there were three men who were not Indians he hoped to see and speak with. The man was not a member of the tribe that was coming there, but could help de Vaca in seeing the men, as he was on friendly terms with that tribe. De Vaca was told to hide at a certain place in the forest, and the man would take him to see the men.

It turned out to be the two men he had been told it would be, but Dorantes was terrified. He had been told that de Vaca had died from illness while with the Capoques, but now he was seeing de Vaca in front of him. Asked by Dorantes what his plans were, de Vaca told him that he was determined to find Christians again, which he hoped to find soon.

Dorantes told de Vaca he had tried to convince Castillo and Estevancio, the black Moorish slave owned by Dorantes, to depart with him to find Spanish people, but had been turned down as neither of them could swim and they knew that they would have to cross water in order to find their compatriots. Dorantes then warned de Vaca that if the Indians knew of the plan to desert them and to search for the Christians that were known to be somewhere south west of their present location, they were sure to kill all of them.

Knowing further that this tribe would go to the west and find the prickly pear fruit they craved as food, Dorantes suggested that they wait for that movement by the tribe to make their escape. As he gave himself up to the tribe, he was given to the family that held Dorantes as a slave, and worked for that family while they waited for the tribe to move to the west and the prickly pear cactus found in the western desert.

After six months of toil, the four men, de Vaca, Dorantes, Castillo and Estevancio, had been separated, and this made it mandatory that an escape be delayed for a year, at which time the tribe again gathered together to harvest the prickly pear cactus.

The four men were aware of the plans for their escapes. De Vaca would leave first, hiding in a staging area a few days before the new moon (which occurred on September 8th in 1534). He waited at the appointed place for the others to arrive, with Dorantes and Estevancio arriving a few days later, and Castillo coming there last. The fruit and juice of the prickly pear were the only food and drink the four men had, although there were rains that provided water while they fled.

They became aware of an Indian tribe traveling the same direction as they, and discovered that they knew of the Spaniards who found their way by a barge along the coastline. However, after coming ashore, all men were killed.

The Indians showed the four men the clothes and arms the men were wearing and carrying when they were killed, and where the barge was still stuck in the sand. The four men continued to help that tribe collect the prickly pear fruit and juice, and await another tribe to meet them from the area ahead which was the direction de Vaca wanted to travel.

Having heard of the help both de Vaca and Castillo had performed as medicine men for other tribes, some of this tribe brought five sick members of their tribe to the hut in which Castillo was housed. Giving him five sets of bows and arrows, they asked him to perform curing rites on the five sick individuals. By the grace of God and good fortune, the touching of the bodies and the prayers said by all four men allowed the five men to rise in the morning as if they had never been sick.

News of this success in healing spread throughout the Indian tribes of the region, and a tribe called the Susolas had some men who had suffered injuries, some sick and one near death. They requested Castillo to come give aid, but he declined.

Then de Vaca was asked, and because of his previous experience of curing the Indian years prior, he agreed to go and attempt aid. Dorantes and Estevancio accompanied him to the men's sides, and by breathing on them and the laying of hands on their bodies, accompanied by prayers and the sign of the cross, the following day they were made whole again; even the man who had appeared dead was up and around.

The various Indian tribes would allow the four men to travel within their areas, performing cures as they traveled, being called to one tribe then another, always being requested for the cures they seemed to perform. The tribe they most were affiliated with were the Avavares, who treated them well, and later, the Arbadaos, whose bodies appeared weak, emaciated, and in a swollen condition.

There were four families that accepted one of the Spaniards to each family, and allowed them to make items to trade to other members of the tribe. The most requested items were mats for their homes and combs used for their hair and for scraping skins of small animals they may have caught or trapped.

Then, too, being treated as slaves, they spent much time seeking out and cutting wood for their fires. The Indians themselves spent most of their time searching for food, not very successfully. The four men ate what little food they were allowed raw, because if they had started a fire on their own the Indians would come and take the food for themselves.

Living with those Indians, in what was to become known as the "Texas hill country" in a completely naked condition, left the men's bodies bleeding whenever they came into contact with any cactus, or any other plants with needles as branches or leaves.

Finally, de Vaca traded some projects he had made by hand for two small dogs, and they were cut up and eaten raw by the four men. This provided them enough strength to leave the Arbadaos Indians, who directed them to another tribe who spoke the same language as they did.

Along the way a rainstorm occurred, sending them into a wooded area for shelter. They attempted to catch and collect rainwater for drinking, but no food was found until they found prickly pear cactus which kept them alive as they searched for the Indians they had been directed toward.

They finally located the pathway they had been seeking, which led them to a community of fifty dwellings. The Indian inhabitants looked at them in fear. Some of them approached the men, feeling their bearded faces, their hairy bodies, and then their own, comparing the two.

Since the men could express themselves using the language skills they had learned from the Arbadaos people, the tribe allowed them to stay overnight. The next morning, the people of that village brought their sick to the dwelling they had offered to the men, asking them to cure the sicknesses of those unfortunates.

After performing their usual efforts of curing the sick, the Indians offered prickly pear pads and the green fruit roasted. Because of their kindness toward the four men, the Spaniards stayed a few extra days trying to help them gather more fruit. While there, a group of another tribe visited the village, and they had arrived from the area in which the four men were traveling.

The Spaniards requested the other tribe for permission to accompany them, and after permission was granted, left the village which had been so good toward them.

From that point on, the four men walked from village to village being asked to perform curing rites at each, with the sick people always claiming they had been cured, whether they had or not. Most of the villages treated them very well, feeding them and sending them on to the next village with gifts they had earned by their cures.

And, with the increase in fame, fortune smiled upon them and they were able to clothe themselves, using the skins of animals to cover their nakedness.

Eventually they came to an area where each Indian man carried a club with which he would capture rabbits. There was a game the men played as they scared up rabbits by pounding the ground in front of the rabbit, which then scurried toward another man who would do the same until the rabbit was killed. In that particular area rabbits were very numerous, and other men went into the forests bringing back many deer, quail, and other game.

The tribe would not eat any of their catch until it was blessed by one of the four visitors. The men ate very well during their stay at that village.

Resuming their westward movement, they entered a mountainous area, probably in the southern part of what is now New Mexico, as Andres Dorantes was presented a large copper rattle with a face cast in a hollow form on the front of it. When asked from where it had come, they indicated from the north, and that much copper, very valuable to the Indians of that area, could be found there.

Also, mica, seashells, and turquoise items were offered to them, but they had no use for them while traveling. Many other gifts were presented, not only to the four men, but also to the people who began guiding them. It was also in that area the men began seeing items made of woven cotton, and foods such as honey, pine nuts, and the very popular prickly pears as fruits, jams, jellies or drinks.

Many of the items were brought to them by the traveling traders who walked from areas in what is now Mexico as far north as southern Nevada, and from the Pacific Ocean to places in New Mexico. As de Vaca, Andres Dorantes, Castillo, and Estevancio walked their way through the mountains of what is now southern New Mexico, they met more Indian tribes anxious to have these medicine men cure the sicknesses of their tribe members.

And the people who accompanied them extracted the wealth from the village they had directed the men to, until they entered the plains of what is now southern Arizona. There the residents of the villages looked forward to the arrival of these medicine men from afar, and gave whatever they had to those four men.

They in turn gave those items to their people who were guiding them to that village, and then releasing them to return to their own tribal country. In one of the villages they arrived at, the men of that village brought to de Vaca a man who had been shot with an arrow that was lodged close to his heart. Although hesitant, de Vaca reopened the old wound with a flint knife and extracted the huge arrow head from the man's body, closing the opening he had made with stitches sewn by deer bone, and covering the area with the hair of a deer hide.

With many prayers having been said to the Good Lord for recovery, the man awoke the following day and said all pain had left his body, the stitches were cut out, and the incision looked no worse than the normal folds in a man's hand. This cure inflated the fame of de Vaca as a medicine man throughout the area, and he, along with the other three men were welcomed wherever their paths led them.

Needless to say, there were many more villages over many more miles of rugged hills, long dry deserts, with not enough food and water to keep the men healthy.

Throughout that hilly and mountainous territory, much antimony, copper, gold, iron, silver, turquoise, and other metals could be found. But they struggled on through areas that were the homes of the Apache bands in eastern Arizona, the Pima people of the central part of Arizona, and the Papago people of southern Arizona. There Castillo recognized an amulet made from a sword belt buckle being worn by one of the Papago Indians.

Asking the Indian where it had come from, he proudly announced it had belonged to the people who had come from "heaven" several years before. They had emerged from the waters of the "South Sea" and had sent lances through the bodies of two warriors before returning to the sea, and "heaven." This information sent tears of joy coursing down the cheeks of the four men who had been praying for an indication of the location of the Spaniards who had preceded their voyage to "New Spain."

The Indian people who were with them at that time were amazed at the feelings displayed by these men, who had once again appeared from far away, but this time they had arrived from over the hills and mountains to the east. The four men, and the entourage that traveled with them, met groups of Indians who had been in contact with the Spanish troops.

They were told these men were plundering the homes of the poor Indians who abandoned their planted fields, then hid away as best they could, being forced to eat roots and bark as they were constantly moving from hide-out to hide-out.

These last two tribes they had found and traveled with, the Pima and Papago, offered everything they had to the four men, whom they thought of as healers, who might convince the other Spaniards to stop their invasions of their families, homes, and planted fields. They guided the four men to the most recent areas in which the Spaniard troops had camped.

There they found indications of where their horses had been hitched, where captured men, women, and children had been sitting, and evidence of chain linking them together. De Vaca urged the three other men to move more quickly on their route to catch the Spaniards ahead of them, but Dorantes and Castillo said they were too tired of hurrying, doubting they would ever catch up to the soldiers ahead.

De Vaca and Estevancio began the next morning to follow the tracks of the horses as it seemed they had moved just a few days before. It took two days of following them before they saw the group of twenty horsemen in the distance ahead of them. Hailing them by shouts and screams, the group finally stopped, turning around to see two men, naked as the day they were born, walking or half-running toward them.

One had a beard, the other was browner, and although they were not recognized as coming from Spain, they definitely were not Indians. Waiting for these strange individuals to come nearer, they heard the man with a beard shout out in Spanish, "Take me to your captain."

The horsemen led the two strange men a short distance to a camp in which their captain waited for their reconnaissance group to return. The captain's name was Captain Diego de Alcaraz. After talking with the captain for a period of time, the captain told de Vaca that he and his men were tired of trying to catch and capture Indians to be sold as slaves, that they were hungry and exhausted, wanting to return to the comforts of their camp at a place the Spaniards called San Miguel, better known as Culiacan, the northern-most settlement in Mexico.

De Vaca told the captain of the location where he and Estevancio had left Dorantes and Castillo, and the captain dispatched three of his horsemen and fifty of his Indian allies, with Estevancio as the guide, to bring the two men to the camp.

Five days later the group returned with the two men and a group of about six hundred Indians who had been escorting the four men for many days and miles. All the while de Vaca had been in the camp, Captain Alcaraz kept requesting de Vaca to order the Indians in the surrounding area to bring food to the camp, and over six hundred Indians came to the camp bringing corn in clay-sealed earthen containers, which was all of the food they had available to them.

The captain wanted to capture and enslave the Indians, but de Vaca and the other three men spoke against it, and left behind the many items of worth they had been given by the many tribes they had been with, and which had been carried by the Indians of those tribes for the men.

Encouraging the Indians to return to their homes, begin their planting anew, and to live as they had before the incursions by the Spanish soldiers, was the next mission the four men undertook. Since it was already March, 1536, and the normal planting time would have been February, they tried to hurry the Indians from San Miguel, but the Indians insisted that it was their duty to take the four men to another tribe of Indians, as they might die if that duty was not completed.

Captain Alcaraz had his interpreters explain that these men were from his home country, and he had the duty of returning them to their own people.

The Indians explained that the four men came from the direction of the sunrise and had performed great deeds as medicine men in helping them, while the Spanish soldiers came from the sunset direction and captured and took away the Indian people to be slaves to the Spaniards.

Finally, the words of de Vaca and the three other men were enacted by the Indians, and most of them returned to their homes and fields. Captain Alcaraz put two of his horsemen in charge of the four men, arresting them as it were, even though they were accompanied by a few Pima Indians intent on passing them off to another tribe before leaving them.

As they marched on, they were directed through wooded areas, so as to keep the men away from other Indian tribes. Traveling in this manner they found no water to drink, and soon seven Indians perished from the lack. They eventually did find water, shortly before entering the city of San Miguel, or Culiacan, where Melchior Diaz had become mayor and captain of the province. Upon hearing of the four men who had lived through the fateful voyage of Narvaez, the news of which spread throughout the Spanish world, Diaz hurried to meet with the four men, and wept with them as their story was told.

All of them gave praise and thanks to the Good Lord for their unholy travels through uncharted and wild parts of an unknown country. Diaz provided for every want expressed by de Vaca and the other three men, apologizing for Captain Alcaraz's rash move to arrest the men and the injustices he put on them, and making references to Nuno de Guzman, the governor of the territory. He requested that the four men rest for several days before returning to the area most recently traveled through, requesting the friendly

Pima and Papago Indians to resume their lives and planting of their crops of corn, beans, and squash. These words spoken to the Indians by the interpreter for Diaz were heard and followed by the Indians, as well as the Spaniards and the Mexican Indians under his command, and that part of New Spain was considered to be civilized.

The four men stayed in San Miguel until May 15th, when they were escorted by a detail of twenty horsemen for a distance. The horsemen were then replaced by six Christians who were taking five hundred Indians as slaves to the city of Compostela, the city in which the governor of the territory, Nuno de Guzman, lived. There, the four men were greeted by Guzman, and treated royally, being given clothes of his own, and excellent quarters in which to reside. Unfortunately, after having lived nakedly for so long, clothes were not comfortable, and for a period of time after their arrival, floors were more comfortable than beds of feather down.

After twelve days, de Vaca and the three other men were escorted toward Mexico City, the former Tenochtitlan, and capital city of New Spain. The route was over nine hundred miles, and this time, the men were mounted on horses, arriving there on July 24th, 1536, being greeted there by the viceroy, Antonio de Mendoza and the Marques del Valle, Hernando Cortes.

The four honored men were given new clothes, as after their travels the clothes were torn as they rode through areas of much cacti and brush. The four were treated as royalty until de Vaca and Dorantes expressed a desire to return to Spain. Upon inquiring of de Vaca, Dorantes, Castillo, and Estevancio, whether they had seen evidence of gold, silver, or other riches, they answered they had seen areas where gold was found in the soil and in building materials.

Asking if any of the four would agree to return to those areas with Fray Marcos de Niza, a Franciscan friar sent to spread the Catholic faith to the Indians, they replied they would not return. Prior to their departure, the viceroy, Antonio de Mendoza, purchased Estevancio, the black Moorish slave from Dorantes.

Chapter 7—De Vaca's Return to New Spain

1540-1545

DE VACA AND DORANTES did return to Spain, although there were many interruptions on the way there. Traveling as far as Veracruz, they waited for a ship to land, but a hurricane blew in, capsizing the vessel.

They returned to Mexico City for the winter, then caught a ship that was pursued by French privateers near the Azores, but the ship escaped to the port of Terceira in the Azores, waiting for other ships to join in a convoy heading for Portugal and Spain. While on this journey, De Vaca mentally went over the mistakes he felt Narvaez made in the voyage and expedition to New Spain.

He felt that he had learned much about the land and its people, and wanted the opportunity to settle this new land for the benefit of the church, the king, and Spain. Upon his arrival, he found that Hernando De Soto had won the appointment as governor of Florida, the appointment he wanted for himself.

On his voyage upriver to his home and wife in Jerez, Spain, he contemplated steps by which he could extract an exploration of his own to a part of New Spain where no one had been awarded a governorship. He heard about Rio de la Plata, which is a broad channel between present day Uruguay and Argentina.

The former governor, Don Pedro de Mendoza, had died on a ship returning him to Spain, and had been buried at sea. Rio de la Plata was a very rich area that sent much silver back to Spain, and was thought to have much more wealth available. In fact, Rio de la Plata meant "River of Silver."

Before leaving Rio de la Plata, Mendoza had appointed his second-in-command, Juan de Ayolas, to rule in his absence. With the debate raging between Spaniard residents, the royalty, and the Catholic Church regarding treatment of the natives in the newly explored lands of New Spain, de Vaca was appointed as governor of Rio de la Plata and lands uncharted north and west of there by the Council of the Indies on March 18th, 1540.

The only stipulation was that de Vaca would become governor if Ayolas was deceased. In order to appease de Vaca, should he find Ayolas alive, he was awarded governorship of Santa Catalina Island (now known as Santa Catarina), and be second-in-command to Ayolas at Rio de la Plata. During the summer of 1540 de Vaca raised funds by borrowing from family and friends.

He bought four ships, loading them with provisions including milk cows for food and milk, flour, salt, and many other types of useful items, including knives, mirrors, scissors, shirts, linen cloth and other items which could be used in trading with the natives. He recruited four hundred soldiers, forty-eight horses, nine priests and friars. Medicines, iron tools, vestments for the priests and friars, other necessary items, and many barrels of water were loaded.

Assigned to the expedition to watch that King Charles V would receive his share of any wealth attained during the expedition were a treasurer, comptroller, and an inspector, all holdovers from the Mendoza expedition. His companion, Andres Dorantes, of the perilous journey through New Spain to Mexico City, accompanied him on this expedition.

There were many problems as the ships left Cadiz, Spain in March, but due to weather issues, waiting for favorable winds in the Canary Islands, and leaks in the largest ship which had to be repaired at the Cape Verde Islands, the ships arrived at Santa Catalina on March 29th, 1541. Only twenty-six horses survived the voyage.

De Vaca took time to formally claim that land for Spain, but the natives were accustomed to greeting European ships at Santa Catalina, as many ships put into port there for fresh water, firewood, and other provisions. In May of 1541, he entrusted Felipe de Caceres to sail to Buenos Aires, the capital of Rio de la Plata, but the ship sailed into storms, and returned to Santa Catalina.

A ship arrived from Buenos Aires with the men aboard telling de Vaca of the happenings in the city they had departed. Ayolas had left Buenos Aires looking for gold on the Upper Paraguay River, appointing Captain Domingo de Martinez de Irala to guard the riverboats while he marched inland. However, when Ayolas returned to the river with native warriors in pursuit, Irala had gone, leaving Ayolas with nowhere to escape.

The men on the ship told de Vaca that Irala was to blame for the death of Ayolas. A power struggle for leadership took place after the death of Ayolas, and Irala was elected governor by the residents. Irala moved the capital of the colony up-river to Asuncion, a new town on a bluff overlooking the Paraguay River, seven hundred fifty miles from Buenos Aires, leaving only eighty settlers behind at Buenos Aires.

De Vaca made a decision to divide his expedition, as he had sent his friend, Dorantes, and a group of one hundred armed men to find out if an overland route could be used in getting to Asuncion. Dorantes used some natives as guides, and after several months reported back to de Vaca that although the first part of the march would be over mountains, the latter part would be through a fertile plain.

De Vaca determined he would lead the majority of men overland to Asuncion, while the ships would carry everyone else to Buenos Aires, ordering that group to wait there for further orders. Overcoming some arguments from Felipe de Caceres that the entire expedition should sail to Buenos Aires, then proceed up river to

Asuncion, he explained that he had been sent to discover and explore, as much as to aid the colonies that had been settled. On November 2nd, 1541, de Vaca, two hundred fifty musketeers and crossbowmen, twenty-six horses, and local native guides began the march into Southeastern Brazil.

The first nineteen days saw them traveling through dense forests and over mountains. Then they came to the plains, where they were helped by friendly natives, who brought food to them daily as they progressed from village to village. De Vaca paid for the food with Spanish knives, scissors, mirrors, and other trade goods. He kept a close watch on the men in his command, making sure that they would not antagonize any of the natives.

As the group progressed, de Vaca became aware of the value this land could produce from cultivation, stock-rearing, and the more than adequate fresh water supply. On November 29th, 1541, de Vaca performed the ceremony taking possession of the land in the name of King Charles V of Spain. In early December, the group met a baptized native, Miguel, returning from Asuncion to his village at Santa Catalina, who offered to show the way to Asuncion, which offer de Vaca happily accepted.

Giving presents to the natives who had been guiding him to that point, he released them to return to their homes. As the group moved forward, they came to forests, steep mountains, and marshy lowlands which had to be cleared of thickets, and bridges had to be built over narrow rivers and over swamps.

Some of the group became ill, and de Vaca paid villagers to care for the sick, leaving them behind. At the Iguazu River, they built canoes, and de Vaca separated the ranks again, sending the horsemen with one hundred sixty foot-soldiers along the banks of the river, while he and eighty men boarded the canoes and floated downstream until they heard the roar of a waterfall they were approaching.

Hurriedly they rowed to shore and carried the canoes around to the river beyond the waterfalls, reentered the canoes, and eventually came to where the Iguazu River emptied into the Parana

River. That is where the horsemen and foot-soldiers, and de Vaca and the men in the canoes met.

A short distance beyond that, the group met a large army of natives, wearing bright paint, and armed with bows and arrows ready to do battle. De Vaca defused the standoff by offering gifts. Pleased with the gifts, the natives helped de Vaca's group to cross the river junction.

The village from which the army of natives had come was just a short distance from the rivers, and they escorted de Vaca and his group to their village, feeding and providing sleeping quarters for them. Asuncion was only nine days from the village where they rested for a few days. A Spaniard arrived, having walked from Asuncion to meet them, as some natives had alerted the Spaniards that de Vaca and his group was on its way overland, and had reached the junction of the two rivers. As de Vaca's group now had a guide to lead them to Asuncion, the closer they got to that city the more Spanish was spoken by the natives.

Along the way during the four-month journey, de Vaca had lost but three men of the two hundred fifty that accompanied him. One man had drowned, one died of sickness, and the last one died when attacked by a jaguar. De Vaca had not ridden a horse, but either walked or rode in a canoe during the whole journey. He had led the group through much of southern Brazil and into Paraguay, not once lifting a sword, musket, or crossbow.

Entering Asuncion on March 11th, de Vaca found that Irala was preparing to lead an exploration party to locate gold up river. De Vaca, being the new governor, found many items which were more important to the community than leaving the residents behind in Irala's search for gold. The first order of business was to re-establish a community at Buenos Aires, as Irala had burned down the community upon moving to Asuncion.

It was paramount that there be a community at the Rio de la Plata, as Spanish ships coming and going needed to know that they need not travel another three months to Asuncion in order to find a

Spanish community. De Vaca sent two boats stocked well with food and other supplies to Buenos Aires, expecting to find the one hundred fifty people he had sent to Buenos Aires waiting for his orders.

As it was, that group, upon finding Buenos Aires in ashes, began floating in canoes downriver toward Asuncion, when they met the boats from Asuncion sent by de Vaca. Receiving the news that they were to rebuild Buenos Aires and occupy it, they turned around and began work on that project.

With all of the food and supplies, they were able to accomplish that feat.

Further addressing issues in Asuncion, de Vaca heard many complaints from Irala and his men who had been planning to search for gold. Where had the supplies they needed for their exploration gone? They were angry that the supplies had gone back to Buenos Aires. Other issues had to be addressed before the exploration for gold could be allowed.

Many of the Spanish residents of Asuncion complained of Irala's governance, such as taxes he placed on them when trading for food with the natives. The natives living around Asuncion were angry that the Spanish men treated the women badly, married or unmarried, and made the native men work as slaves. Also, the natives were paying the Spaniards for protection from other nomad native tribes who were warlike, attacking the villages, carrying off food, burning the homes and massacring villagers who had food and other supplies.

Each issue was dealt with by the steady, but firm, rules set up by de Vaca. The taxes were abolished, there was to be no more trading of women, and work done by the natives was to be compensated by the families who received the benefits of that work. The orders went out with a six-day moratorium, and anyone not complying spent time in locked stocks.

He punished the Spaniards leniently, and quieted the natives' complaints with gifts. The people who had been accustomed to the liberties allowed by Irala complained bitterly among themselves, but de Vaca remained firm in his judgements. He was also intent on the conversion of the natives to the Catholic religion, designating a place within the community for a church and a house for the priests. Many conversions to the Catholic faith by the natives occurred during de Vaca's time as governor.

There were only two occasions when weapons were used against natives, the first being against a tribe that attacked the natives who lived around Asuncion, and after that, one of the native tribes attacked Asuncion while de Vaca had led the small army against that first tribe, defeating them, and buying their friendship with gifts. The second instance was put down by Irala, ordered by de Vaca.

After he had cleared up the more pressing issues, de Vaca turned toward the search for gold. He was careful on how, where and who would be accompanying him on the expedition. His plans were based on diplomacy, and information gained by men who had searched this area before, but some had perished while in the task. De Vaca sent Irala on a discovery mission on October 20th, 1542 to the west of Asuncion, but during his absence, many issues arose that commanded de Vaca's immediate attention.

First, the boats de Vaca had sent to Buenos Aires returned with news that the Spanish settlement on the Rio de la Plata had failed due to repeated attacks by natives living near there. The Spanish people there had suffered through attacks, near starvation, and an earthquake that killed fourteen settlers.

The remaining residents scrambled aboard the two boats and sailed to Asuncion. Although disappointed in the failure, he was happy to see many of his friends who had accompanied him from Jerez.

Then, in February, 1543, a native accidently brushed by and set fire to a thatch wall of a home, igniting a large number of homes in Asuncion, destroying up to eighty percent of the community. The loss of provisions, including food, clothing, livestock, and housing was disastrous during the four-day fire.

When Irala returned, he told of a good prospective area to find gold near the border of what is now Brazil and Bolivia. However, he also found all of the provisions that were planned to be used for the gold expedition had been destroyed in the fire.

Shortly thereafter, one of the natives who lived near Asuncion came to de Vaca with the story that two friars had taken a number of women with them. De Vaca sent two soldiers after the fleeing friars and the women, and upon their catching and returning the group to his presence, found that there had been a conspiracy against his rule, and the friars were surprised to see de Vaca still alive.

The three royal officials sent by King Charles V with the Mendoza group felt they were overlooked in the governance of the colony. The friars had letters they had hoped to take to Spain, and in the letters, requested that Irala be returned to governor.

The three officials and the notary who had prepared the letter were imprisoned, but Irala was not punished as de Vaca needed him to guide the expedition to the area Irala considered as the best for finding gold.

On September 8th, 1543, a very long procession of boats and canoes carrying four hundred Spaniards and one thousand two hundred natives aboard ten boats and one hundred twenty canoes left Asuncion, following Irala in the lead boat along with de Vaca and thirty-eight other Spaniards. Initially, the group ate well as they moved toward the west, but as they came to an area where many native tribes lived, de Vaca split the group into two so as not to disturb the natives in the areas they were approaching.

De Vaca marked the trail his group was taking with wooden crosses, and he took formal possession of Puerto de los Reyes, where he also ordered a church and fort built. While this was being done, he sent two Spaniards to the north to find natives who traded in gold and silver, hoping that they could lead his group to their sources. The men returned a few months later having traveled many miles to an area at which they found a native of one of the tribes that was accompanying de Vaca's group.

He volunteered to guide de Vaca and a smaller group to the area where gold and silver were traded, but after five days he became lost. Most of the provisions had been used, and the natives ahead were not friendly, so the group turned back to Puerto de los Reyes. Before turning back to Puerto de los Reyes, de Vaca sent out a small group headed by Francisco de Ribera to find the route to the places where the "Lords of the Metal" were located.

But they returned to him with news of their two hundred ten mile hike through the wilderness, as well as suffering from many attacks by native tribes on the way there and back, but they were unable to find the sources, nor the fabled "Lords of the Metal."

Waiting for a better time to mount another search, many people within the fort became very ill, with one Spaniard and several natives dying. De Vaca became so ill that he could not understand the plight the men were trying to explain to him. The natives surrounding the settlement attacked the fishermen and hunters that were sent out for food, even attacking the fort, killing fifty-eight soldiers during one attack.

Finally in February, 1544, de Vaca realized that diplomacy would not settle the problems with the nearby natives, and he declared war against them. The comptroller, Caceres, worded a strongly written letter to de Vaca, demanding that Puerto de los Reyes be evacuated, and everyone return to Asuncion. De Vaca had to agree that rather than staying there with all of the sickness getting worse, returning to Asuncion was the right thing to do.

Before leaving, he ordered all slaves taken by the Spaniards and the friendly natives that had accompanied his group be returned to their tribes, which further alienated the Spaniards against de Vaca, but was appreciated by the unfriendly natives. De Vaca reminded the Spaniards of the king's orders that no natives were to be removed from their lands, but the Spaniards considered the women as their personal property, and began to plan the overthrow of de Vaca's governing.

As the Spaniards and friendly natives sailed back toward

Asuncion, the banks along the river concealed many warriors of the natives' tribes, raining arrows and spears at the boats.

With most of the Spaniards sickened, including de Vaca, the soldiers strong enough to aim and shoot the muskets kept the warriors from entering the water to fight with the occupants of the boats. All this while resentment against de Vaca simmered, with the expedition failing to yield any wealth and the slaves and women being released from their bonds to the captains and the other officials.

Upon their arrival at Asuncion, the officials and captains, including Irala, staged a coup on the evening of April 25th, 1544, breaking into the bedroom of de Vaca, rousting him from the bed, screaming, "Liberty! Liberty! Long live the king!"

They dragged de Vaca into the street, wakening the town with their cries. Taking him by force to the house of the royal treasurer, Garci Venegas, then shackling him inside a small storage room, they built walls around that building, and stationed soldiers that were trusted to keep de Vaca imprisoned there.

The royal officials appointed Irala as the new governor, who then imposed strict laws. Irala and the officials scuttled all boats so that men who might support de Vaca could not return to Spain and report the mutiny. Friends, relatives from Jerez, and priests who preached against the arrest of de Vaca were arrested. In order to stop the growing resentment to the escalating arrests, Irala threatened to behead de Vaca.

The standoff only ended after de Vaca wrote a letter saying, "Better to go back to Spain under arrest than that on my behalf a single drop of blood should be shed."

Meanwhile the rebels looted de Vaca's personal property, rewarding valuables to supporters, and inking out, on letters he had written intended for the king, misdeeds committed by the captains and officials. False claims against de Vaca were written up during that summer to be presented to the court in Spain.

On March 7th, 1545, the officials and soldiers came to the cell, picked up de Vaca, carrying him to a ship that had been built to carry him, still in chains, back to Spain for trial, and judgement. Unknown to the rebels, a small space had been hollowed out by the carpenters to hide papers defending de Vaca's governorship, and those had been placed there by the friendly carpenters.

Many problems on the voyage to Spain occurred. Among them were the food that de Vaca was given contained poisons. He refused to eat for four days, but ate a remedy he had hidden from his captors. This was helpful in regaining his health.

Then a terrible storm battered the ship so badly that his captors, even the royal officials, were so scared they filed off the chains binding de Vaca begging his forgiveness. After the storm had abated, they even offered to throw the condemning letters they were carrying back for use in the trial overboard, but he refused to accommodate them.

With the restrictive chains removed, he was able to walk the ship enough to remove the letters that had been placed into the secret hiding place by the carpenters, and conceal them in the clothing on his body.

Upon reaching the Azores, de Vaca was placed aboard a different ship, and although the officials arrived in Spain ahead of him, de Vaca was freed on bail, even after the accusatory letters from both sides were presented to the court.

However, in court at a later time, he was convicted and imprisoned again, and over the next eight years he had his titles stripped from him, was sentenced to be banned for life from returning to the Americas, and was ordered to serve five years in the service of Spain in northern Africa—supplying his own horse. Then, being released from the military service sentence, he was finally released to roam throughout Spain.

Soon, relatives of his in Jerez requested him to represent them at the royal court, followed by the city council of Jerez paying him to perform work on its behalf. De Vaca had restored his reputation. He found time to publish the story of his time spent in New Spain on behalf of Spain.

Although there is no proven date of death for de Vaca, it is said that he was supposedly buried in the tomb of his grandfather, Pedro de Vera, the brutal conqueror of the Canary Islands.

Chapter 8—Fray Marcos de Niza, Estevancio and the Search for the Seven Cities of Cibola

THE VICEROY, ANTONIO de Mendoza, organized an expedition into the upper reaches of New Spain in hopes of finding the "Seven Cities of Cibola."

These were the fabled places where gold taken from the churches of Spain by the priests for protection against being taken by the attacking Moorish armies, was to be found. Legend spread that the gold was put on ships which put out to sea traveling westward to places unknown.

With the discovery of the new world (the Americas), the Spanish kingdom, which had defeated the Moors in the 1400's, sought to bring back the riches to their shores. With the words spoken by de Vaca, and the other three men, of having seen gold and other valuable items on the ground and in the walls of buildings they had passed by, the viceroy thought he would become rich and famous if he could uncover the gold, and send some of it to the treasury in Spain.

Fray Marcos de Niza had been sent to New Spain in order to convert the pagan Indians to Catholicism. This had been his main mission when sent by his order, the Franciscan priesthood. After the word of gold being sighted in the area of northern New Spain, plans were made for Fray Marcos to leave for that territory, and be guided by Estevancio, the black Moorish slave, who chose to accept that position rather than the plight of a slave doing hard work under brutal men.

As the two men started from Mexico City, Estevancio became concerned for his life, and began to adorn his body with a feathered headdress and carry rattles, as worn and carried by chieftains of villages he had passed through.

Also, many women of the Indian tribes had heard of the wonderful healing miracles the four men had accomplished as they had walked through the area before, and began to follow Estevancio thinking he might be able to do the same. With a growing throng of people following Estevancio, Fray Marcos had watched enough of the circus Estevancio was performing, and told him to advance one day ahead of him, sending back a cross the size of which would tell him of the find for the day.

As they entered villages ahead, Estevancio would be greeted by the chieftains, and he would ask them for their most desirable women and drink. Day after day, the group walked many miles, stopping overnight, Fray Marcos de Niza staying outside the villages, while Estevancio looked for villages in which to eat, sleep, drink and enjoy the pleasures of the women he was given.

This went on for some period of time as they walked up into the interior of what is now New Mexico and Arizona. At some point in either of these two now recognized states, Estevancio entered a village in which the leaders said "no" to his demands. At that village, he was supposedly killed by the men of the village. Whether that is true or false is left to the imagination. History is written that he was killed in one of the Zuni villages alongside the river now known as the Zuni River.

As most expeditions of that time would have followed rivers from which they could drink fresh water, it would stand to reason that Estevancio would have followed that river which stretches down from the mid-western edge of New Mexico into the far eastern edge of Arizona. Being that what it may be, the Zuni villages were located along that river.

Whether the village was along the river in Arizona or New Mexico is unknown. Whether Estevancio was killed or not is not for us to know for sure. Could he have been tired of being a slave, or tired of being the guide for Fray Marcos de Niza, or could he have been tired of the entire expedition, and just became a resident of the village?

According to Fray Marcos de Niza, the people following Estevancio returned to him, informing him that Estevancio had been killed. Nothing is said that those people who had reported the killing stayed with the priest, or left him. The question remains as to the actions of the priest after hearing of the killing of Estevancio. There were three possible things he could have done after that.

The first would be to turn around and head back to the viceroy with nothing to report. The second would have been to enter the village in which Estevancio was reportedly slain, possibly being killed as well. The third possibility was to climb a hill outside of the village and peer into the village, checking for any valuable items to be seen. The third possibility is the one he reported to the viceroy. He said that he had seen gold, silver, copper, and turquoise in the walls of the homes there.

Adding a footnote to the above description of the location of the supposed killing of Estevancio along the state lines of New Mexico and Arizona, there have been earthquakes that occurred between the time of Estevancio and Fray Marcos de Niza's expedition in 1538/9 to more present days, possibly changing the course of history and the rivers.

A personal theory of mine is that if Estevancio had walked the same route as he and the three other men walked down toward Mexico City in reverse, Estevancio may have walked up to the northward-flowing San Pedro River.

That river starts ten miles south of the US/Mexican border below the now city of Sierra Vista, Arizona, and joins the east/westward-flowing Gila River, that flows just south of what is now Globe, Arizona. As you will recall, the Pima and Papago Indian people had helped the four men while traveling through their areas. The Gila River was their main source for water.

The now city-owned archaeological park of Besh ba Gowah in Globe, Arizona might have been the village that put an end to Estevancio's guidance of Fray Marcos de Niza. Besh ba Gowah is a small Indian village, dating back to the 1100 AD period. The walls of the buildings still standing are filled with colorful stones that reflect sunlight when the sun falls on them.

Globe is built on hills, so that if Fray Marcos did look from one hill into, or onto the village, he would have seen the colors of black obsidian, copper, mica, peridot, and turquoise in the walls and on the ground. A colorful and mind-bending eyeful. Yes, it might have been!

Upon leaving that area, Fray Marcos may have walked southward to where the Gila flows westward; there was found, carved into a large boulder on the far eastern corner of what is now known as South Mountain park in Phoenix, the following inscription: "Fr Marcos de Niza corona todo el Nuevo Mexico 1539."

It was judged to be a fake sometime during the 1940's, but as a famous comedian of that era said, "Vas you dere, Charley?"

Walking back to Mexico City, Fray Marcos had to make up his mind what to tell the viceroy, Antonio de Mendoza, when he stood before that magistrate to tell him of the results of the expedition. He still had a choice, either to tell him they had found nothing, or that he had seen great wealth during the time he was gone.

He decided to tell the viceroy that Estevancio had been killed by the men of a village in the northern area of New Spain, and that he had climbed a hill across from the village, and had seen jewels of many colors including gold in the walls of the homes in the village, and even on the ground on which the Indians walked.

The words of the priest were good enough for the viceroy, and he ordered an army to be raised by Francisco Vasquez de Coronado, a thirty-year-old governor at the city of Compostela. Before ordering the expedition to begin, Mendoza requested from King Charles V authorization to expand the territory under his command. The approval came to Mendoza on January 4th, 1540, and his nomination and appointment of Coronado was approved.

Anticipating the approval would be coming soon, Mendoza alerted Coronado, and Coronado began gathering the army. It was a magnificent army to behold as they rode their horses and marched from the city of Compostela in February, 1540. Mendoza, who was always trying to best Cortes's fame, thought at last he would be able to accomplish that feat, and for that reason, he had put a great deal of his capital into the expedition.

The army consisted of upwards of eight hundred Spaniard soldiers, accompanied by over eight hundred Mexican Tlaxcalan Indians who walked along the flanks of the army, and three wives of three soldiers who accompanied their men.

Of course, Fray Marcos, astride a mule, led the army on its way northward. A second Franciscan priest, a Fray Juan de Padilla, who would become the first priest martyred by natives in what was to become part of the United States, was assigned to the effort. The expedition started carrying its own food, but was to be supplied with additional food by ships of Hernando de Alarcon, which sailed from Acapulco.

However, confusion on where those ships were to meet the army, meant they missed connections completely. Alarcon sailed up the coastline of the Gulf of California, but never entered the Colorado River near the present city of Yuma, Arizona, where he was supposed to meet the army.

The speed with which the army was moving upset Coronado, so he detached a group of his soldiers that were on horseback, and having Fray Marcos join him up front, Fray Marcos led them to the city where he said that Estevancio had been killed.

Upon seeing the city from another hill, Coronado saw no gold, nor any other things of worth, although the walls did sparkle in the sunlight. He became very upset, and as they entered the city, they were met by arrows, fired by the many men who were armed with long bows. This battle lasted a very short time as the weapons of the crossbowmen and musketeers soon took control of the Indian bowmen, and the Spaniards had won the battle.

Coronado was wounded in the battle, and not wanting to hold back the expedition, sent Don Pedro de Tovar as leader into the rest of the area considered to be Cibola. Following the directions Fray Marcos had received from the Indians whom had been with Estevancio prior to his entry into his final Indian city, the army rode and marched into the other six cities which were expected to be part of the seven cities of Cibola, finding nothing of worth, but having to fight the warriors of those cities.

As they reached the last of those cities, the army entered into the area of the Hopi tribe in the northeast area of what is now Arizona. Short skirmishes took place there, after which the Spanish spoke with the Hopi who indicated a great river to the west of where they lived, and Tovar took this information back to Coronado, who then dispatched a squadron led by Garcia Lopez de Cardenas to investigate.

Fray Juan de Padilla accompanied Cardenas, and they both looked down upon the river from the high bluffs above, and seeing nothing noteworthy to report, rode back to tell Coronado that the river was found below a huge hole in the ground, so deep, that no one will ever have an interest in attempting to get to its banks. That scene was described by Cardenas from the south rim of the Grand Canyon.

Millions of people from all over the world visit there each year, proving that reports of first glimpses should not have been taken as gospel.

After the fruitless visits to the seven cities to which Fray Marcos had directed the Spanish army of Coronado, he was sent back to Mexico City as a shamed man, but still retained his title of provincial superior of the Franciscan missionaries in Mexico until his death in 1558. Coronado was again injured in combat against one of the Zuni Indian villages in 1542, and returned to Mexico City reporting to the viceroy that nothing of interest was found during the exploration of the northern territories of New Spain.

It was said that Coronado explored parts of the states of Kansas, and returned through the corners of Oklahoma and Texas. Coronado was accused of mismanaging the expedition, which affected him psychologically, and Cardenas was sent back to Spain in irons, sentenced to prison where he died.

While Coronado's expedition was in Kansas, a few horses got loose and that is where the thousands of wild horses got their start in North America. While in Kansas, Fray Juan de Padilla was killed by the Wichita tribe in 1542, and became the first martyr of the Catholic religion to die in New Spain.

Other expeditions stretching across the areas of what is now known as the southern states of the United States were sent out from Mexico City, and there were numerous Spanish priests of the Franciscan order who did their best in trying to convert the Indian nations to Catholicism, some of whom were quite successful.

Much of the history of New Spain between 1542 and 1681 has been lost to ignominy both by the forces of the Spanish military and the Catholic religion.

Much of the abuse of power and mistreatment caused the colonization to continue without much opposition.

Chapter 9—The Exploration of Northern and Western New Spain

1529-1600

THERE WAS ANOTHER war taking place in what is now considered to be western Mexico. It was being fought by the natives of that area against the incoming Spaniards. A brutal conquest of that area was led by Nuno Beltran de Guzman with an army of Spaniards searching for gold and wealth.

It took but a few years to subjugate the native people in that area using horses, muskets, crossbows and swords against the longbows, slingshots, and the machetes used by the natives. That region became known as Nuevo Galicia after a region of Spain. Nuno had been a special bodyguard for King Charles the V until the king became suspicious of Hernando Cortes possibly short-changing the crown from a share of the riches Cortes was finding in Mexico, and becoming too powerful within the country, or as it was known, New Spain.

Sending Nuno to oversee the proceeds Cortes was accumulating, Nuno was given authority to conquer the western part of that continent. After conquering that region, he became the governor of the province of Panuco from 1525 to 1533, and the governor of Nuevo Galicia from 1529 to 1534. He was the founder of the city of Guadalajara in Mexico.

As governor of Panuco, he came down hard on Cortes and his supporters, stripping them of property and rights. During the conquests, Nuno took thousands of native prisoners, sending them to various Spanish holdings both in New Spain and to European Spain. This was not tolerated by the other appointed governors and religious leaders who had him arrested in 1537 for treason, abuse of power, and mistreatment of the indigenous people in his territory.

He was sent back to Spain in shackles, imprisoned there for one year before being released and was again made part of King Charles V bodyguard, until King Charles abdicated the throne, and King Phillip replaced him in 1556. Nuno Beltran de Guzman died in poverty in Spain in 1558.

A man who served as a conquistador in the service of Beltran was Cristobal de Onate, a man who was to become very wealthy in New Spain. Having been born into a wealthy and important Spanish family, he was given the very influential job of being the assistant to Rodrigo de Albornoz, auditor, one of the five royal officials sent by King Charles V to oversee the government of Cortes in New Spain.

Arriving in New Spain in 1524, he married into an important family to Catalina de Salazar de la Cadena, daughter of a high-ranking officer of the royal treasury for the colony. As a member of Beltran's conquistadors, he traveled over much of the western part of what is now Mexico, finding much of it having beauty and riches, to which he returned after leaving the military and becoming governor.

He found very rich silver mines in what is now known as the state of Zacatecas, becoming one of the wealthiest Spaniards in Mexico. Although he served under Beltran, he was not a brutal man, but rather, treated everyone with whom he worked with kindness and respect.

He often fed the people who had little, and, for their betterment, bequeathed to the villages and cities in his areas some of the wealth he had accumulated. He died on October 6th, 1567 at his home in Panuco, Zacatecas, Mexico. Many streets in the towns he had been governor over still have his name on them, as he was well thought of, and much admired.

In order to bring to New Spain a new name, that of Father Eusebio Kino, we must go back to 1521, when during wartime, a young Spanish aristocrat and soldier by the name of Ignatius of Loyola, was helping to defend the citadel of Pamplona when a cannon ball broke his leg.

While he was recuperating, he began reading a religious book about the early saints of the Catholic Church. Thinking of himself as becoming as dedicated to the church as they had been, he took up a religious education at four different universities of Spain and France over eleven years.

At each university he accumulated men about him that were thinking the same as he, that they must become humble and chaste. After vowing to live within those disciplines, the group traveled to Rome to introduce their new order of priests to Pope Paul III, offering their services to him and the church. Accepting the group in 1540, the pope named the group the Society of Jesus, and assigned them to service throughout the Christian lands of Europe. In 1541, Ignatius was named society superior general.

During that time, the Protestant religion was being introduced by Martin Luther and John Calvin, and the various orders of Catholic priests were out to save souls of Christians who might be tempted to bolt the Catholic Church, and introduce people of other lands to the new religions. The Society of Jesus became known as the Jesuit order and grew swiftly, and the pope assigned some of the new priests to outposts in New Spain.

Because of the university educated men who first joined Ignatius in the Society of Jesus, they were more accepted by the people of higher status, while the Franciscans appealed more to the poor. The first of the Society of Jesus priests who traveled outside of Europe was Francis Xavier who was sent in 1542 first to Portuguese India, and later to Japan. In 1549, another of the Jesuits was sent with the appointed governor general of Brazil.

This began a long procession of Jesuit missionaries to places around the newly discovered lands of the world. At the time of the death of Ignatius in 1556, the Society of Jesus numbered over one thousand Jesuit priests.

Father Eusebio Kino was baptized in the church his parents attended in Segno, Italy on August 10th, 1645. His true name was Eusebio Chini, but because his name in the Spanish language sounded more like Kino, he is known by that name.

While he was recuperating from an illness in 1665, he made a vow to his favorite saint, Francis Xavier, to add a second name to his own, thus becoming Eusebio Francesco Chini. He joined the Society of Jesus in 1665, after his recovery from the illness, and was educated into the society at several universities, Freiburg, Ingolstadt, and Landsberg in Austria.

He received his Holy Orders as a priest on June 12th, 1677. He was ordered to go to New Spain that same year, but missed the boat because of illness and had to wait a year before making the trip. Father Eusebio was a very observant man, interested in many things besides religion. In early 1681, a thesis he had written about a comet was published. Later that year he sailed to New Spain.

Father Kino's first mission was to lead the Atondo expedition to the Baja peninsula of the Las Californias province of New Spain. He established a mission named San Bruno in 1683. After a drought lasting until 1685, the mission was abandoned by him and the other Jesuit priests who had been ordered there after he had established the mission.

Everyone from the mission returned to the viceregal capital in Mexico City. On the morning of March 14th, 1687, he left the town of Cucurpe, which at the time was considered the "rim of Christendom" to establish a series of missions. The first eleven missions he established were located in what is now known as the state of Sonora in northern Mexico.

The twelfth was in what is now the state of Arizona, and was called Mission San Cayetano del Tumacacori, and was initially set next to the Santa Cruz River along the east bank. However, that was moved to the west bank in the 1700's as the Apache and Yaqui Indians kept attacking the mission, stealing the cattle and crops from the priests and lay people who lived and worked there.

Even after that move, and the fact that a Spanish settlement had been built just a few miles north of the mission, the attacks would come so quickly that by the time the soldiers would arrive the Apache were gone.

Finally, even the new mission was abandoned, moving all of the pews, pictures, and other valuables to the mission which was the next that Father Kino established south of Tucson called San Xavier del Bach.

That one had to be moved as well, just one mile south of where he had established it as the Apaches burned it down. It was rebuilt by a Franciscan friar, who took over the mission when the Jesuits were recalled to Spain. One of the reasons for the recall was that the king had placed taxes on all completed governmental and religious buildings.

The priests had intentionally left part of the building incomplete, such as one of two towers remaining flat without the crown. This is what happened at San Xavier del Bach, and you can still see one tower with its steeple, the other flat roofed. That huge church was built by a Franciscan priest, Father Juan Bautista Beldarrain, who was sent there to build it in 1751. Father Kino established eleven more missions stretching all the way to California.

On his return from California, while approaching San Xavier del Bach mission, some of the Pima native tribe took him to an abandoned village with a three-story house built of caliche mud which he named "Casa Grande" (big house).

It was built in the 1300's, and there were several smaller homes built of the same materials in the village. In 1938, the large building was protected by a large umbrella-like metal covering placed over it by the US government when it was declared a National Monument.

While Father Kino was establishing missions in New Spain, he was in contact with sixteen bands and tribes of Indians, including the Apache, Pima, Tohono O'odham, Quechan, Yuman, Yaqui, and ten more groups. Father Kino died on March 15th, 1711 at Magdalena de Kino, in Mexico.

Chapter 10—Padre Junipero Serra and Lt. Colonel Juan Batista de Anza

1713-1788

MIGUEL JOSE SERRA was born in 1713 in Petra, Spain, and at sixteen years of age joined the order of the Franciscan friars. Educated by them, he received his Holy Orders in 1738, and continued his education earning a doctorate in theology in 1742. By then, he had become a great preacher and educator, and began teaching, serving in that capacity until receiving orders to travel to New Spain to spread the Catholic religion throughout Central and North America.

Arriving at Vera Cruz in 1750, he and his companion, Franciscan priest and former student of his, Francisco Palou, walked two hundred fifty miles to Mexico City.

During that long walk, Serra injured one of his legs, from which the pain never left throughout the rest of his life. Upon arrival in Mexico City, he became part of the University of San Fernando, preaching and teaching off and on until 1767, when he volunteered to lead several Franciscan priests to Baja, California and establish missions along the coastline.

Altogether, he established nine missions from San Fernando de Velicata south of San Diego in July, 1769 to the San Carlos

Borromeo de Carmel mission at Carmel by the Sea, California, which he organized in 1770. This last mission was founded after Serra had boarded a ship and sailed up the coast to a landing at what was to become Carmel by the Sea, and because of the beauty of the land, the ocean view, and all of the other beautiful sights in the area, Serra decided to establish that mission there.

During his time in California, it is said that he converted as many as four thousand six hundred native Indians, with six thousand Baptisms having been performed throughout the missions up to his death. He oftentimes ran into issues with the Spaniards who traveled to California, residents and soldiers alike.

In trying to protect the natives from the bad behavior of the Spaniards toward the natives, he would admonish them. When the natives would misbehave, he would administer corporal punishment. Although the present mission buildings were not erected until 1797, he remained at the San Carlos mission until he died on August 28th, 1784.

He is buried beneath the floor of that mission. His efforts were recognized by the Catholic Church in 2015 when he was named a saint by Pope Francis during the pope's first visit to the United States.

The first of the people written about in this book who was born in the Americas is Juan Bautista de Anza, who was born on June 7th, 1736 in the area of Fronteras, Mexico, which is now part of the state of Sonora, Mexico. His father, with the same name, served Spain in the service of the military.

Young Juan was first educated in Fronteras, then went to the college of San Ildefonso in Mexico City. He furthered his education at a school for future military leaders, then went back to Fronteras to enlist into military service. Moving quickly up the ranks to captain, he was sent on missions to what is now the state of Arizona. In 1760 he became the military commander of a small garrison at a village next to the Santa Cruz River called Tubac, just a few miles north of the mission of San Cayetano de Tumacacori.

Tubac became the first walled-in city-fortress in what is now the United States of America. Unfortunately, as was previously described, it was far enough from that mission to allow the constantly aggressive Apache warriors to attack the mission, kill the priests and lay people who worked for them, steal the cattle, horses, and produce from the planted fields, and leave before the Spanish soldiers arrived just a few minutes later. This forced the priests to remove everything of worth from the mission and move the religious items to the mission just south of Tucson at San Xavier del Bach.

In 1774, de Anza was ordered to establish an overland route to San Francisco in the northern part of California, the western-most part of the Mexican New Spain territory. With but thirty-four soldiers accompanying him, he made his way there through extremely hot, dry deserts, over mountains, and across the Colorado River, returning by much the same route.

Gathering people interested in settling near the Pacific Ocean at San Francisco, he organized another group consisting of two hundred forty men, women, children, and livestock, to make that same journey in 1775.

They left the city of San Miguel in the state of Sonora, traveled north along the Santa Cruz River past the San Cayetano de Tumacacori mission. Their next stop was at the walled-in city-fortress of Tubac, just a few miles north of the mission, where de Anza had been military commander before the expedition in 1774.

This was a chance to acquire provisions for the long and treacherous journey through territory that was attacked constantly by the Apache bands of Indians, although it was inhabited primarily by the Tohono O'odham and Pima tribes, both of whom were primarily agriculturists, and had accepted cohabiting with the Spaniards.

The expedition followed the Santa Cruz River to just west of the Casa Grande ruins which had been found and named by Father Eusebio Kino in 1694, where the expedition turned west and met the Gila River, which they followed to the crossing of the Colorado

River near the present-day city of Yuma, Arizona.

The Quechan Nation of Native Americans became good friends of de Anza during both of his trips through their territory, helping the expeditions to cross the Colorado River by building tule (cattail bushes) rafts.

Traveling straight west from the crossing, they wove their way between mountains before turning northward, passing south of the present-day Los Angeles, and following the coastline northward to what is now San Francisco, arriving there on March 26th, 1776. Although he led the expedition to San Francisco, he was not responsible for establishing the city there. Upon his return to Mexico City in 1777, he was appointed the governor of the Nuestra area which is now the state of New Mexico.

He retained that appointment until 1787, when he was appointed the governor of Tucson, but died on December 19th, 1788 before he could assume that appointment. He died in Arzipe, Mexico and is buried at the church of Nuestra Senora de la Asuncion in that city.

There were many more very important people that helped establish the Spanish heritage in North, Central and South America, but these have captured my imagination, and I hope yours too.

Thank you for reading a very important part of history for the countries in all three Americas.

www.ingramcontent.com/pod-product-compliance
Lightning Source LLC
Chambersburg PA
CBHW022142240626
47153CB00007B/2472

9781949267396